AZALEA HOUSE

AZALEA HOUSE

CLARE CASTLEBERRY

Jacket Design by L1graphics

Published by Winding Road Stories

Print book interior design by A Raven Design

ISBN#: 979-8-9850815-0-3

CONTENTS

1

My birthday fell on Friday the thirteenth that year. I used to ignore those omens as a child, but now I look for symbols everywhere, searching for the hidden truth buried deep within the universe.

The March air in South Louisiana was brisk. Mushy snow covered the ground like spilled snowballs, a rarity for the area. On the morning of my birthday, the snow diminished to sleet.

As icy rain tapped on the window, I stared through the halo of lit birthday candles until everyone in the background became glowing orange. Mid-March in Louisiana was supposed to be a high time for change: seasons turning, warming weather, and new blooms. But the earth stalled that year. The symbols and omens hung on with spidery fingers, signaling colder, dark times.

Turning sixteen heightened my anxiety. In 1996, the digital landscape shifted seismically under my feet—multiculturalism, alternative media and the World Wide Web were changing the way I saw the world. Those rapid currents couldn't even keep pace with the changes taking place within me, as I held onto my childhood with clumsy fingers.

I blew out the birthday candles, and smoke twirled around the intricate rose-shaped icing Momma had so meticulously prepared.

"See what's in the bag first, Marianne," my uncle Joseph said as Momma cut the cake. I pulled the contents from the plain paper bag: a white lacy bra and panty set. Someone whistled. My body burned with embarrassment.

"Jesus," Momma said as she rolled her eyes. "You'll need to hold that over your chest to see if it fits," she told me.

I glanced across the table at my brother Marcus. He flushed and looked down at his feet, fidgeting with his crutches.

I could feel my face burning with embarrassment as I went into the other room to see if the underwear fit. I overheard Momma telling Uncle Joseph that the set wasn't appropriate for his niece, but he justified the gift with a price tag.

"Go apologize, Junior," Momma said to my uncle. "You embarrassed her."

"I told you, call me Chance." He had this thing lately about not wanting to be called Joseph—or worse, Junior.

"Joseph," she said, her tone more authoritative, "Go apologize."

I held the cup over my breast in the mirror of the living room armoire as my uncle came in.

"I'm sorry if you were embarrassed," Joseph said as he entered the room. He got closer, the vodka on his breath as strong as ethanol. My stomach flip-flopped, but I remained still with my shoes anchored to the floor as if they were filled of concrete.

"I couldn't stop thinking about what you'd look like in that," he said in a lowered voice only I could hear.

As the chattering in the other room became louder, he got closer. He put his hand on my hip and then let his fingers trail up my belly, up to my breasts, and up over the sports bra I wore. I was still in denial about having breasts and had already outgrown the starter bras Momma had bought me.

"You would look so good in that. I hope you'll think about trying it on for me one of these days," he said, his mouth right up against my ear. His other hand moved down the front of my pants, doing that thing he always did when he came for holidays. I hated holidays because of him.

I pushed him away and ran back into the kitchen where the cake was.

"Don't eat too much of that," said my Grandmere Lily. "You don't want to lose your figure."

"Mom. Stop it," Momma said. She looked at me with pleading eyes. *Tell them to go away*, I tried to convey with my thoughts.

But my throat closed and as much as I wanted to say it, I couldn't, because it would be impolite

What a Sweet Sixteen party. My brother, my parents, my aunt and her new young husband, her daughter Vivienne, my drunk Uncle Joseph, and my Grandmere Lily and Granddaddy. Why had they come? Why couldn't we just have *us* there: me, Marcus, Momma, Daddy and even my friend Chloe?

My father looked at me with soft eyes. "Have as much as you want, Marianne. It's your birthday." He came up behind Momma and slipped his gangly arms around her waist and kissed her on the cheek. They looked so beautiful together. My parents had been through everything together: they started a band called Spellbound Hearts, toured the world, even bought back our old family home with the money they made. I hoped one day I would experience that kind of love.

"Well, the twins would be what, twenty-one years old now? I'm sure their party wouldn't be as awkward as *this*," my grandmother said as she drummed her fire engine red fingernails on the table.

"Lily, stuff it, okay? Have a piece of cake. A little sugar might do you some good," Granddaddy said. He dished out a large hunk of cake and plopped it on the paper party plate in front of her. Icing landed on the sleeve of her black linen shirt—a small dot shaped like a star—but she didn't notice. Instead, she clicked her tongue and rolled her eyes before pushing it away. Granddaddy winked at me. I gave him a quick, small smile.

My parents, Janelle and Abel, had won my harsh

grandparents over with their good deeds, their wealth, beauty and fame. My brother Marcus and I were still outcasts to them, though Granddaddy was warming up to us more these days. Until now, we were the odd ones, banished to live on the outskirts of the family. I could barely bring myself to talk, and Marcus had trouble walking because of his mild cerebral palsy.

We couldn't escape the shadow of our dead twin brothers, Brendan and Benjamin. They were buried on the edge of the property of our old family home, Azalea House, when they were five. At the mention of the twins, Momma glanced at me, her usual soft green eyes going cold for a split-second. I hung my head. I had only heard about them in passing; I knew they died before I was born, but once I found out they were buried on the property, it changed things between me and my parents.

"You know it's true," my Aunt Julia said underneath her breath to her husband, Troy. Her daughter, Vivienne, snickered. Troy, my step-uncle, rolled his eyes.

"I heard that, Julia," Momma said. "Let's be civil today, okay? Please?" Something in her tone must have worked, because the mood in the room shifted from somber to tolerant.

Momma, Janelle, was the nicest member of our family. With her auburn hair and bright green eyes, she won the jackpot in looks, drawing admiring gazes from men and women. Despite the constant attention, she remained gracious and sweet. She frequently put out the fires set by the emotional arsonists in my family

Uncle Joseph downed yet another glass of vodka on the rocks. He was a con man, my father always said—the kind who was involved in real estate, but could never really tell you exactly what he did.

Aunt Julia and Vivienne exchanged knowing, snarky glances. My Aunt Julia had a habit of making snide comments about Momma, and lately, about me. No matter how much makeup she slathered on her face, Julia could never match Momma's beauty. Julia was the plain one. Instead of the beautiful chestnut curls Momma had, Julia's hair took on a wiry, Medusa-like appearance.

Her green eyes were as soulless as glass bottles, set too far back in a pockmarked face she shellacked with makeup. And she didn't have any of the talent Momma had, though she insisted on keeping her maiden name so she could easily be associated with Janelle Easton, the bright and beautiful songstress from Spellbound Hearts.

Julia was a religious studies instructor at a community college in town. I had no idea how a person like her wound up with Troy, my twenty-five-year-old step-uncle. Troy and I locked eyes for a second, before he looked down, then away and rubbed the back of his neck. I glanced over at Vivienne, who smiled and flipped me off.

Oh, Vivienne. The bane of my existence. She was a bully to the core, popular at her school in town, a cheerleader, and always quick with a comment about me or anyone who didn't live up to her standards. We were friendlier when we were little, but something changed when Vivienne started modelling. Her personality became abrasive. She once made a cameo on MTV's House of Style when the show came to New Orleans, and that moment made her a local celebrity amongst everyone our age. After that, she started making fun of me for being too quiet. It escalated into tripping me during family gatherings or coming up with elaborate ways to embarrass me.

My grandparents were alright. I liked my grandfather aside from the odd comment that older people make when they no longer edit what they say. My grandmother and I met eyes for a brief second. She was studying me as I studied everyone else, with a judging, cold air. I was deathly afraid of her and of Julia. They had the same steely gray edge to their eyes.

I can't explain why I couldn't talk. I never had a problem talking to my brother or Momma, and Chloe, my one friend at school. But I didn't have much to say to my dad, and nothing at all to the rest of the world. It was as if my words were caught somewhere in between my chest and my tummy, and they would never come out. That place always felt tight and sore, and the sensation would worsen when someone asked me a question.

My grandmother and my aunt made the biggest show of me not talking.

"She's just slow," Aunt Julia liked to say with the slightest smile. "And Marcus is physically handicapped."

"You need to take her to the doctor," Grandmere Lily would tell Momma. "She may never finish school at this rate. Your son, too."

Their words stabbed me in the heart. Momma told me and Marcus that we were smart. I was ahead in reading, and he was ahead in math, but it never mattered to my extended family.

I finished my cake and disappeared to the sanctuary of my room, hoping the rest of my family wouldn't notice, but Marcus did.

"Marianne," he whispered, his crutches tapping on the old hardwood floor in the hall behind me. "Are you okay?"

I shook my head, went into my room, and let its cool darkness wash over me. He followed me and closed the door.

"Do you want to go into the woods?" he asked.

Even though Marcus was three years younger, we had a psychic connection. At thirteen, my brother was a genius at computers and all things logical, but he believed in the unknown and untouched just as much as I did.

I opened the window and he followed me outside. I had to walk slower so Marcus could keep up, but I didn't mind. We shut the window and escaped into the comforting darkness of the evening. We breathed smoke like fire dragons in the cold. The slushy snow lingered on the ground like bad memories.

We veered left and meandered down the trails my father kept cut for us. I looked up at the glittering stars before they slid behind gray cloud curtains and sighed. This was our only freedom from the velvet prison of the big, beautiful red castle-like house that kept us caged for our childhood years. Momma didn't like it when we went into the woods or anywhere else but school, but Daddy quietly encouraged us to wander. He cut trails for us all through the dense pine and oak forest. He weaved in labyrinths and created dead-ends and hiding spots and everything a child could dream of.

"Was Joseph gross again?"

Marcus was the only person I ever told about Uncle Joseph and the things he did when he had too many of his vodka drinks.

"Yes," I whispered and nodded. When I did talk, most people couldn't hear me. Momma and Marcus were among the few.

Marcus said nothing. There wasn't much else to say. My uncle would leave me money after those little incidents, hundreds of dollars I was always too afraid to touch. I kept them in a lockbox in my closet amongst all my dolls. I never spent a dime. Never even counted them either, but the thousands of dollars stacked in the box became a growing reminder of how often these things happened.

The snow still clung to the trees like birthday frosting. Marcus and I walked through the woods, listening to our shoes crushing the remnants of snow under our feet, enjoying the clean smell of the pine trees and the crispness of the chilly evening. But soon, someone would come looking for us. We were supposed to be socializing like normal kids, as if talking to my deranged extended family was normal at our age.

We were getting close to the twins' graves, and a sense of unease wormed its way into my mind.

"Let's go back," I urged, and Marcus nodded. We went back in through the window, and it was like entering a portal to reality, away from the magic of the night and the outside world.

Someone banged on the door and I jumped.

"Go away, Vivienne!" shouted my brother. My brat of a cousin was always trying to inject herself into our private conversations. She was so nosy I was surprised she had knocked at all.

"Your momma and daddy went out because they're sick of you!" screamed Vivienne.

"Stop it, Vivienne!" yelled my aunt. "Marianne, Marcus, your grandparents and uncle left, and your mom and dad went for a drink. They'll be back in an hour. Let Vivienne in your room,

Marianne. You can't just shut her out all the time. She's your family, too."

Marcus rolled his eyes and looked at me for the okay before he opened the door. I nodded, hesitant, but too afraid of creating a scene.

She barged in. "Your parents don't like you because you are too stupid to talk, Marianne. But *I* know the truth. You just think you're too good to talk to us."

"You're an idiot, Vivienne, and you're right—she doesn't want to talk to you because you're annoying. Why do you want to come in here anyway?"

I put my hand over my mouth to stifle a giggle.

"Vivienne," said a voice in my doorway. It was Troy, my aunt's new husband. God, he looked so young, yet Vivienne seemed to be a constant source of stress for him. By the way his brows knitted together and his fingers curled into fists, I could tell he didn't care for her so much. Maybe he saw her more as an annoying little sister. He was only nine years older than us. "Vivienne," he sighed again, "leave them alone. It's Marianne's birthday."

"Marianne, Marianne, Marianne! I'm so sick of you. Why would I want to hang out here, anyway? You're both *geeks*!" She whirled around and pushed Troy aside.

"Pleasant, isn't she?" Troy said, casting a lingering glance before he left the room.

We closed the door to my room again while Vivienne wailed outside, loud enough for us to hear. She was bored, wanted to go home, and wanted to go out with her boyfriend. She wanted new lingerie, too.

"God, Vivienne is so annoying. I feel sorry for Troy. He didn't know what he was getting into," said my brother.

"Money?" I whispered, and Marcus laughed. Though Aunt Julia made a respectable income as a professor, she always needed more, it seemed. There were little tidbits Momma gave Aunt Julia from the band royalties throughout the years. And Julia always seemed to need money for new car payments or clothes or something, and she always played on Momma's heartstrings.

Time seemed to struggle to move along, as if hindered by the cold. We finished a jigsaw puzzle.

"Mooooooom, I want to leave! This house is creepy!" It was Vivienne again, parading up and down the hallway in front of my room.

"It's been two hours. Where are they?" Troy asked. He was close, probably on the stairs. They must have gotten up from the living room and started roaming around the house, probably in search of money or valuable trinkets.

"Marcus, something is wrong. My head hurts—bad," I said, a little too loud. My cheeks burned because I didn't want Troy to hear me.

I knew they just went out to get away for a little while, but they would have come back to see us off to bed. Marcus and I stared out the window, but the car never came down that twisting driveway. My aunt and Troy chattered away in the other room in an antsy tone. They were eager to leave.

Nine o'clock, and we were still waiting.

Anxiety gnawed at my stomach.

"Look!" Marcus cried out, having caught sight of a car turning into our tree-lined driveway. "That's them coming now."

But it wasn't their car. It was a white sedan, and there was a light affixed to the top. It was the state police.

I opened my door and looked down the stairs and into the foyer. The two state troopers approached the front door and rang the doorbell. The officers asked Julia if she was a relative.

They apologized and said there had been an accident. My parents were involved.

I held Marcus's hand, and we walked down the stairs and into the foyer, dazed.

"My sister?" whispered my aunt. "She's... dead? Are you sure?"

"Ma'am," said a female officer, her voice very solemn, "I'm

sorry to bring you such terrible news on what looks like a special occasion," she said as she looked around at all the decorations.

"Well," Vivienne said, "it *is* Friday the thirteenth." She looked over her shoulder at me.

"Vivienne, shut up," Troy said. I appreciated the anger in his voice.

Marcus's eyes went dark and haunted. I could no longer see the blue. His crutches clattered to the floor. He gripped my hand so hard I winced. Then, he screamed.

It didn't seem possible. Momma had been sitting at the kitchen table earlier, and my father was standing next to her. They only went out for a minute. There was no way they could be dead.

"Get out of our house!" Marcus screamed. "Go away! They're not dead!"

But they were. I could tell by the look on the officers' faces. Marcus let go of my hand and collapsed on the floor as I began to cry.

Reality set in like the sleet settling into the grass outside. We would never hear Momma's laugh or my dad's corny jokes. We would never hear Momma sing or my father strum the guitar. Never again would we have those nights where we sat around the living room together as Momma and Daddy played songs from Spellbound Hearts—raw, stripped acoustic versions, not like the ones everyone else heard on the radio. We would never look into Momma's intelligent, caring eyes and would never again see the way my father's hair curled when it got too long.

I helped Marcus up. The hollowed out look of shock and grief darkened his eyes even more. I was sure I looked the same. We would only have each other. The rest were family by blood. But they didn't have the special bond Marcus and I shared, or the one we shared with our parents. The thought of being around Uncle Joseph and Aunt Julia without Momma felt like an open wound. I also feared for Marcus. He had just turned thirteen and was mature in so many ways, but he was still clinging onto childhood ideals. He wasn't ready for this.

I ran from the foyer and out into the sleeting rain. It stung my face as I sprinted faster and faster, further into the woods. The trees showered tiny little crystals of melting snow. It was fully dark now, but I knew the woods as well as I knew the house.

I ran until I reached the twins' graves. I ran from all the things that tore out my heart. I beat my fists up against a pine tree until I could smell the rich sap, beat until my knuckles were sticky with blood and the nectar from the tree. I cried rivers of tears for my parents who should be alive, and for Marcus, who wouldn't know the comfort of a parent through his sure to be difficult teenage years. And for myself. Why did they have to die today, with my birthday as a perennial reminder? Why couldn't they grow old and gray?

And what would become of us? What would become of this house now that they were dead? Would we go into foster care? I dreaded it all. It made my chest and stomach ache.

I gritted my teeth, clenched my fists and denied it was real until Troy brought me by the wreck yard the next day to see the car. That old Lincoln Town Car with its colossal size and shape had twisted into a nearly unrecognizable hunk of metal. There were papers scattered everywhere inside. In the backseat, there were yards of fabric strewn about. And in the front, blood. Blood on the dashboard. The steering wheel. Pooled into the carpet. Handprints on the passenger side window.

And it had all happened right in front of Azalea House.

The tire tracks marked the scene of the crash. They stayed there for weeks after the mud dried. I visited that site often to listen for their voices.

Momma and Daddy had gone for a quick ride and almost made it home. In the curve right before our driveway, Daddy lost control on the icy road and the car careened into the ditch in front of the house. All that time, I could have run down there to the end of the driveway. I would have seen the car, could have pulled them out in time. We never heard a car crash; the house was too set back off the road. It was terrifying to think they could die so close to home. Just a minute or so later, and they could have turned right into the driveway, and the worst part of my birthday would have just been a wrecked car, Vivienne's snotty attitude and my perverted uncle's roaming hands. I would have accepted that.

Daddy died instantly, but Momma struggled to escape the wreck. You could see the bloody handprints where she banged on the window for help, before she bled to death.

In the days after my parents' deaths, no one knew what to do with us. Marcus and I didn't want to live with our grandparents, and they didn't want us to live there, either. They wanted to travel to Florida or go on cruises with their friends. I certainly didn't want to live with my uncle. So, that left us with one choice. We could go live with my Aunt Julia and Troy, along with Vivienne, in the next town over.

Or, we could stay in the house, and they could live with us.

Mostly, we just wanted to run away.

2

Crows covered the leaden sky in small inkblots. My eyes followed them as they landed on a bare tree that resembled some sort of great witch's mane, tendrils dry and wild. From faraway, the crows' calls sounded like a conversation concerning my parents' funeral. I paid attention to the crows instead of the coffins before me for fear of breaking down in front of my brother.

Before us were two stone angels, their arms embracing the grave markers. Their features were so lifelike, when I shifted on my feet, I swore I could see their eyes following my movements.

My grandparents and my aunt made the decision to have my parents buried in town. I had hoped they'd be buried at Azalea House, near the twins, so we could visit their graves more often.

There was movement beyond the tombs. Twin bodies, a fleeting glimpse among the drab, gray grave markers. I wasn't sure if it was my own imagination, or if there were ghastly figures of some sort attending the funeral, too. The orbs zigged and zagged throughout the markers in an almost playful fashion, and instead of filling me with dread, they became a welcome curious distraction. The preacher continued to drone on about lives lost too soon and the immense talent that would be committed to the earth.

I refused to think about their beautiful bodies buried beneath the soil. I could not empty that image from my brain of murky, damp roots tunneling down into the rich, decomposing earth and infiltrating Momma and Daddy's coffins. Were the coffins airtight? Could anything get in? Here in Louisiana, water most definitely could. The thought of us burying them in the earth instead of an above-ground tomb filled me with dizzying worry. Would their graves be robbed? Would fans of their music make their resting place a makeshift party?

Visitors tried to make it a pleasant cemetery, but it was no use. The heavy rains and sleet had wilted the flowers, leaving red roses black and bruise-like, and white roses like brittle bones. Even the angel-faced statues were more ominous under a slate-gray sky, their features hollowed out by dim light.

Off in the distance, behind the headstones, I could hear the laughter of children, two identical voices. The voices had been haunting me since I was twelve. On my birthday that year, my best friend Chloe bought me a Ouija Board. Ever since then, I swore I felt a connection to the twins. Instead of listening to funeral prayers and speeches, my mind escaped into those memories from four years ago.

We had a crawfish boil for my twelfth birthday, as people in South Louisiana tend to do for any spring gathering. My family came out and I opened presents I didn't want. Barbies, horse stuff, a little floral stamping kit. The metal albums and the black clothing I hoped for never materialized.

But my best friend Chloe came through. She always did.

Chloe found a Ouija board at a garage sale and spent her allowance on it. It was her way of one-upping me for the Prince cassette I'd splurged on for her birthday.

She thought it would help me talk more if I asked the Ouija

board questions. I was often reprimanded at school for not saying a word. Selective mutism. That's what they called it. I always kept my head down, absorbed in a book, and only talked to a few people. Chloe said perhaps if I practiced talking to people who weren't there, my ability to speak to real people would improve.

But to me, the twins really were there. And the board didn't just get me to talk. It made me scream.

Chloe had wrapped the board up in a comic from the Sunday newspaper. There was a purple bow on top.

I opened the present and stared at the image on the box: disembodied hands slightly levitating above a weird, heart-shaped object. It reminded me of a movie I had seen, some sixties black and white film about an astronaut's severed hand that fell from the sky and pestered people. The box itself had tattered edges, and the lady's hands were adorned with chunky hippie jewelry like my mom always wore. I desperately wanted to be like my mom: chatty, pretty, and able to pull off all that fashionable jewelry. She had a ruby ring she always wore, a large gemstone surrounded by gold filigree ivy. I greatly wanted to pull off something so mature-looking and elegant. I studied my baker's pink bedroom with its frilly white curtains and glassy-eyed dolls and sighed. Twelve was too old to have dolls or receive stupid games for my birthday.

Chloe had a smug, mischievous expression on her face. She was six months younger and like a little prankster sister. She twirled her whitish blonde hair and grinned. I would not be surprised to see the box full of roaches or snakes.

"Come on, Marianne. Open it," she said. I shook it first, just to be sure there were no live creatures skittering around in the box. Inside was a board with letters and numbers, and the heart shaped plastic thing.

"It's a planchette," Chloe explained, and demonstrated how to use it. "You talk to ghosts. You ask a question, and it spells out the answers through the little window here. You just put your fingers on it and talk and it does the rest." She held up the plastic thing. I didn't want to touch it, but she gave me that look again, like *I'll never leave you alone unless you do it.*

It moved as soon as we put our fingers on it. I snapped my arms back at my sides and shook my head.

"Come on," she said. "Let's do it. Ask it a question."

"Who is here?" I wanted to get this over with, so we could do something else. She just wanted to move the plastic thing again and scare me.

The planchette shuddered, then moved. *U-S*, it spelled.

The lights flickered. The room dropped to a wintery temperature, despite the early spring humidity outside. The windows fogged over.

"You win," I said. "Let's watch a movie."

I didn't realize our fingers were still on the planchette. It moved to *NO*.

"Who is 'us'?" Chloe asked.

"Okay, I'm scared, you win. Didn't you hear me?"

TWINS, the board spelled.

"Prove it," I said, still afraid yet curious.

I thought the game would stop there. But it had just begun.

Two pairs of blue tennis shoes appeared just underneath the door, followed by hushed child-like voices. I screamed, and so did Chloe. The owners of the blue shoes laughed and ran. The lights in my bedroom flickered again.

I put the planchette on top of the board and stored it underneath the bed. Chloe was sweating, her blue eyes wide, her face flushed red.

"You weren't moving it?" I asked her. I was sure she was. She shook her head. If she wasn't scared, she was doing a fine job acting.

I swore I wouldn't touch it again. When Chloe turned around and left, the back of her shirt was dark with sweat.

But like moths and insects drawn to the windows at night seeking light and warmth, I pulled out the board again, mesmerized.

The planchette began to move.

LISTEN.

The blue tennis shoes appeared under the frame of the door again. I tip-toed over to peek, then yanked the door open. I caught a fading glimpse of them as they rounded the corner to the front door. It opened and shut with little noise. The warm night air filtered in, wet and putrid as a deluge. I wrinkled my nose and pressed on, still not knowing why, and followed them into the darkness.

Twigs and leaves crunched under my shoes as I followed their laughter. Blackberry brambles clawed at my arms and legs. Soon, I was deep in the woods, and there was nothing to guide me but dim pinprick stars high in the sky. I stood in a small clearing, listening for a sign.

We are here, they said.

"How did you die?" I asked.

But they did not want to tell me how they died. They told me their names were Brendan and Benjamin.

The next day, I sat at the kitchen counter as Momma put together a roux for a gumbo, her bracelets clinking together as she stirred, creating a rhythmic song.

"Momma," I said, wishing she would make eye contact with me. "Brendan and Benjamin told me to tell you not to be so sad about them passing away. I just thought you should know."

She finally looked at me. Her eyes were round and wet, and she tossed the wooden spoon she'd been using straight into the pot and ran to the back of the house. Her sobs echoed through the halls as the roux burned and smoked on the stove.

She didn't speak to me for three days. It wasn't until the third evening around the time she came in to say goodnight that she finally asked how I knew those names.

"The twins. You know. They told me on the Ouija board," I said.

"Brendan and Benjamin were two twin boys I had before you," Momma said with that wet softness in her eyes again. "They died before you were born. Tell me the truth, sugar. How did you know who they were?"

"I told you," I said. I pulled the covers up close. I didn't like it when Momma's eyes welled up like that. "They told me on the Ouija board."

Momma took the board out from under the bed. I followed her and stayed out of her line of vision as she tossed it into the trash, then took the garbage bags out to the end of the driveway.

Why did she do that?

A week later, the board was back in my closet. I dropped my dress on the floor as I was taking it off the hanger. I remembered Momma throwing the board in the trash.

I left the dress on the floor and opened the box. Brendan and Benjamin said they missed me too much and wanted to talk to me again. They also said not to tell Momma and Daddy they brought the board back.

But I told Chloe at school that day. They didn't say I couldn't tell her.

That weekend, she came over, and we hid in my room to talk to the twins on the board. She made me put a towel against the crack under the door, though.

"Why did you get this for me again?" I asked her as we talked under a blanket tent.

"I told you. I thought it might get you to talk more," she said as she yawned and stretched. She wasn't taking it as seriously as I was anymore. "When I used it, it said to give it to you on your birthday. So I did."

"Chloe," I said.

"What?"

"You don't think that's weird?"

"No," she said, her eyes round and blue. "Is it?" Her voice was getting shrill. I was just about to tell her to keep it down when Momma burst in and ripped the blanket off our heads.

"I told you not to mess with that thing!" Momma shrieked. She grabbed the board and stormed out of my room.

Chloe glanced at me and shrugged. "Can we do something else now?"

After Chloe left, I stared out my bedroom window as my parents argued in the driveway. The air conditioner was on full blast and it was hot and humid outside. I used my forearm to wipe the fogged window clean. They motioned towards my room and mentioned my name several times.

I pressed my fingernails into my palm. When I released, there were tiny half-moons there, dotted with blood.

"I *did* throw it away," Momma screamed. My dad pointed a finger at her. She pushed him away, and he grabbed her and said something I couldn't hear. He then walked around to the driver's side of the car and started it up and peeled out. The car spit gravel up into the air and my mom cursed.

But I didn't need the board anymore anyway. What I didn't tell Chloe was that I didn't need to board to hear Brendan and Benjamin. They talked to me as if they were sitting in the same room. At first, it sounded like static, or trying to listen to several radio stations at once. But their voices became clear after I did what they taught me: I stayed very still and cleared my mind of my own thoughts.

They told me a story about water creeping up across our driveway, pooling around potholes and low spots. They told me about swimming in that water.

In the rainy summer months, the floods came with a fury, the putrid brown water swirling around all our Creole cottages and devouring everything in its path.

There was a slough in front of Azalea House that filled up fast. It was full of cottonmouth snakes and gators, but when it flooded, everything crept up too close to the house, threatening to invade it.

Brendan and Benjamin told me it was late in the day when it happened. The sun set behind full and rich cypress trees, orange glints filtered behind the screen of green needles. But it was still light outside. Just enough. There was a damp, humid odor from puddles collecting in the driveway, and my nose burned as they described it. It blended with the sickly-sweet scent of swamp blossoms and the fermenting ditch. The aroma was unsettling, but combined with all the sounds and imagery, it was beautiful and comforting in its own way. The slough teemed with activity and life, a sensory overload. Birds sang and swooped in and out of the ditch in search of an abundant green treasure: grasshoppers. Cicadas sang their eerie spring chorus in a continuous, raucous crescendo.

The twins stepped into the warm flood, cautious at first, but were soon splashing and laughing, speaking to each other in their secret babbling twin language as they always did. But the laughter didn't last for long. Hands held them down. In my mind's eye, there was an image of a person, but I could not make it out through the veil of murky liquid.

I didn't want to hear about their suffering any longer, or think about someone holding them under, alone in the dank, fetid flood without any adult supervision.

Satisfied that they had gotten their point across, they let me sleep.

But not for long. The next morning, I was outside again, following their voices to the clearing in the deep woods.

Dig, they said. I used Momma's garden spade and cleared the earth until I uncovered their tiny little coffins. I used the blade of the tool to wedge open their wooden resting places. Both skeletons were curled up in a fetal position. I gathered the fragile remains of one twin and carefully placed them next to his brother, pushing the skeletons together until they were touching. When my parents found me kneeling in the mud, I didn't even hear the twins' screams anymore. I felt at peace. Their voices faded away into whispers.

I didn't want to believe any of it. The twins wanted me to know they were there, buried somewhere close to Momma's heart. She never let them go, kept them so close they became a secret.

The funeral service came to a close and as people shifted on their feet, ready to get away from this dreariness, I felt my uncle's eyes undressing me from across the graves. As he approached, the odor coming off him reminded me of rotten lemons and ethanol. I turned my head, glaring at Marcus to fend him off.

"Uncle Joseph," Marcus acknowledged. He put himself between me and Joseph, spreading his crutches out.

"You know, you really ought to call me Chance," Joseph said. "That's what everyone calls me."

"I am not calling you that."

"Come on. Let me talk to your sister."

"Anything you have to say to her, you can say to me, too," Marcus said. He did not move. Joseph had to either cut through a large group of people to get to me or try to skirt around the holes in the ground.

"Y'all know you can count on your old Uncle Chance for anything you need, right?" He swayed a little as he said it.

There was a presence behind me. "How about we wrap it up for today, huh? Alright, buddy?" It was Troy.

Joseph narrowed his eyes and swayed again. "I'm not your buddy. And by the way, I should be living in that house now, taking care of these kids."

"Not happening. Their grandparents are staying at Azalea House until everything is sorted out," Troy said. The thought of Joseph living with us filled me with horrid dread. I had only really connected with Troy once in my life, but his interference meant a lot to me at this point. Joseph was the last person I wanted to deal with.

"You stay out of this! You're just a damn kid!"

Joseph charged at Troy, nearly knocking Marcus straight into Daddy's grave. He had to splay out his crutches to catch his balance. A sickening thwack beside me let me know Joseph was sober enough to get a hit in. I had rushed to Marcus's side. By the time I turned around, Troy had Joseph pinned on the ground.

"Junior!" Julia yelled from somewhere in the crowd.

"It's your sister's funeral," Troy was saying in a low voice. "Are you going to get it together? You going to act right?"

"Alright, alright," Joseph croaked, and Troy let him up. Joseph dusted the grass off his blazer and laughed. "Just a little horsing around," he said to a stunned group of onlookers. Vivienne was among them. She shot me a brief, slight smirk.

How dare she. Anything to disrupt my life pleased her, even the death of my own parents.

As the funeral ended and we walked away from their graves, I couldn't help but think my parents were with the twins now. Maybe they weren't all buried together, but they were with each other in spirit.

And I couldn't help but think I wanted to join them, too.

3

Though we wanted to leave, Azalea House wouldn't allow it. It did everything it could to keep us there, as if it missed having visitors from back when it was a boarding house. Painted blood-red with large, blinding teeth-like columns, a grand front porch and a cupola that looked like a crown, the house felt alive.

Our grandparents decided that Julia, Troy and Vivienne were to move into Azalea House because it was "in our best interests." But what Ed and Lily really wanted to do was to forget this whole thing, to live out the rest of their lives splayed out under the sun, reading paperbacks and drinking gin and tonics.

On the day my aunt, step-uncle, and cousin were to arrive, I woke with the sun. I stood at the edge of our driveway, looking up the hill at Azalea House, shrouded by early mist. A new sense of doom filled me and twisted my heart.

Something rattled in the bushes, shaking the leaves in a moccasin cadence like a rattlesnake. I backed away, Azalea House in my peripheral vision, its murderous red exterior like a forewarning of more bloodshed.

The shaking stopped.

I swallowed and called out, "Hello?"

A titter of quiet laughter followed. I walked in the opposite direction, to my right, into the garden. I always found peace in the garden, as if Momma was there and still tending to her beloved plants.

The plantings and flower arrangements around the property created a jewel-filled necklace around Azalea House; red, purple and pink, so strategically placed, a dizzying kaleidoscope of colors. Marcus complained about the constant perfume, claiming they made him drunk. On bright spring days, I knew what he meant. Sometimes the scent was so intense, I had to retreat to the woods escaping into the piney clean aroma to reset my palette.

Momma had planted roses in a myriad of colors and shapes and sizes. Instead of lining out scores of them with their own name tags like grave markers, she let them grow wild along the picket fences. Their fragrance was intoxicating and heavy. Purple wisteria climbed up trellises and arches, creating royal entrances to different parts of the gardens. My favorite were the gardenias, which Momma so painstakingly kept free of insects. In the summer, the pearly white buds would unfurl like seashells, then explode into thick, smooth petals that burst with an exhilarating perfume. Everywhere one looked in the garden, something bloomed, no matter the time of year or weather.

I entered and sat down on one of the stone benches. The chilly air defied the hot summer day. The shade of the garden required one to wear sleeves, even during the hottest hours. I inhaled the garden's ancient mossy fragrance, the smell of an old back corner of a forgotten cemetery, where lichen grew upon the graves and ivy tendrils crept across stone angels. From the corner of my eye, one of the tendrils twisted like a snake. When I looked, ready to flee, it was a mere leafy tentacle, still as the air.

The wind chimes sounded, and footsteps pattered from behind a wall of green.

"Who's there?" I asked. Breathy giggles suggested not one person, but two.

"What do you want to tell me?" I asked, trying to summon the twins, while hoping they would stay hidden. They often made their presence known in sickening and sometimes shocking ways, like leaving muddy footprints or smears of food behind. I supposed that was the way of two five-year-old boys.

The silence broke as a tug on my hair yanked me backwards. When I turned around, the bushes shook like pom-poms.

"That's enough," I asserted, standing with my hands balled into fists. "Say something or leave me alone!"

After a few moments of silence, I opted to head inside and face my family's impending arrival. Marcus would be questioning my whereabouts if I didn't show.

As I exited the labyrinth garden, a trickle of blood led the way.

"Hello?"

A faint, keening noise responded. I tried to squint my eyes to avoid seeing it or to run past it, but it burned into my brain nonetheless. There at the exit were two doves, both with their heads missing. I ran inside as fast as I could.

Marcus and I sat with our grandparents until Aunt Julia, Troy, and Vivienne arrived. Granddaddy tried to make idle conversation around the breakfast table. He and Grandmere were wearing travel clothes, locked in denial about their dead daughter, ready to set out to the Bahamas as soon as my aunt arrived.

"Doing anything fun this summer?" Granddaddy asked, as if our parents hadn't died.

"Coping," Marcus said. He got up and tossed his cup in the sink and the clattering noise echoed throughout the house, disturbing the inhabiting spirits and shattering the awkward silence.

I took in all the little details of the house to distract me from my pounding heart. What would Julia do to this place? Would she take us away from here?

I knew something else besides the twins waited and watched from behind the screen of branches. I had no idea if it was the devil or something else, but everywhere there was sunshine and happiness, a glimmer of darkness lurked somewhere near it. When I watered the flowers, I sometimes caught a glimpse of blood on them. It gleamed so brightly, almost as if it was red wax, and the contrast on those white and pink flowers was dizzying. I would blink, only to see the blood disappear. And there was laughing beyond the trees, deep and sinister, not from a specific place but just all around the house. It felt to me as if the house was expressing itself.

Maybe it was the juxtaposition of souls that had come and gone there. Azalea House had seen its share of suicides, murders, robberies, and crimes that have been lost to memory with each passing decade. I once read stories about a haunted derelict hotel in Los Angeles that had seen many people pass through. Once the hotel got a taste of something bad, it thrived on it, as though the negative event were like a drug. People might find a story like that silly, but I knew exactly what they meant.

It did not matter how shiny I tried to make the objects in the house. It did not matter how many flowers I planted, how many light bulbs I changed. Azalea House still had dark corners that crept into the mind and made one see or hear things no human should experience. I had changed one bulb in the foyer where an angel statue sat, some old cemetery relic that came from New Orleans from the early 1700s. As soon as I finished, the bulb snapped. When I turned around, that godforsaken angel had a wicked grin plastered on its face, whereas before it was always serene and wistful. The longer I held its gaze, the more its smile widened until its face split in half and a black hand emerged from its mouth. As the spidery tentacle-looking fingers wiggled out, I blinked, and when I opened my eyes, the angel's face was once again serene and peaceful. But every time I changed that bulb, it rebelled and blew itself out.

Nothing could shake the strong presence that had its hold on the house. Its black threads infiltrated every corner of the property, and its grasp was so strong, I could feel its squeeze.

The stained-glass red and pink windows cast little Valentinelike kaleidoscope patterns on the marble floor. I did my best to avoid stepping on those little colorful projections. They looked too much like blood spatters to me. And outside, the wind chimes tinkled, as if they knew all my secrets and were whispering them back to me. They had, after all, the best view of the house from all four corners.

We had the largest house in the whole area. The rest of the village had a smattering of old swamp homes or trailers, so our house was out of place, yet such a large part of the little fishing village's history hinged upon Azalea House.

The house was built in the 1800s with lathe-shaped wooden forms and complex, almost jigsaw-shaped intricacies. The posts and railings had unusual wooden designs and curved brackets and scrolls were placed at the corners. The building had served as a store and briefly as the village courthouse before someone bought it in 1900 as a gift to my great Aunt Betty, an eccentric but locally famous musician who turned it into a lively boarding house that operated until the fifties. When she died, my grandfather and my other uncles inherited it and decided to sell it, but after Granddaddy was the last man standing, he regretted his decision. He recalled the times he spent there with great nostalgia.

"Your great Aunt Betty was such a wonderful storyteller. And she played guitar, and shaped those stories into songs," he would tell me with a certain misty recollection in his blue eyes.

I had once found a picture of a group of people sitting on the porch of Azalea House and brought it to Momma.

"Oh, that's your Great Aunt Betty," she told me. Betty was dressed in a frilly, long-sleeved white number and a wide-brimmed hat that shaded her eyes and gave her a very mysterious quality. She was poised with her guitar. I imagined her fingertips had hardened just like Daddy's from strumming all day, entertaining guests.

I could not imagine that Aunt Betty, my Momma, and myself were all from the same stock. I was so quiet, it was as if my family used up all the words in songs, and there were none left for me to speak.

"I so wish I would have been able to meet her," she lamented. "She was a musician, like me. And your father. But I feel like she lives on in this house. We wrote the Wild Hearts album here, your Daddy and me and the rest of the band. Finished it in less than a month. So I feel she is here with us even now, helping us."

I had gasped in fear at that thought. "This house is haunted, isn't it, Momma?" I asked her.

She laughed in the same way she always did when something struck her as funny—closing her eyes and throwing back her head like it was pure ecstasy to hear something so hilarious.

"Not all ghosts are bad, sugar."

"But some are?"

For some reason, she never answered that question.

Granddaddy sold the house to a rabid teddy bear collector who filled it with bears of every size, shape, and color. He was gay, and his partner moved in with him after a year, which apparently caused quite the stir in the village. When the famous members of Spellbound Hearts offered him a pretty penny for the house, he happily packed up his bear collection and moved back to San Francisco.

So the old home was back in the family once again. But since our parents died, the fate of the house was up in the air.

After their deaths, I spent many days just wandering the property, numbly soaking up the warmer spring days until the sharp decline into summer, which was right around the corner. Grandmere Lily and Granddaddy Ed moved in temporarily until a decision could be made about what to do with us, but I certainly didn't want to go back with them to Arkansas. Grandmere still resented us because in her mind, we weren't as perfect as the twins. I knew life with her would be miserable with her constant nitpicking and snide comments. Granddaddy would try to make it tolerable, sure, but I knew he wouldn't be successful. Grandmere was as mean as a snake, and everyone feared her fangs, even Granddaddy.

I got up from the table and put my breakfast dishes away.

"Go check on your brother," Granddaddy said behind his

coffee cup. I nodded. I could tell they didn't want to leave on a bad note; they expected us to be cheery and optimistic as they left for their vacation. I flashed him a quick smile to put his mind at ease.

I tapped on Marcus's door. "Marcus? Do you want to go outside?"

The door swung open, and he emerged, dressed and ready. Together, we escaped the cool confines of the house.

Marcus and I usually spent a lot of time in the woods, but it was rare for us to do that in the summers. Going outside was often too brutal, but the harsh reality of a home without Momma and Daddy was even more so. So, we sweated it out in the surrounding woods and swamps around Azalea House.

The swamps vibrated with life. Spiders, bugs, and creepy crawly things made the tall grasses shiver. Marcus loved to check on them to make sure they were well, and any creature that didn't seem so went straight to the makeshift animal infirmary in his room.

The summers got meaner and muddier from the flash torrential storms that rolled through, and all the swamp things were hyper vigilant and angry. I believed it was because the sun damn near drained the life force out of every living creature and left them starving for something. Everywhere I went, mud sucked hungrily at my shoes, insects accosted me, and films of sticky spiderwebs covered my body when I walked, as if the swamp was trying to keep me from escaping.

The woods were not much of a retreat, but we managed to make things more hospitable. There was a vine that hung down like a cradle, and we could sit in it and swing. Sometimes the pond was a welcome relief from the heat, too, but it scared us that year. It was snake infested because Daddy wasn't there to control the population, so there were dozens and dozens of them, sometimes intertwined together or slicing through the swampy waters like fairy tale sea serpents from my books. It made it all seem so alive, like the swamp was one big living creature.

Marcus and I took some sort of comfort in that. The hot

swamp, with its sickly-sweet allure, was at least alive. And when we found out Julia, Troy, and Vivienne were going to be moving in with us, we started making the woods our home away from home.

Julia lived in a deteriorating condo in the city and deemed it too small. I was sure she knew if she sold our parents' house, she could buy anything she wanted. So they moved in with us.

Marcus and I walked around the trails three times before we were both soaked in sweat.

"Let's go back," I said. Marcus just looked at me, his eyes dark. "Let's get it over with. Then we can come back out." He followed me, and as Azalea House came into view, we heard gravel crunching under car tires.

4

We sat in the living room with my grandparents, as Aunt Julia, Troy, and Vivienne walked in. My heart sank as their luggage hit the floor. Aunt Julia immediately started babbling to Troy about the things she would change.

"It's way too dark in here," she said. She complained the dark corners and intricate details would be such a pain to clean, and she didn't like the style of this or the way that looked. Momma would be so heartbroken to know all the hard work she'd put in this place would be undone. Julia seemed committed to erasing her memory.

The greed in Julia's eyes lit the marble, the copper, the statues on the property. I was sure she was assessing their value and how it would calculate into a new car or clothes. Vivienne copied her every move, following her mother's eyes, studying her cunning ways. They were so alike, especially in the way they appraised you like you were some sort of antique. Valuable or worthless? Their eyes would let you know in an instant.

Troy stared at the floor, dazed. I inched forward until my shoes were in his frame of vision, then his eyes drifted up my legs, my hips, waist and breasts...and there they lingered. I crossed my arms over them. I dressed in baggy clothes that day, yet he still stared. The obvious way he did it angered me. My face grew hot and sweat pooled at the band of my sports bra. I caught his eyes and he flushed, too.

Vivienne's eyes darted around to every little collectible thing, her perfect lips quirked up into a devilish smirk, her dark eyes gleaming with mischief. I could see the fire sale in her eyes.

Troy seemed passive and resigned, and when he did look at us, I caught a glimpse of softness in his eyes as he saw us, our eyes still red and puffy with loss.

My father had created those labyrinths in the dense woods for my brother and me to hide from each other and play chase. But as the years went on, we used them to escape when family came to visit. And once my grandparents left on that hot June day, it was the first place we intended to go.

I nudged Marcus. We loped out of the house while Julia, Vivienne, and Troy settled into our Azalea House.

Marcus and I walked with a dreadful, silent communication between us. No amount of talking would make this better: Julia, Vivienne, and Troy were living with us now. And that meant we would have to endure an entire summer with Vivienne torturing us, and maybe my aunt as well. The only thing we could do was walk underneath the hot, shaded pine needle-laced sky and draw strength from the "friendly" ghosts here.

"No one is looking out for us, Marianne," Marcus said, breaking the silence. His words cut through the humid air like a machete. I already knew what he said was true, but his saying it out loud solidified our new reality.

We were getting close to the twins' graves. In the South, it wasn't unusual to bury relatives on an estate. But it *was* unusual that no one said much about the twins.

I had seen ghosts here. I had heard them. And I had told Marcus all about them. He listened with some interest, but now I knew he could tell I was thinking about contacting our parents, bringing them back from the dead, or something too weird, too esoteric for him.

I knew it terrified him. And it terrified me, too. But just like everything dark about life, I had to open it up and look inside it. Marcus was more likely to leave the dark elements alone, but I couldn't look away. His world was down here on earth, taking care of the local critters and learning everything he could about computers. My world, on the other hand, was full of fantasies, books, writing stories, and painting pictures. And the ghost stories of Azalea House helped fuel my world.

Though there were happy stories about Azalea House, there were many horrific ones, too.

There were travelers who had committed suicide here, back when it served as a boarding house. People passing through or getting away from something felt they had run out of options, and this was their last stop. There were also many others who were chased down in vengeance, who had run off with a lover, or with someone else's money and paid the price.

The story that terrified me the most was that of the twins. They had never been touched by an adult's filthy hand, and they were not moody like me. They could speak eloquently even at a young age.

But they died when they were only five years old.

Then my parents had me.

And three years later, they had my brother.

It was a mystery to my brother and me—how had they died? If they spoke so well and were so vivacious one minute, how could they be dead the next?

Once at school, I had dredged up an article that they were kidnapped and murdered by one of the gardeners at the house, Carter Leblanc. He was in jail for his crimes, and no one else spoke of the twins. There was a faint black-and-white photo of the twins in the newspaper article. The photo Momma gave the newspaper was of the two identical boys hunched down, playing with the same Tonka trucks.

The only things my parents would reveal is that we had twin brothers who had passed away before we were born. But in the attic, there was a half-finished playroom. The walls were not up yet, the bathroom wasn't finished, and my parents eventually used it for storage. My brother and I would dare each other to go up there alone, but we never did. The only time we'd ever go in there was with each other.

We knew the twins were buried on the southwest corner of the property. To get there, we had to meander through the labyrinth of paths, and then forge our own trail through the dense patch of pine trees and blackberry bramble. There, in a little clearing, were two small white pillars marking their graves, each with a little angel with wings carved into the headstone. There was nothing else to indicate who they were, when they were born, or when they died.

I waited until after my thirteenth birthday to ask about the twins again. This time, I was sure Daddy would tell me more.

"Daddy, how did the twins die?" I asked. My cheeks flushed and my palms dripped with sweat. I had to know.

My father had been driving us through the blackberry bramble in our tractor. We were supposed to pick berries for a pie Momma was making. After I asked, my brother shot me a look of disapproval.

"You shouldn't ask questions like that, dear," Daddy said, but he didn't look at me.

"But why not?"

"It hurts your Momma's feelings to remember those things. But the twins are gone, and you and your brother are here now, and all is well. Don't worry about the twins, because that is in the past and the past is gone. Okay?"

"Okay, Daddy."

But that conversation never satisfied me.

Marcus and I walked through the labyrinth twice before I realized it. When we reached the corner of the property where the twins were buried, I took the narrow, marsh grass lined path to the graves. The ground was low on the path, but the twins were buried in a high spot. Momma and Daddy were both familiar with the lay of the land, and so was Aunt Betty, apparently. Momma had the twins buried in this spot so their graves wouldn't become saturated with water and come out of the ground, like coffins sometimes did down in New Orleans or other parts of the swamp that were below sea level. And Aunt Betty knew damn well the front part of the property down by the road was low-lying, so she always made sure she had a pirogue ready when it flooded so she could pick up guests arriving at Azalea House.

"Marianne, why do you want to go back there?" Marcus asked. There was a strain in his voice. Marcus didn't care too much for going off trail unless he was assisting some animal, and he didn't dilly-dally outside as much as I did. He didn't care for going through the mud on his crutches, and he didn't like the marsh grass stinging his skin as he walked. He swatted away an insect.

"Go back home if you want," I said. But I knew he wouldn't. He was always by my side. Part of it was growing up together and the fact that I helped Marcus when his crutches got stuck, or he needed help getting around. He followed me out of habit.

We walked for what seemed like another hour, but the high Louisiana heat had a way of doing that to anyone outside in the sun's wrath. The cicadas' mating call rose and fell, a cacophony of white noise. In front of me in the high grass, things jumped and slithered. Finally, we arrived at a slight clearing where the ground was higher, and the sweet relief of shade greeted us. There were two large white oaks towering above us, their leaves and branches screening the bright sky.

I cleared grass and old dead leaves away from the twins' graves.

"Marcus," I said. I breathed in heavily. The air was so thick it was like water was catching in my lungs. "Do you think Carter Leblanc really killed the twins?"

"That's what the news article said," he said as he dusted mud off his jeans. "And Momma and Daddy never liked to talk about it much. There are a lot of rumors going around all the time about it, though. Like Carter Leblanc was framed. Or the twins are still alive but were abducted by rabid fans."

"What?" I asked, alarmed. Could that last one be true? I had not heard that one before.

Marcus shook his head and adjusted his glasses. "I doubt that's true. But there's probably more to it. Maybe Leblanc demanded a ransom or something. Who knows? It's in the past."

"I want to talk to them on the Ouija board," I said, but more to myself.

"Ha! I knew it." Marcus shook his head.

"Not to talk to Momma and Daddy," I said. "To talk to the twins."

Marcus gave me a long look. His eyes seemed even larger and bluer through his glasses.

"Okay, Marianne," he said. "But no weird shit." He wagged a finger at me. "And I want to do this in the house. It's too hot out here."

I shrugged and turned to go back to the house. Marcus followed. We opened the door and crept through the shadows, trying to avoid making too much noise. The television in the other room blasted some interview with my parents' old band mates. I put my hands over my ears and trudged off to my room. The drummer and the bassist were nice enough guys, but I didn't want to hear any stories about my parents right now—at least, not from non-family members.

I closed the door, put the blanket over the crack and pulled the board out. Marcus lit a white candle and we settled in. We put our fingers on the planchette and looked at each other. It had been a while since we had done this, well before our parents died.

"Who is here?" I asked.

The planchette shuddered. I stared at it. My eyes shifted over to the candle. It danced in the still air.

"Who is here?" I asked again.

Three small movements forward, then the planchette shot across the board so fast, our fingers fell off.

But it kept moving.

U-S, it spelled out.

"Fuck this," Marcus said. He reached for his crutches. "I'm out."

"Marcus!" I hissed. My heart was still pounding. "Wait! Please."

He turned back to me. "Marianne," he said. "That thing was moving without us! Nothing like that has ever happened to us before. And a lot of weird things have happened with that board."

I knew what he meant. He was referring to the first time he and I had talked to the twins on the board. When they explained who they were, we asked them for proof. It was quiet for a time, but footsteps approached and when we crouched down and looked through the crack underneath the door, there were two pairs of identical blue sneakers there, just like I had seen with Chloe. I didn't dare open the door. It was proof enough for me.

Marcus also knew about the board coming back after Momma threw it away. He wasn't there, but he believed me. Those were the two most prominent incidents so far. There had been giggling and knocked over objects, but those two incidents floored us.

"Just come and sit down. Nothing will happen."

He gave me an unreadable expression and gently set his crutches down and settled back into his spot. He cracked his knuckles before placing his fingers back on the planchette.

R-I-N-G, the planchette quickly spelled out.

I looked at Marcus. He shrugged.

"Momma's ruby ring?" I guessed.

Y-E-S.

"She lost it over Christmas."

Marcus nodded. "Where is the ring?"

It took a long time for them to spell out the answer, but it didn't surprise me one bit.

V-I-V-I-E-N-N-E-B-O-X.

We didn't get to look for the ring for a few days since there was so much hustle and bustle going on with the move. I had never seen so many articles of clothing in my entire life. Their wardrobes took up entire bedrooms, and Julia already had an architectural specialist come out. There were people measuring, holding up swatches of color, and chattering.

We both retreated to our rooms and didn't come out until we were starving. It was morning, and the air was on full blast. I shivered as I got out of bed, and, putting on my robe, slipped out the door and into chaos.

Momma had all these chandeliers restored from Azalea House. Someone came out, took them down and cleaned them, painstakingly polished them and replaced fixtures and crystals. Julia had those replaced with track lighting.

"What is this crap?" Marcus asked, gesturing at the lights. He was also in his robe, but he had more of a princely air about him with his spectacles and grand gesticulating.

"It's track lighting," she said, her glasses perched on the tip of her nose. "It's very modern."

"It makes this look like an autopsy table," Marcus said, bending down to run his hands over the plain white coffee table in the middle of the room. "And you painted it…"

"It's beige," she finished for him. "What else do you children want?" She called us "you children" even though Vivienne and I were about the same age.

"You're replacing all the stuff in here, but what about the gardens? Why not have someone come out and maintain it, at least?"

"That's a good idea," she said with a slight sneer. "Why don't you two take care of that?"

"Are you serious?" Marcus swung one of his crutches across the room in an arc, nearly whacking the coffee table. Terror flashed in Julia's eyes. "With these?"

"Your sister will help. Now, run along."

Being outside all day wouldn't be so bad, so I pulled at Marcus's robe sleeve, and he and I went to our rooms to get dressed.

"I'm not doing this shit, Marianne." He clomped down the stairs behind me.

"We can wait until the evenings, avoid them at dinner and work out there while it's cooler," I said. "Come on."

We made our way through the foyer. I rifled through a stack of mail while Marcus sat down and pulled his shoes on. I flipped through and opened a few Hallmark condolences that all said the same thing. Bills still in Daddy's name went into another pile. Just seeing his name had me choked up again.

Seeing a letter addressed to Julia from Greener Pastures Christian Boarding School tightened my throat even more. I flipped it over and showed it to Marcus.

"Open it."

There was a brochure inside, advertising it as a premier Christian boarding school for teens in crisis. I sat next to Marcus as we scanned it. The husband-and-wife proprietors wore plastered-on, ultra-white grins. I put my finger over their mouths and couldn't tell from their eyes if they were scowling or smiling.

Marcus and I read in silence. The brochure mentioned equine therapy, nature-based therapy, and reparative therapy. I glanced at Marcus. He had a dead, vacant look in his eyes. He was still grief-stricken, but there was something about his expression that made me want to wipe it away, as if it would be easy, like cleaning smudges from the windows.

I balled up the brochure and threw it in the trash.

Outside, as we pulled weeds silently, Marcus in a cool spot in the shade and me out in the last rays of the bright summer afternoon sun, I wondered about what the house would look like with years and years of Julia's decorating touch. Momma had bent over backwards to have it maintained as it was, and now Julia was modernizing it with things she thought were trendy but would be obsolete in months.

I hated going in the house now. Everything was ultra-frilly and floral from the patterned window treatments to the bottoms of the chairs, kind of like it was her antidote to how grungy we were. There were plates, little trinkets everywhere with colorful accents. I was sure the garden would be enough, but Julia made sure to inject it in every corner of Azalea House now. And she wanted to put in carpet, too.

"We have to stop this, otherwise she's going to take over our rooms next," Marcus said while yanking up weeds with gusto. I just stared at him, unbelieving. "You think I'm joking? You better lock your door. Otherwise, your room is going to end up with the Laura Ashley treatment."

I couldn't imagine my dark bedroom brightened by Pepto Bismol pink paint, but Julia would do it just to spite me. My bedroom was me, with a plain white down comforter, hardwood floors, a purple medallion rug and my own wild abstract watercolors scattered about on the walls. I could daydream in there for hours, a real escape from our reality. It wasn't the woods, but it was the second-best thing I had.

"I'm thirsty," Marcus said, swiping at his brow. "Let's go inside."

We came up on the door as the light began to change from sunny yellow to faded lilac. When I turned the handle, it didn't budge.

"It's locked," I said more to myself. I rang the doorbell and listened. There was a faint murmuring of the television coming from the depths of the house, but no footsteps. I rang it again.

When I turned, Marcus had a knowing look on his face. "She did that on purpose," he said, slipping into his best nasally Julia imitation, continued, "If you don't like the house, fine. I'll lock you out."

I pounded on the door.

"I'm really thirsty," Marcus whined in his usual tone. I suggested we just sip out of the hose since it was clean well water anyway, so Marcus followed me across the gardens.

"It's pretty out here at sunset anyway," I said as we wiped our mouths.

Marcus shot me a look of mock disgust. "You always try to make light of any situation, don't you? She locked us out of our own house."

He was right, as usual. I sat on the garden bench and gazed out at the woods as the sparkle of fireflies lit up the black silhouettes of the trees.

Momma was into the esoteric, and sang about it in her songs, often writing dictation from seances. Gossip columns ate it up, but the '70s and '80s were well into the age of Aquarius and it was becoming more accepted. Still, the things she would tell me seemed intimidating. She told me I could change the weather or always materialize something in my life, so long as I remembered my own potential. I tried to find books about it at the library, but they were scarce. Not having Momma around as a guide made my vision blur with tears, so I tore my gaze away from the dark woods.

What did it mean to materialize things in my life? Had Momma known she was going to die young? She knew I had a sixth sense–I proved it to her that day I told her I knew about the twins. Had she died to get away from me? Was she as afraid of my power as I was of hers?

"Let's go in through my window," Marcus said. "That way, we don't have to face them. I'm pretty sure I left it unlocked."

I followed him through the lengthening shadows of the garden to a great flowering Gardenia bush that always reminded me of a body wash Momma used. She always smelled of gardenias. She must have loved that scent so much. She had a bush planted right next to her bedroom window, so she could open it, allowing the white scent to flow into the room. But now, the flowers had a faint rotting stench, musty and rich.

Marcus fiddled with the window until it swung open with a loud shrieking sound. We were both covered in a thin sheen of sweat with little pinpricks of grass and stickers. Outside, in the woods, I swore I heard a thin peel of children's laughter.

Surely, the twins weren't the ones to lock us out. It had to have been Julia or Vivienne, and if confronted, they would claim it had been a mistake.

I left Marcus to brood and shower while I strolled the hallways, taking in the final decorative accouterments left behind:

Momma's antique lamps, the Persian rugs, the baroque themed Gothic furniture, and her purple Victorian lounger that she used to sit on to read. Sometimes she'd be there for hours, reading and writing down little things in her notebook, then staring out the window at the woods with a wistful expression on her face. Who or what was she thinking about? When we would ask, she said she found inspiration in books for her songs.

She read a lot of romance, the kind with the buff guys with long hair on the front, as well as Gothic novels. When I read a few of those books and looked back over Momma's lyrics, it made sense. The band was sort of synth-goth, so I imagined she drew inspiration from the wooded surroundings and all those dark romance novels.

Julia would get rid of all of it. I thought about trying to hide things to save them. If I begged her, she might have let us keep a couple of things. But by God, she was redecorating this house, and she intended to get rid of all the dark Victorian details and 'spruce it up.'

I worried about our future with Vivienne lurking about and Julia as the mastermind of everything, the one with the husband who wasn't much older than us.

Julia and Vivienne were the cleverest allies. We were getting locked out of the house more often during those hot summer days. Vivienne would lock the door so we couldn't get in, and Julia would say something like, "Oh, goodness, I totally forgot that you were outside." Something in the way her overlined lips quirked up into a little smile and the way her eyes narrowed revealed that she enjoyed it.

Besides Vivienne sneering at me constantly, my aunt would always buy three of everything—or just enough for three. Troy would often say he was going to save his for later and would instead split it in half and divide it between Marcus and me.

Those days we were locked out of the house were the worst. We banged on the doors and windows. Troy was drinking so much he often passed out, while Julia watched television or read her trashy romance novels. Vivienne would sit in her bedroom, peering out the stained-glass window, laughing at our desperation. She had nothing else to keep her occupied during those longest summer days. There were no modeling gigs for her, so she delighted in tormenting us. We had to drink out of the garden hose. Our stomachs growled and sweat pooled in crevices we didn't know we had.

And the insects outside were overwhelming. It seemed the bugs were at their fullest prehistoric size by August, bounding around with such vigor that they would fly at Marcus's face. They never bothered me. I declared myself Queen of the Dragonflies one day while the sun dipped down past the overgrown lawns, a hundred or so blue and green iridescent bodies floating around me. Marcus just sat back and shook his head, baffled at how I let them land on me. But I lapped up any sort of positivity I could in those days.

And after I was drained of that, I searched for something else: Momma's ring.

5

"Don't do it."

"I'm just going to go in there and see if it's in her jewelry box, Marcus. That's it."

I crept down the hallway to Momma's old sewing room, which was now Vivienne's room. It was larger than my room and had an attached bathroom.

Vivienne still had clothes strewn everywhere. Gucci, Prada, Fendi—Julia obviously spared no expense dressing up her model daughter, and she made sure she was always dressed to the nines herself. That money had come from my parents, though. Julia made a decent income as an instructor, but it was not enough to afford the clothes they wore.

Marcus was too afraid of going inside, so I told him to wait for me in the hallway and be my lookout.

Vivienne had several jewelry boxes: one for bracelets, one for necklaces, and finally, one for rings. The ruby ring shone like a beacon, even in the darkness of Vivienne's room. I removed it and tip-toed out of her room. I wouldn't mention it until she did.

I flashed it to Marcus when I got out into the hallway, and he flashed a scowl of recognition. We went to his room.

"How did you know the ring was in there?" he asked once the door was shut.

I stared at him, befuddled. "What do you mean? The twins told us."

He gave me a sideways glance. "You're not trying to mess with me, are you? You didn't move the planchette yourself?"

My mouth fell open. "Of course not!"

He studied my face. "Okay. I believe you. But another promise: you won't conjure our parents. If they want to come through the board, fine. But don't summon them. It's too much for me," he said, his voice cracking. I had to hold back a fresh bout of tears. I dealt with my grief as best I could by crying in private, but the tiniest things would set me off again.

Days went by—hot ones that forced Marcus and me to remain inside. We kept quiet, woke before everyone else to grab breakfast, made our own sandwiches, and stayed up late after everyone went to sleep so we could eat leftovers. Julia didn't seem to care, and Vivienne just gave us the death glare if we came in contact with her, especially if House of Style was on and we dared to walk past the living room. We would often see her mimicking the models' movements on the screen as if she was a robot. Last year, she was on it once for about ten seconds twirling in some nearly see-through white bikini and it made her a local celebrity among kids our age. She was famous enough locally to get a few catalogue gigs, but so far, it was her biggest credit as a model.

Not long after the twins told us about the ruby ring, they told us about something else hidden away: a secret staircase.

A-T-T-I-C C-O-R-N-E-R, they spelled out on the board.

My brother and I climbed the stairs to the attic and went where the twins told us. He clung tightly to my side as I led the way. We stepped beyond where the wall should have been and carefully balanced on the floor beams to avoid the cotton-candy-like insulation. Once we reached the corner, I moved some of it aside with my shoe and shone my flashlight around.

There was a square outline on the floor. I used an old toy shovel to pry it up.

A plume of dust blew up into the air, and my brother and I both sneezed. Something shuffled in the darkness and my heart leapt in my chest. I turned the flashlight on. Sure enough, there was a staircase leading down into a dark abyss.

Why was this here if there was a main staircase that went into the attic? Was it the original staircase to the attic? Where did it lead?

I started down the stairs. Marcus gasped and grabbed the hem of my shirt.

"You're not going down there!"

I looked at him, confused. "Of course I am."

"But you'll leave me up here!"

"So come with me," I said with a shrug.

Marcus whined faintly and shuffled closer. He set his crutches aside and reached for me. I took his hand, and we descended the stairs together.

They seemed to go on forever, and at the end, there was nothing.

"There has to be a point to these," Marcus said. His voice trembled and I could tell he was trying to be brave. "Maybe they connected the rooms to each other when it was a boarding house?"

"Maybe Daddy added it in?"

"Daddy wouldn't just build a staircase to nowhere," Marcus said. "Everything he built had a purpose."

Marcus was right. I tapped on the wall in front of us and it sounded hollow. Marcus and I both glanced at each other. I felt around in the darkness and pressed the wall to see what would happen. Eventually, I found a space that wiggled. I pushed.

It was a door that opened into a dark hallway.

It was quiet except for squeaking sounds off in the depths of black. Mice, probably. I steadied my light, and we went on.

We ended up at a doorway with a crystal knob. I looked at Marcus before I opened it. His forehead was beaded with tiny sweat droplets, but his hand was like ice. I squeezed it. I wedged it open carefully, but it caught on something. Something soft.

Clothes? I focused the flashlight. Laundry—from my parents' closet. We were somehow in my parents' closet, which was now Julia and Troy's.

I moved carefully so as not to make noise. Marcus realized where we were and let go of my hand. It was dark except for a little sliver of light underneath the door that led to my parents' old bedroom. I could see some of Julia's stuff scattered around: her purses, her shoes, her clothes.

Did Daddy build the staircase up to the attic in case they needed a hiding space? Maybe Daddy made it so he could get up there quickly in case something happened. Maybe my parents forgot about it. Maybe it was here the whole time and Betty used it to easily go back and forth between rooms. Maybe Daddy didn't even know about this passageway?

What a strange sensation, almost like we were doing something illegal by being there. Now that we knew where it went, we'd have to go back out. Otherwise, Vivienne would find out what we were up to.

I ushered Marcus back to the staircase. He didn't budge.

"I don't want to go back out that way," he whined. I put my finger to my lips and grabbed his hand. I pulled the door closed and stayed quiet. We crept back up the stairs. Never had I been so happy to see the attic again.

"The twins are going to fucking *haunt* us, Marianne," Marcus said. I didn't like the sureness of his tone. It made my heart catch in my chest.

We went through the attic and out the door to the other staircase. When I opened the door, none other than Vivienne was on the other side.

"Oh, great. *You* again." Marcus rested his fingers on my back and gave me a light push, urging me to shove past her.

Vivienne put her hands on her hips. "What were you doing up there?" I hated the way she cocked her head to one side. I wanted to knock her head right off and see it go bowling down the stairs. I fantasized about the angle while Marcus did all the talking.

"Why are you always following us? Don't you have, like, boys to talk to?" Marcus pushed me a little harder, and I backed up against him. I was sure Vivienne would hit me soon. It hadn't happened since she moved in, but I knew it was coming. I sucked in a breath and scooted past her without much incident, but her little needle-like fingernails punctured me as I went down. It would likely bleed. Marcus stayed behind.

I pounded down the stairs and out the back door, knowing what would come next. Marcus probably planned to whack her with his crutches after he questioned her about Momma's ruby ring.

It was humid outside, misting and foggy.

I ran through the wet grass and into the fallen leaves covering the ground in rusty red and brown splotches. I ran over puddles and around ant piles and crawfish huts. The frogs sang a loud presence song, chanting for more rain.

I had to see if I could glean anything else from those graves. I'd dig them up to see if they were still in there if I had to. I had done it before. For some reason, speaking to them on the Ouija board made me feel connected to my parents, to their past. It was hard to believe they had lives before Marcus and I were born, but maybe if I uncovered more of their past, I could let go of their deaths.

Now there were two places we could keep secret from Vivienne: the graves (and most of the woods, Marcus would say) and the passageway in the attic. She must never know about the passageway.

I could run, kick and punch. Marcus could use his crutches and his wit. We each had something going for us.

I reached the graves nearly drenched, but my muscles tingled with relief after the sprint. I knelt in the wet grass and cleared weeds. I ran my hands over the gravestones as I tried to pick up anything, anything at all. I closed my eyes and let my mind go. Nothing yet. Maybe they really were there with us in the attic, guiding us, showing us the way.

A full moon was due, but the sun still shone fiercely through inky storm clouds, even though it was after four o'clock. I pulled up my sleeve and pressed a bit of blood from the wound left by Vivienne's fingernails, letting it trickle down my hands. I pressed my palms into the ground, hoping my blood would connect with them and bind us all together as siblings.

Trust us, I heard. *Trust us. Keep it a secret.*

A strange pang of missing them filled me, even though I never met them. They were dead, and maybe they were haunting us, but they helped us today. For what we needed the most in this situation was an advantage over Vivienne and my aunt, anything we could get.

When the three of them first came to live with us, I just wanted to run away. But afterward, I didn't want to leave the twins there. Something bound me to them, but we needed to get away at some point. What was I going to do with Vivienne and my aunt taking over the house? We had to convince them to leave. I was sure both Marcus and I wouldn't survive in boarding school. I silently said a prayer to the twins to protect us and show us the way, just like they had done by telling us about Momma's ruby ring and the passageway.

The rain picked up at some point, and now the scratches on my arm were bleeding more, the red running down my arms in little streams. It didn't matter to me. I believed the blood drawn by Vivienne, trickling down into the graves of the twins, would give me more power. I placed one hand on each grave and let the blood run down into the earth. I thanked them silently for what they had told us. I had a feeling the passageway would uncover more secrets in the future.

When the sun set and the bugs started bouncing around in the high grass, I decided to go back to the house.

There were media vans parked outside. Reporters were all crowded around the front, and my aunt was talking. I drew closer, hiding in the shadows until I could hear what was going on.

"I am saddened by Janelle and Abel's deaths," Julia said. I peeked around an old oak and could see she was dabbing her eyes with a silk handkerchief. "That's why I have come here to take care of their children."

Sure. I rolled my eyes.

"Will you be living at Azalea House permanently?" a reporter asked.

"For the time being. But as you know, this is an old house with a lot of history. There are so many terrible memories here, and I believe the children would benefit most by being in boarding school. They have been sheltered by their parents so much that they both have...*difficulties.*" She sobbed.

I clenched my fists. How dare she say that about Marcus and me. And boarding school?' So she was planning on sending us off to some Christian torture chamber, some place that would alter our identities and make us fall in line.

This house belonged to us. We couldn't leave the ghosts of Aunt Betty and the twins. Maybe my parents were still here, too. It seemed so wrong to leave the final resting place of the twins, and after so much work my parents put into this house, shouldn't it stay in the family this time?

"As you know," the reporter asked, "Carter Leblanc will soon be released from prison..."

"*What?*" my aunt proclaimed. Her face was no longer twisted with what I suspected was feigned sadness. There was a titter of conversation and gasps from the crowd of reporters.

"Are you worried about the safety of their children once Leblanc is released? Will you be sending the children to boarding school this fall?"

My aunt snapped her mouth shut and rolled her eyes around. "No, no, it would be too much of a shock to them right away. And why would we run? *I* am not afraid of that lunatic! Let him come here so I can show him what I think about what he did! He should be the one to leave, not us. We will leave when we're good and ready." My aunt nodded as if that settled it, but I could tell the reporter caught her off guard. Good. Any slight against Julia was a win in my book.

I ran back to the side of the house and tapped on Marcus's window. He opened it without looking.

"Marcus, you have to check to see if it's me before you open your window," I warned. "The media is outside."

He adjusted his glasses and stared at me. "I know. They're broadcasting it on MTV. Look," he said.

There was my aunt, and then Vivienne, looking self-righteous and trendy in her tight black jeans, Gucci belt, and new blouse. She must have spent hours straightening her hair, because it was shining underneath the media lights. Troy stood slightly out of frame, and I wondered if it was on purpose. My aunt had a serious expression with her pursed lips and narrowed eyes. She was dressed in some Alexander McQueen number.

"Oh my God," I said. "They don't even try to look humble."

"And there you have it," some reporter with perfectly sculpted eyebrows said to the camera. "Back to you, Hunter."

"Since the revival of Spellbound Hearts' music after the death of their founding members and their tragic history, Janelle Easton's niece, Vivienne Easton, has seen a surge in modeling jobs."

They flashed a picture of Vivienne in an obviously over-edited photo spread for some brand I had never heard of.

I rolled my eyes. "Is this for real?"

Marcus nodded. "People became enthralled with the story of the accident, then there was an interest in their music once again. And people are latching on to Vivienne because she's pretty or whatever. And it all just so happens to coincide with the release of Leblanc. Now you're up to date." He turned off the TV and looked back at me.

I put my hand over my stomach. I could not believe the media came all the way out here to interview my aunt about my parents. They would have hated the media showing up to their home. They rarely gave interviews at all, and Azalea House was their sanctuary. I didn't want it tainted with Vivienne's poisonous narcissism, and I didn't want my aunt capitalizing off our pain.

"I feel sick," I said.

"She's doing what she can to popularize this house and get interest from buyers, I'm sure," Marcus said. He reached under his desk and fiddled with something, resulting in a metallic clicking sound.

"But wasn't there a will?"

Marcus turned to me a pained expression on his face. He removed something brown and wiggly from under the desk. "I don't know. Either way, we're fucked," he said.

He had a female mallard duck in his hands.

"Where did you find her?" I asked. I wanted a break from thinking about the house and Julia.

I supposed that was why Marcus pulled out the duck—to keep me from getting too upset. He was always rescuing critters he found on our walks through the woods and swamp. At any given point, there were birds, kittens, lizards or various other living things he saved and brought back to life. I wondered if he would become a veterinarian one day, but he seemed to nurture the animals out of obligation, not passion.

"Out by the pond," he said as he checked a bandage on her foot. "She was caught in some blackberry bramble, but her foot looks better." The mallard clucked happily as Marcus stroked her. She seemed content and nuzzled the crook of his elbow. I smiled. Momma always loved that about Marcus and I wished she could have seen this.

But then again, I wished I weren't so nostalgic.

"She's going to sell this house and it'll be out of the family again," I said.

Marcus shrugged. "Maybe we could buy it back?"

I thought about it. "Maybe."

Marcus threw me a look. "Marianne," he said.

"What?"

He rolled his eyes. "Do you really want to stay here for the rest of your life? Don't you want to get out and explore the world? See what else is out there?"

"Sure I do. But I'm afraid. I can't talk and..."

"Of course you can talk. You're talking to me right now."

I shook my head and looked at my mud-caked shoes. "You know what I mean. It's safe here. It's what I know. The twins are buried here. And our parents loved it here. I kind of feel like it would, I don't know..."

"Keep them alive somehow?" Marcus looked pained again.

"I guess."

"I'd really like to get out of here. I barely need my crutches anymore and I want to go someplace where they won't beat the shit out of me for being different. We can hold them all in our minds, Marianne. But we can't keep things going for someone else."

I sighed. He was right, as usual, with his logic and common sense. What would I do around here in old age? Run a boarding house? Raise children? I couldn't even wrap my head around the idea of getting married, much less having the responsibilities of a boarding house and a family.

It was too much to think about. My head started to spin, and that queasy feeling came on again, so I changed the subject.

"How did you get past Vivienne on the stairs?" I asked.

"How do you think? Shoved her aside with these bad boys," he said as he gestured to his crutches.

"Did you get in trouble?"

He put the duck back in her cage, turned back to his computer and typed a few things. "No, but I assume it's coming at some point." There was a certain carelessness in his voice, which I was glad to hear. The less emotional he got about our situation, the better. I was emotional enough for the both of us.

I decided to go back out into the woods again before the last light faded. It was better to wait until everyone cleared out of the kitchen before going in there and getting something for Marcus and myself. I was less likely to encounter my aunt or cousin, who would always glare at me for being in the kitchen—*my* kitchen.

I felt like I wasn't allowed anywhere else in the house except my room. Vivienne and Julia had spread their stuff out in every room: there were bottles of nail polish, cosmetics, wine glasses, or little trinkets that told me they'd just been there. My stomach growled as the sun set through the pine trees. Another storm cloud opened and unleashed its fury on the Azalea House grounds. I walked back, my wet clothes clinging to my body.

6

I would likely have to find a way to sneak into Marcus's room, as I assumed he would surely be grounded for whatever ended up happening on the stairs. When I neared the house, I went to Marcus's window instead of going through the back door. I knocked lightly, and he opened the drapes briefly before opening the window and letting me in.

"I told Vivienne we were up in the attic talking to demons again. I don't think she'll dare go up there," he said. The room was draped in a curtain of incense smoke. Marcus had likely lit it to clear negativity out of the room.

"Aunt Julia came and talked to you?"

"Just talked. That was it."

"Just talked?" I was suspicious. Julia never 'just talked' to us about anything.

Marcus pushed his glasses up. I could see a little glimmer of mischievousness. "Having crutches isn't always a bad thing."

"Vivienne didn't bust her head open on the stairs or anything?"

Marcus sighed and shook his head. "Sadly, no. Just a bruised elbow and a knocked knee. She'll be fine, but I got sent here with no dinner, as usual. And Vivienne will be able to call all her friends and will get lots of sympathy, I'm sure."

"So you didn't eat anything?"

Marcus shook his head. I clenched my fists. Julia had Troy make these elaborate dinners for her, but they never shared with us. We had to scrimp around and eat cereal or nothing at all.

"Be back later," I told him. He went back to his computer and I crept out the window and around to the back door.

"Where the hell have you been?" my aunt barked as I walked in. Troy shrunk back in his chair. I noticed he was looking through a fashion magazine, and Vivienne was sitting very close to him.

"I was avoiding your daughter, as usual. We were trying to come down off the stairs and Vivienne scratched me," I said as I gave Vivienne the stink eye. She was trying to cozy up to Troy, probably to show off some salacious modeling photo.

"I didn't!" Vivienne let out a little pleading whine and looked at Troy for help.

"See?" I said and pointed to the scratches. "I'm not lying. She's always following us around and then makes a swipe at either me or Marcus. Marcus just retaliated." I turned to my aunt. "You really shouldn't send Marcus to his room without dinner. It's neglect."

My aunt turned red in the face and Vivienne wailed, "She probably did that to herself!"

Troy grabbed her hand. He glowered. "She's got blood underneath her fingernails, for Christ's sake!" Troy pushed her hand away and Vivienne glowered at him like he'd betrayed her in the most tragic way.

"Troy, do not take the Lord's name in vain," Aunt Julia said.

I looked my aunt dead in the eye. "I want a plate for me and one for Marcus. If you withhold food from him again, I'm calling child protective services."

Surprisingly, my aunt stepped aside, but not without an eye-roll first. I was so stunned for a moment that all I did was stand there in shock. Maybe the child protective services thing was a solid threat from now on.

I brought Marcus a plate and his eyes grew wide with astonishment. Not only had I brought him two helpings of everything, I'd managed to sneak a piece of cake on the plate as well.

"Wow! What'd you do, shove a knife in her face?"

"No," I said. "I threatened to call CPS."

"Good one," he said with a full mouth. God, he was so frail. As soon as he finished the plate and started on the cake, the color in his face returned. Still, his lanky arms stuck out at odd angles beneath his black t-shirt. If my aunt kept punishing him by withholding food over all these asinine things, he would waste away to nothing. I had to do something. Knocking Vivienne down the stairs looked like it drained all his energy.

As he stuck the last bit of cake in his mouth, I threw my arms around him. He tensed at first, then relaxed and put one of his skinny arms around my shoulders.

"It cannot go on like this," I said.

"I know."

"Tonight, when they get ready for bed, I'm going down the other stairs and I'm going to eavesdrop on what they say."

Marcus pulled away from me. He pushed his glasses back up his nose. "No, Marianne. You can't do that. What if you get caught?"

"Then I can at least say I tried."

"I'm going with you."

"No, Marcus. You stay here. Let me go down the stairs. I'm not afraid."

He looked a bit defeated, but he nodded.

I took his plate and left him to his computer stuff. I'd have to face Vivienne in the kitchen, but I somehow felt empowered with the knowledge left to us by the twins, the blood I'd shed on their graves, and the CPS threat.

She was waiting there for me at the kitchen table when I walked in.

"You and your faggot brother are going to pay."

"Don't call him that."

"Faggot! Faggot! Faggot! What are you going to do?"

I threw one of the plates at her head and it shattered into a thousand pieces right above her. She screamed. My aunt came running in.

"Moooooom! Marianne is trying to kill me!"

I didn't deny it. I did want her dead. God help me, I really did.

My aunt grabbed my arm. "You psychotic little bitch! You are going to clean up this whole mess right now, you understand? And the whole kitchen. Spotless!"

She dragged Vivienne out of the kitchen, but it was enough time for Vivienne to throw a sarcastic grin over her shoulder. I sighed and started on the kitchen.

Someone else was there, though. I turned and saw Troy watching me. He had a weird look in his eyes.

"Need some help?"

"Julia will kill you."

"I don't give a fuck about Julia."

I looked down at the ground because I couldn't decide what else to do. Troy walked over and loaded dishes into the dishwasher as I rinsed.

"I'm glad to see you and your brother finally standing up to Vivienne." His eyes undressed me. "Your clothes are still wet." He cast a brief glance at my nipples.

"I didn't have time to change," I said, and pulled my shirt away from my breasts. "Marcus was hungry."

"Let's finish up in here. I want you to bring him another piece of cake."

I looked down at Troy's shoes. "Julia is going to be really angry with me and Marcus if you're nice to us."

He stepped in closer towards me, so close his warmth and spicy scent enveloped me. "I told you," he said, taking another step closer, "I don't give a damn about Julia." He took me by the arms. My skin prickled into goose flesh. He pulled me in closer.

"I'm only nine years older than you are," he said.

"It still makes you too old. I'm sixteen. You're twenty-five. And you're my uncle."

"Not by blood," he said, his mouth mere inches away from mine.

"Troy," I said, staring him in the eyes, "let go of me. I want to finish cleaning and get back to my brother."

He huffed, let me go, and helped me finish the rest of the kitchen.

Exhausted, I tip-toed through the shadows and back to my brother's room. He had a black tent over his screen, and he typed furiously.

"What the hell are you up to?" I asked as I set the cake in front of him. He immediately began demolishing it.

"Hacking into Vivienne's Hotmail account," he said. "God, she is such a vacant and air-headed bimbo. She used 'Houseofstyle' as a password. She's too dumb to figure out the passageway."

"Shh!"

"What?" His mouth was so stuffed full of cake I could barely understand him. He slapped his hands together to dust them off, which sent a cascade of cake crumbs into the keyboard.

"Can I see?" I asked. He waved me over.

It looked like every other email I'd seen, except she'd sent naked photos of herself to about a hundred different agents. I doubted Julia approved, but she was a hypocrite when it came to Vivienne.

"How are you able to see all this?"

He just grinned at me, so I sneered back.

"Open that one," I said. The subject of the email was, "It sucks here."

Marcus read aloud, '"My Mother has gone totally crazy. I really wish I could have met my real dad. In a way, I'm glad my aunt and uncle are gone. I hated seeing Abel and Marianne so close. She doesn't even have to open her mouth and she gets everything.'"

Marcus paused and looked at me for a reaction. I didn't move, so Marcus continued reading:

"'When I talk, everyone gets upset. Marianne doesn't say a word and she gets everyone's attention. It makes me crazy, so I say things just to stir people. Everyone is attracted to Marianne. Even Troy likes her. I mean, he's married to my mom for God's sake.'"

Marcus let it simmer for a minute. I read the rest of the text on the screen, which droned on about modeling jobs, about being hungry, about wishing she were back in the city.

"My, I didn't realize she could think that deeply," Marcus said.

"Troy *was* looking at me like that again," I told Marcus.

"You look like you're trying out for a wet t-shirt contest on Bourbon Street, that's why."

I punched him on the shoulder, grabbed his plate and left.

We needed to get out of here. I still wasn't sure if what Julia said was true, if we'd get to go back to our regular schools in the fall. I hated thinking about being shipped off to some boarding school where I didn't know anyone, while Julia did God knows what to this place.

I brought the dishes back to the kitchen and tip-toed in the darkness. All was quiet. There was a large grandfather clock off in the living room, tic-tocking away the time, and wind chimes tinkled off in the distance outside. From the looks of it, Marcus and I were the only ones still awake.

I washed the dishes and turned back to go up to the attic, but something caught my eye in the reflection of the counter. Something in the foyer. Was it one of Marcus's rescued creatures? I crept in to look, ready to scoop up whatever beast was creeping around to return it to the safety of Marcus's room.

What was there, standing right in front of the door, caused me to clap my hand over my mouth. I fell to my knees. The hair on my arms stood up and every inch of my body broke out into cold goose flesh. When my eyes adjusted to the dark, it was like my muscles came unwound, and I wanted to simply pool into the floor and disappear.

The pale, almost lilac tone of their skin was the first thing I noticed. Then the smell hit me: putrid yet almost rosy, like someone was trying to cover up a terrible odor with some sort of flowery scent. The sickly-sweet smell of rot caused my stomach to roll, but I was glued to the floor, my knees like iron anchors.

The twins. Who else could they be? Their clothing, matching plain t-shirts with blue jeans and blue sneakers were faded and streaked with mud. The full moon shone through the front door and illuminated their features, which I wished I hadn't seen.

Under their eyes, there were dark violet half-moons, the same color as their lips. There were hollowed out pits where the eyes used to be. They were as still as mannequins.

I choked out some sort of half yelp.

They opened their mouths simultaneously, as if to scream, but all that emerged was a low croaking sound, gurgly and wet, like their throats were blocked. The sound was so terrifying I wrenched myself up off the floor and bolted up the stairs.

I resisted the urge to barge into Marcus's room. Vivienne might hear the door, and I didn't want to scare the life out of Marcus. I knew it would render him sleepless. I decided to wait until morning.

But morning couldn't come soon enough.

I hurried to my bed and wrapped myself in the covers, shivering from shock. Just when I began to tell myself I had hallucinated, that gurgly wet sound returned. At first, it was so faint I thought it was my own mind playing it back in a loop to scare me into insomnia. But the sound got louder, like it was coming up the stairs.

There was nowhere for me to go, and my body tingled with electricity. That sprint from the foyer to my bedroom caused every muscle to wake up, and adrenaline still coursed through my veins. I could run, but where? The strange sound was right outside the door. I closed my eyes and put my hands over my ears. If I waited long enough, they would leave me alone and I could sleep.

I stayed that way until my eyelids were sore and my ears ached. I let my hands drop. The only sound was the hum of the air conditioner.

I listened. I opened my eyes and looked around the room. End of the bed, dresser, desk, rocking chair—all of it seemed normal. Shrouded in darkness, yes, but normal.

The air conditioning cycle ended. I could not hear the wind chimes.

There was that sound again. This time, it was *in* the room.

It was a death rattle, followed by shuffling sounds.

I looked around the dark room, frantic. I caught that stench again.

"Leave me alone," I croaked. I curled myself up into a ball.

And then they were there, both identical little rotting dolls, their jaws open into dark maws. Something thick and viscous poured out of their mouths in a torrent, something that resembled the black swamp mud we kicked off our shoes at the end of the day.

When they reached for me, I screamed.

I don't know how long I screamed, but my throat was raw. Troy burst in and flicked on the lights and it seared my vision and disoriented me; I wasn't sure how everyone else in the house ended up in my room.

I was shaking and sweating, my arms and legs numb. I had such a surreal synesthesia experience, all I wanted to do was shut my eyes. Every time there was a noise, my brain associated it with a color for some reason. The only pleasant color was blue, and I concentrated until I realized it was Marcus talking.

"You just have to accept it. Like a Chinese Finger Trap. Don't fight it or that will make it stronger," he said. There was pressure on my hand valley point, and my eyes focused to see it was Troy. Marcus was talking me through it. I started to breathe deeply, but the tremors still carried on.

"Just a nightmare," Troy said to Julia. My eyes had adjusted to the light enough to notice Julia was making a face, and Vivienne was behind her, laughing.

"It wasn't a nightmare!" I shouldn't have said anything. My voice sounded thin, hysterical. I put my hand over my mouth.

"Marianne," Marcus warned. I didn't want to give anyone else any indication Marcus and I were fooling around on that board.

"Okay, whatever," my aunt said. I could tell by the look in her eyes she resented the fact I had interrupted her beauty sleep. "Troy, let's go back to bed."

Troy followed suit. He turned and gave me one more concerned look over his shoulder before disappearing. Marcus and Vivienne lingered in the doorway.

"Poor crazy Marianne, losing it after her rich parents died," Vivienne said with a sarcastic grin. "Tsk-tsk. It's really too bad. Maybe Mom needs to send you off to a mental institution."

"Shut the fuck up, Vivienne, or I'll tell Julia about the ring you stole," Marcus interjected.

Vivienne's facial expression changed from sardonic to shock. She lifted her eyebrows in feigned innocence.

"Stole? I *found* a ring..."

Marcus shook his head. "No, you didn't. You stole it, you greedy little whore."

"What did you do with it?" Vivienne barked. Now she was angry.

"That was Momma's. We took the ring back and hid the rest of the jewelry in a place you'll never find because you're too stupid. Now slink back to your room." Marcus shooed her away with his crutches. Vivienne pushed them away, and they clinked against the door frame.

"You both just wait until school starts," she said. She flashed a look at me before retreating to her room.

"We know about everything that happens in this house, you vacant-headed bitch," Marcus called out after her. I was really stunned at how quickly he had stood up to her. He didn't seem to care if he pissed Vivienne off. Her door slammed.

"What happened?" he asked me.

"I saw something. The twins." I could see his eyes searching my face. For a minute, I could tell he wondered if what Vivienne said was true: did I really need to go off to a mental institution? "I really did," I said.

"Is it possible you're just stressed and you were dreaming? Maybe knowing Leblanc is getting out has you thinking about what really happened."

"No," I said as I shook my head. "I was standing up in the kitchen when it happened. I saw them in the foyer. I came upstairs and they followed me here."

"That sounds scary," he said. He tromped over to the bed and sat down. "Are you alright?"

I nodded.

"Maybe we should hold off on talking to them?"

"I think it was a sign to keep going," I said. "They want to talk. That's why they've been helping us. They told us where Momma's ring was. They told us about the passageway. They came to me looking horrid, to tell me something about how they died. There's a reason for that."

Marcus fidgeted. His eyes darted around the room. Did he believe me? The last thing I needed was everyone in this house thinking I was crazy.

"You've been keeping up with everything," I said. "Why is Leblanc getting released?"

Marcus shrugged. "He did his time and got out on parole. There wasn't a lot of evidence, anyway."

"What do you mean? I thought the news article I read said the police found the twins' bodies in the trunk of his car?"

"The cause of death was drowning. So that means even if he did kidnap them, he didn't kill them. They think they died when the floodwaters came and swept the car away. There were no other injuries."

"You've been reading about this," I said. I had to admit I was flabbergasted. Every time I brought up the twins, Marcus changed the subject. So he really *was* interested in this whole case.

"I also think that he was arrested and convicted because he's an outcast." Marcus shrugged. "It's just a hunch. But maybe that's why you're seeing them. Maybe you're right, maybe that's why they've been talking to us."

"Then who do you think did it?"

He shrugged. "Joseph."

I hugged my knees to my chest. "No."

"Yes. Daddy always said he was trying to swindle money. He told me that before the twins were born, Joseph asked him if he wanted to rob a convenience store. He's a criminal, Marianne. Look at what he does to you."

I blinked, still processing that bit of information.

"Maybe it was an accident and Julia helped him cover it up. She's always standing up for him."

I couldn't think of anything to say. If Carter Leblanc was jailed for a crime he didn't commit, and our drunk asshole of an uncle was responsible, then the twins haunting us made some sense.

"You've been isolating a lot," he said. "It will cause more trouble for you when you go back to school."

"I know," I said. My throat began to close.

"Well, I've got some good news. Trixie laid some eggs a while back," he said, his expression shifting into pure delight. "They're due to hatch any day now."

"Your duck?" My throat relaxed again. I guessed I made some sort of face when my throat closed up and Marcus was accustomed to it over the years. He always knew when to change the subject to something lighter.

"Yes!" he said. I smiled at the excitement in his voice. "So we'll have some baby ducklings for the pond. I wonder if we could find someone to help clear out all those snakes. Anyway, get some rest and come in and see the eggs in the morning."

He hugged me, and we stayed like that for a minute. The summer days were so long lately, and the grief still gnawed at my heart like little worms. I was exhausted, so as Marcus closed the door, I curled up. With thoughts of a clean, serene pond and cute baby ducks swimming around in my head, I was finally able to drop off to sleep.

But my dreams were plagued with ghosts. Bloated, cold fingers reached out for me in the darkness. I tossed and turned. I replayed Momma and Daddy's death in my head until I had a clear picture, which played out in my dreams. The background music was one of their songs, a short duet they had written, performed with just her voice and his guitar, with him singing the backup lyrics. It was one of my favorite songs.

Someday, I will break.
Cracks and nicks, starbursts and spiderwebs
Fissures creeping....

In my nightmares, the song never finished.

It was interrupted by that awful death rattle.

7

Days later, I was still thinking about that song. I had never thought about it much before. I really liked the little melody that went along with it, but the lyrics never struck me until that morning.

What horrible pain they must have felt, losing two beautiful children, then having to keep it together for the media and for their band. They both retired from the music industry when Momma got pregnant with me, but now it seemed evident they never really recovered from losing Brendan and Benjamin.

The intense rush of seeing the twins exhausted me. I assumed what I had was an anxiety attack. I had them before at school, but that night's episode was like running a marathon.

I had been sleeping until after ten. I woke up much earlier on the twins' birthday.

I eased out of bed and put on clothes. The whole process took so much effort I was ready to lie back down again, but I made my way to Marcus's room to look at Trixie's eggs.

Marcus had created a comfortable environment for her, and her foot was healing well. He decided to let her hatch her eggs in the cage. Once hatched, he said, he would release them into the pond.

I made my way downstairs to fix some tea. It was storming outside, so I would have to find a reason to lock myself in my room to avoid seeing everyone else. I really didn't want to face Vivienne after last night.

To my shock, I found Troy sitting in the kitchen, alone. A strange sense of disassociation crashed over me, like I was about to leave my body.

"Are you okay?" he asked. The words floated out of his mouth and formed into a strange gray cloud. I put my hand on the counter top to feel its cool surface and stared at a large ceramic chicken Momma always kept as the centerpiece. I tried to pick out every one of its little intricate details.

"Marianne?" he asked again.

I put my hands on my temples. "Please," I said, not really knowing what I was begging for.

It was difficult to answer all those questions when that fear came on. I never realized what it was until much later. My palms would start to sweat first, then wet patches formed underneath my arms, soaking the pits of my shirt. A knot would form in my stomach and chest, blooming there, and the fear would rise and catch hold of my throat. My ears would ring, or I'd hear a rushing sound, like a waterfall. Then my vision would blur—the worst part and the best at the same time. It was like an abstract Rorschach image would come into each corner of my eye and bloom together like watercolors. The rest of the room would be inked out. Later, I figured it was my own body protecting me from fear of people in the room. When they spoke, I would see a strange fog come out of their mouth and it was always a different color for every person, almost like an aura.

It was like this for me every day, and it got worse and worse over time until I swear it ate a hole in my stomach. I couldn't eat and had stomach pains so intense, they would often keep me up at night. I'd toss and turn, dreading the next day, but dreading the time after school, at dinner, even more. It seemed like every day

Marcus and I had to endure some sort of torture, that we were destined for it no matter how hard we tried or what we did. School was just a few weeks away. I dreaded it. I knew Marcus did, too.

There was really no one else in the world we could trust. Maybe Granddaddy, but he was out gallivanting around with Grandmere Lily, so that was a moot point.

Troy was the only person that actually listened to us. Did he care? He seemed to.

Two years ago, Julia had brought him to the house for some holiday. I think it was Easter. Troy and I immediately clicked: I didn't know what it was about him, but he was one of the few people I found it easy to talk to. He was pretty quiet the way I was, and I thought maybe he was dealing with his own emotional wounds.

I was fourteen at the time. I caught him pouring some of my Uncle Joseph's vodka into a glass half-full of orange juice. I walked into the kitchen to grab one of Grandmere Lily's pies, which were always horrible, but we intended to serve it anyway to avoid a confrontation.

"You're not going to tell on me, are you?" he asked.

"The less Uncle Joseph drinks, the better," I said without even really thinking about it. He laughed.

"You're funny. But I can see why you keep quiet," he said. He took a long swig of the drink and went on to fix another. "It's kind of crazy around here."

"Why do you put orange juice in it?"

"The sugar mixes with the alcohol and gives you a stronger buzz. Want to try it?"

I shrugged. "Sure."

That was the first time I drank anything, but Troy and I giggled and exchanged quick glances throughout his stay. Marcus was the only one who noticed and kept his arms crossed over his chest for the rest of the day, but he didn't say much about it afterwards. He knew very well about the happenings between Joseph and I, so he never brought it up.

Over the years, and especially that summer before I started sophomore year, I felt Troy's eyes on me more often. It was not in an Uncle Joseph way. It was more curiosity.

As I recovered from that weird disassociation sense, I said to Troy, "Just give me a minute."

"Vivienne and Julia are out shopping," he said. "Take your time."

I knew what he meant by his tone. It was flat, non-pressuring. He also appeared to be drinking a glass of juice, but I could tell by the way he was hunched over at the table that it wasn't just juice.

"Okay," I said. I took a few deep breaths and made my way over to the cupboard.

"Let me do that. Sit down. You look pale."

I was too tired to protest, so I sank into one of the chairs. It was my usual spot at the kitchen table, right across from where Momma used to sit. Marcus would always sit to my right and Daddy would be diagonal to me.

"You know, I was pretty young when I lost my parents," Troy said as he shuffled around the kitchen.

I patted my face with a paper towel and looked at him, shocked. "Your parents died?" I asked.

"Not exactly. But they disowned me."

Anger bloomed in the pit of my stomach. "Well, mine *did* die, Troy."

"I'm sorry," he said, shaking his head. I could tell then he was really drunk. "That's not what I meant. I mean I was about Marcus's age when my dad left, and my mom gave me up to my grandparents to hook up with other guys. So I relate to not having someone around is what I'm saying." He glanced up at my flushed face, then down at my breasts again.

"Well, now you have Julia," I said. I was not feeling this whole bonding thing he was trying to do.

"Not really. Julia has me. But if I'm on my own, I'll fail."

I stared down at his feet as he brought the tea over.

"I'm glad you're talking to me," he said as he put the mug in front of me. "I'm really hoping for some sort of friendship with you and Marcus."

"Not exactly connecting with Vivienne, are you?" I said. I couldn't believe the sarcastic words coming out of my mouth, but I was genuinely perplexed at his relationship with Julia. "Why did you marry Julia, anyway?"

He shrugged. "Why not? She takes care of me. I met her when I was lost in college. She's an attractive older woman who sets me straight."

I looked down at his drink.

"What? There's nothing else to do around here."

"Aren't you supposed to be preparing the house to be sold or something?"

He sighed. "Look. Try not to worry about that too much right now. I talked her into staying at least through Christmas."

I looked out the window and finished the rest of my tea. It stopped raining, so I decided to go outside.

Every time I walked down the hill and faced the house, it seemed menacing, so blood-red, its white columns like great fangs. I could have sworn it was alive, threatening us to stay or face its wrath. As the days slid into one another, the house seemed to grow darker and more threatening, as if it were rebelling against all the lighting Julia put up inside. Julia and Troy would never keep its glory alive. They would have to hire help, because they surely wouldn't do it themselves. Would they appreciate the mosaic effect the stained-glass produced as the morning light shone through the windows? Would they relish the way the azaleas came in matching pink and red hues? What about the antiques, the paintings, the family photos? Julia seemed willing to trade our family legacy for a new car and a closet full of this season's designer clothes.

The end of summer days were typically bright and hot by the time the sun greeted the day, but not on this day. Misty and muggy, a gray curtain hung in the air and obscured the woods. Still, I trailed through my path, over the mossy gray stones and out through the garden, my hand caressing the tops of tall weeds. Burrs clung to my jeans and morning dew caked the cuffs, but it was familiar and comforting. I stopped by the twins' graves and pulled weeds, letting them slip through my fingers as I trekked back to the house.

I had snatched one of Troy's orange juices to drink on my walk. I wasn't keen on orange juice, but I got a small shiver of pleasure out of stealing and drinking them. I set the bottle down to untie my shoes. I was careful about taking them off at the door to avoid Julia's wrath.

Out of the corner of my eye, two spidery white hands crept out from under the porch steps to grab it. I got down on my hands and knees, the cold dew biting into my jeans, and peered down under the house. Damp debris, a patchwork quilt of morning sun and shadow, and little toddler hands, scrambling out of view. I caught a flash of auburn hair, brilliant as russet fall leaves. It was just like Momma's.

I couldn't go inside—not after seeing that. Every other time I had contact with them, it was a fleeting glimpse, a whisper of laughter disappearing down the hallway, or seeing their horrific dead forms. But on this day, I had actually seen them as they were before they died, their skin as white as paper, their glorious heads of hair. I sat on the steps and listened, my ears pricking at every bird chirp or falling leaf. I closed my eyes.

All at once they were upon me, their faces sticky against mine, their damp smell, musty and forgotten, assaulting my nostrils. I opened my eyes and watched through the veil of my lashes, catching glimpses of coppery hair, of black blooms of rotting flesh. The door rattled behind me. Their little fingers stiffened with the prospect of discovery, and bright pin-prick needles clawed at my neck. Then, their weight shifted away from me.

"Marianne?" It was Troy's concerned voice. "What are you doing out here?"

I looked into his eyes framed by the pale, hollow face. I opened my mouth to tell him I saw the twins but shook it away.

"Your neck," he said, his eyes dark and glassy. When I brought my hand up to my neck, there was something warm and sticky there. Blood. When I went inside to look in the mirror, there were tiny half-moon crescents scattered about my flesh from their tiny little fingernails.

So they were real. They had to be. But that damp smell was so dizzying, there was something to it. It smelled so fetid and mingled with something else acrid and tangy—like it was mixed with a hefty dose of fear. If Carter had strangled them, of course they would have been afraid.

I could not help but wonder why they had pushed me back on the stairs and attacked me like that. Were they jealous I had lived past the age of five? Did they hate me? I had to know. That summer morning, with only Troy and Marcus stirring in the house, I pulled down the board again and brought it back outside where I had seen them on the front steps. I felt like they might talk to me, since the world was still silent.

"Why did you scratch me like that?" I asked, my fingers trembling on the planchette.

S-C-R-A-T-C-H W-H-E-N H-U-R-T, they spelled on the board.

"Who hurt you?"

S-H-E D-I-D.

"She?" I asked, but I felt their presence stir and dissipate like a fog. Were they talking about mother?

A faint keening sound came from underneath the stairs. I had not realized it was probably a perfect hiding place for them. They could hide there and observe the driveway and the entire front lawn of Azalea House, which would help them see the comings and goings. I put the board up and went outside again. There was that damp smell again, but just as I caught it, it went away. I pushed my way under the stairs, wincing at the slimy leaves and mud, and turned around and positioned myself so I could see through the slats. No wonder they sat there. It offered a perfect view of the driveway. Just as I was about to climb out from under the stairs, Julia's car pulled up. Julia's heels click-clacked up the steps. The keening sound again, like a nervous whine, came from behind me. I turned around and searched in the shadows for their twin figures again, but there was only a flash of decayed, pale skin and russet hair.

"Who is 'she'?" I asked. Silence. "You won't talk to me? Not even on your birthday?" Again, silence.

My favorite spots were the attic and the twins' graves. Those were the two places where Marcus knew to find me.

But there was another place, too, one no one knew about. I walked there, the ground squishing beneath my shoes.

The land was on a slope. It was rumored there used to be an Indigenous village quite close to Azalea house, settled because it didn't flood. The driveway dipped down the slope, and the house was on the high ground. When it rained a lot, the slough would fill up, and we'd have to take the boats down to get to the main road. People often parked their cars along the highway, so they could escape by boat and then drive away.

I had found the highest point on the land. If I sat there and faced directly west, there was an obvious clearing with a direct view of the pond and beyond. Daddy never explicitly talked about it; it was always something he maintained. Sometimes I thought the tribe told us to do things, and we did them without even thinking about it. Maybe a chief ghost had been telling Daddy to keep the sunset clearing there this whole time. I even imagined Daddy going to that spot, that it was his secret place, too, and he never told anyone. I felt lucky I had found it and appreciated its view.

There was an old log to sit on, too, worn in one spot. I imagined Daddy sitting in that spot, wearing it down over the years, pondering, smoking, watching the sun set in the summer when the storm clouds were out. What did he think about? Loss?

Because that's what I thought about when I sat out there. Once the sun was set and the myriad of colors shaded into night gray clouds, it really got to me. Another day done, another day without Momma and Daddy at Azalea House.

But there was something about that spot. It was private. It was far away from the house and even the twins' graves, so far I was free from the chatter from their ghosts or the living. I could be alone with my thoughts, but sometimes those were more terrifying than anything I experienced out in the woods or anywhere else on the property.

The truth was, I didn't know what I felt anymore. On one hand, I thought my parents dying would get me away from this place, and on the other I wanted to stay on and continue the legacy. But there was something sinister hanging around that house. I didn't know what exactly, but the twins seemed to know.

I vowed to sit in that spot in the evenings until I had some answers.

Julia's Mercedes was back when I reached the house. My heart sank into my stomach. I was hoping they would stay gone until dinner, but it looked like they had cut their shopping trip early.

As I approached the house, though, I heard screaming and crying.

It was Marcus.

I broke out into a run and dashed into the house. The crying was coming from the living room.

"What happened?" I asked, looking around and nearly hysterical myself. Troy was seated, his head in his hand. I didn't know if it was because he was drunk or if it was because he was dumbfounded by some bullshit that had happened—or both. Julia had her arms crossed over her chest, and Vivienne had her usual sardonic grin, that same one I always wanted to slap right off. Marcus was wailing.

"She killed the ducklings!"

"What?" I twirled around to face Vivienne. "What'd you do?"

Vivienne shrugged. "They invaded the house, and they shit everywhere."

Inky blots crept across my field of vision and a ball of hot rage built up in my core. I charged at her, ignoring her screams. Before I could even think about it or stop myself, I had fistfuls of her hair, and I was pulling and pulling.

There was a vague sense of her beating fists against my body and my aunt's hands trying to pull me off. Troy's shouting and Marcus's wailing were muffled. All I could see was my own fury. It turned me into a wild animal, and Vivienne was my prey. I would rip her to shreds and eat her if I had to.

Finally, someone pulled me off and once I stepped back, the damage was satisfying. I had a chunk of hair in my hand. I brought it to my face to see if it was real and could smell the expensive shampoo she used. I also noticed I had blood underneath my fingernails. Vivienne had several cuts on her arms, but alas, I had not injured her face. That was unfortunate. Part of me really wished she would return to school with gnarly scars, courtesy of me. I was sure no one would ever give me grief again if they discovered I had kicked her ass.

It was Troy who pulled me off her and walked me outside. He held me gently by the arm. We walked all the way to the pond, out onto the pier. I was breathing hard, still high from the adrenaline shooting through my extremities in electric jolts.

Troy held me by the shoulders and looked at me.

"Did she get you?" he asked. I shook my head.

Then, he pulled me close and hugged me. I was confused. He smelled like sandalwood and citrus, which was probably from all the screwdrivers he'd been drinking. Still, he smelled wonderful. Something strange coursed through my body, an alien sensation I had never really felt before.

"Marianne, I'm so sorry. If I could do it all over again, I would not have married into this family. I'm going to stand up for you both from now on, you hear me?"

I didn't say anything. I just let him hold me.

"What are you doing? She *attacked* me." I cringed at Vivienne's high-pitched shrill.

"Why did you kill those baby ducks? What reason did you

have, other than to torture your cousins?" Troy said as he hugged me tighter. "Don't come near her. You deserve every scratch you get."

"Mother has been working *hard* on that house and any vermin Marcus brings here is just going to ruin everything," Vivienne said. She had her arms crossed over her chest, her jaw clenched.

I pushed Troy away. "You did that to hurt him," I said to her. "There is no other reason."

"So what if I did? You're going to end up a lonely loser, Marianne," Vivienne said to me with her usual smirk. Even with her hair mussed and her mascara running, she still looked beautiful, as if she'd been purposefully disheveled for some photo shoot. It disgusted me.

"Vivienne, you could not be more jealous if you tried," Troy said. *Wow*, I thought. Maybe he really did mean it when he said he would stick up for us. Or maybe it was all the drinks he'd had.

"Me? Jealous of her? I don't think so. She's the one jealous of me. I'm the model. I'm the one on TV. I'm famous. She can barely string sentences together."

"You are cruel, vapid, and vacant-headed. You have no talent to speak of, so you get by on showing your ass," I said. Where did that come from? Had I somehow channeled Marcus smartassery?

She clenched that perfect jaw of hers again and darted towards me. After a strong push, a lukewarm sensation enveloped me. The bitch had shoved me into the pond. I opened my eyes for a second, completely taken aback, and saw her figure, wavering through the watery filter, standing over the pier. Troy raised his arms in a 'what the hell' gesture.

I flailed. It took me a beat or two to realize what had happened, why their figures were so distorted. I blinked my eyes, and a wild thought flashed through my brain: I shouldn't have tried to open my eyes in the pond. It was murky down there; it burned.

Something golden caught my eye. I blinked hard to clear the muck away from my already sore eyes, but it was still there. I composed myself and instead of coming up for air, I swam towards the object.

There were two of them. I swam closer and reached out to grab them. I closed my eyes—the water really burned—but after fishing around in the slimy mud for a moment, my fingers touched something cool and metallic. I held them tightly in my hand and came up for air.

I could tell, from the corner of my eye, that Vivienne was waiting to see what I'd do next. But all I could do was clear the water from my eyes and inspect what I'd seen.

At that moment, I completely forgot about Troy, about Vivienne, and even Trixie's babies. I was solely focused on the strange objects I'd found.

Two identical bracelets. Two tiny golden circles. Two pieces of jewelry. I blinked. I ran my thumb across them, noting the smooth metallic texture, interrupted by indentions. An inscription. I rubbed the slime away and squinted at the lettering on each of them. There were gemstones set in the metal, too.

In perfect, looping cursive the names emerged: *Brendan* on one of them, *Benjamin* on the other.

8

I could barely tread water, I was so shaken by what I held in my hand. Vivienne had stormed off rather than deal with Troy, but Troy stood there with a puzzled look on his face.

The bracelets clearly belonged to the twins. What the hell were they doing in the pond? Did they lose them before they died?

I swam to shore with the bracelets gripped tightly in my hand. They damn near pulsed with warmth and vitality.

"What are those?" Troy asked.

The voices in my head told me to keep it a secret.

"Nothing. Just some of Daddy's old fishing lures, I think," I said. I cupped them in my hand so he couldn't see. He helped me out of the water.

"Are you okay?" he asked. His forehead was a road map of worry, so he was either a great actor or he was really concerned about me.

"I'm fine," I said. "I'm going to shower and check on Marcus."

I walked away from the pond as fast as I could, my shoes squelching with water. I wrung the water from my hair before I stepped inside but didn't bother to take my shoes off. Fuck

Vivienne and Julia. If they were bothered by it, they could clean it up for all I cared.

The shower was blissful, and I stood in the jet until the tap ran cool. I got out and put on a fuzzy robe and headed to Marcus's room. I knocked. No answer. I entered with caution. The room was dark, but he had lit a candle on his desk. He was curled up in bed on top of his covers, his face completely blank. Trixie clucked with apprehension from her spot underneath the desk. I sat on the bed beside Marcus.

"I'm sorry," I said. I couldn't think of anything else to say. He sighed and curled himself into a tighter ball. "Do you want anything to eat?"

He shook his head. I imagined he wouldn't be hungry for a while. I knew my own appetite was destroyed.

I curled up beside him and held his hand. He squeezed it. We stayed like that until the room grew darker and the sun set outside.

Eventually, he sat up and rubbed his eyes like he didn't want to think about it anymore.

"Guess what I found in the pond after Vivienne pushed me in?" I asked him, sensing he needed the distraction.

He sniffed and rubbed his eyes again. "A gun?"

"No. It's more interesting than that." I opened my palm and showed him the gold baby bracelets. He held them up to the candlelight and looked at them, then turned on a lamp for a better look.

"Holy shit," he said. "These were in the pond?"

I nodded.

"Why would they be there? I have a strange feeling about it. Don't you?"

I nodded again.

"I'm willing to get on the board again to see what they say," he said. My heart skipped a beat. I ran to fetch the board and brought it back to his room. The twins' cold, haunting presence wrapped around me, soothing me but terrifying me at the same time, ready to unlock their secrets.

But they would only speak to us in riddles, as if they wanted us to discover something on our own.

S-E-C-R-E-T-S P-U-Z-Z-L-E

"Who killed you?" I finally asked. I was getting frustrated.

Marcus and I looked at each other.

"They want us to figure it out," Marcus said. "That must be the puzzle. It's why you saw their ghosts."

S-T-A-I-R-C-A-S-E

"Well," I said, "we have a whole month of summer left. What else are we going to do?" It was too hot to go outside nowadays anyway, and Julia didn't seem to be keeping track of our activities.

"Why don't we just leave this place?" Marcus pleaded. I could tell the heaviness of everything going on was really getting to him.

"And go where?"

"We should poison them," Marcus said, his eyes wide.

"And go to jail?"

"We're minors," he said as he adjusted his glasses. "We'd get out soon enough."

"And this house would be gone," I said. "Vivienne would sell it. Or Joseph. We have to do something," I urged. "We can't just leave the twins."

I thought of them out there in the woods, alone and crumbling in their graves, their tiny child skeletons and domed skulls so empty, their spirits lost in the maze of trees. Marcus's eyes sparkled as if he knew what I was thinking.

"You're right," he said. "We can't. Not until we find out what really happened to them."

The twins told us about the staircase for a reason. I had to go back there and listen in on the sort of things Troy and Julia talked about.

That night, I waited until Marcus became immersed in whatever he was doing on the computer, and Vivienne was locked in her room, likely looking for herself in fashion magazines. I made my way up the stairs without a light. It seemed so ominous, the way the perspective shifted and narrowed in the dark. Once inside the attic, I could hear the little whispers of the twins. *Don't be afraid*, I thought I heard them say in unison. I meandered around old toys and boxes and made my way to the hidden staircase. Once inside, I could hear Julia and Troy talking. I walked so as not to make the stairs creak.

Once inside the closet, I looked through the peephole. And I had never seen my aunt dressed like that. It shocked me so much, I slapped my hand over my mouth.

She sauntered around the room, wearing a shiny black latex catsuit. When it caught the light, it glowed electric blue. She wore five-inch heels, and her posture opened up, making her seem even taller than the heels made her.

"You do what I say, not the other way around," she said. Her tone was the same one she used with me and Marcus.

She was talking to Troy, though. He was sprawled out on the bed, hands tied to the headboard, ankles bound to the other end. He was completely naked. He had his eyes closed and his penis throbbed.

"You're thinking of her, aren't you?" my aunt asked with venom in her voice.

I had never seen a naked man in person before. Something horrifying and confusing stirred me, and that secret place between my legs clenched.

No. It was Troy. However nice he was, he was my aunt's husband.

But I could not pull my eyes away.

Was this sex? It seemed to be. She kicked up her high-heeled foot and dug it into his torso. He groaned and ground his hips up into the air.

I had never seen anything like it. I had stayed up late watching midnight movies, where they showed men on top of bare-breasted women, undulating in ecstasy while jazz music carried on in the background. That was the only version of sex I was familiar with. It never occurred to me there was any other way.

What wild thing dwelled in Julia? What kind of animal curled into a slumber while she wailed about spirituality, and then came roaring out in high heels at night, in this bedroom? It was like there were two Julias that lived inside one other, one who wanted control over the world through religion, and another who used sex to control Troy.

Mesmerized, I pressed my fingers deeper into the wall, wanting to infiltrate it so I could get a better look. I had never viewed Julia as someone to emulate, to look up to. But there in that black, shiny latex, she seemed Amazonian, almost superhero-like.

I wanted to know what it felt like to wear that catsuit. I vowed to sneak into that room one day and try on her clothes. Could I channel the same feral animal that Julia had? What would it be like to step into those high heels of hers and take on an alter ego? What would happen if I crushed Joseph under the weight of my heel? Could I keep Joseph off me?

Part of me wanted to stay, to see the ritual to its conclusion. But I knew it was wrong to watch. I slowly stood up and tip-toed back up the stairs. But I would make a practice of this. I wasn't ready to stay down there for the rest of the night and witness whatever crazy sex games they were playing, as much as I wanted to understand the rules of it.

I focused on the twins instead. How had they died? No one would say anything about it. The only thing I knew was that they died when they were five, and they died at the same time, apparently by the hands of this Carter Leblanc guy. It pained my parents too much to talk about it, that was for sure.

The only thing that made sense in my shattered, teenage brain was that they were murdered. Why else could the vibes around the house be so tormented? It wasn't just the lives lost long ago. Something continued, something sinister, and something very close to me and Marcus. This house and this land witnessed things. It had stories. I needed to figure out what they were. I knew that solving the mystery was a way out of all this misery and pain.

There was an accident, something that happened back here on the Azalea House grounds. Did the clearing have something to do with it? Would I have to dig up the twins to see if they were still resting there in their graves? It was like they followed me everywhere, their voices trailing behind me. I would turn around and catch a fast glimpse of them. Sometimes I wondered if they were still alive somewhere.

But I would get a sense of things when I sat on that old log that overlooked the pond. Their deaths had something to do with that pond. When I sat there, echoes of their screams skipped across the water. I caught little reflections of light that made me think someone was out there, struggling, flailing around and begging for help. Something happened out there, something so memorable and terrible that Daddy created this clearing in the pine trees so he could sit and reflect.

That night, I had vivid dreams. There was cold all around me, something that made me buoyant and made me float. It could only be water. But it wasn't relaxing, and it wasn't like swimming in a pool. And I was always afraid of the water for no reason. I didn't swim at all until I was six or so, and Momma had to threaten to take all my toys away so I'd go to lessons.

In the dream, I struggled to flip over on my backside. My vision was disoriented, wavy. A figure stood on the shore, watching me while I was underwater. The view changed. The perspective shifted, like there were two of me. Then there was an overwhelming sense of not being able to breath. I flailed my arms to come up to the surface of the water. But there was a hand there, and it pushed me down until the water was ice-cold, murky, and dark. As I went deeper, I reached out and found the grip of someone else's hand.

But why? I never actually had a bad experience with water. I was, for some reason, unjustly afraid of it.

Had someone let the twins drown? Who was the figure standing over the water in my dreams? Who could I even ask about it? No one told the truth in my family, anyway.

It was possible Granddaddy would tell me about it. But I would have to wait. We wouldn't see them until Thanksgiving. I could call him, but I was always so nervous on the telephone. And it seemed like it would be a better question to ask in person, anyway.

The next day, I woke up and decided to spend the whole day in the attic. It was storming when I woke up, and Vivienne and Julia were off getting their hair done anyway. Troy was sprawled out on the couch, watching MTV with his usual screwdriver beverage. Marcus busied himself with hacking into Vivienne's Hotmail account and reading emails. So I was safe to explore on my own for the day.

The attic was filled with dust and decay. And secrets. Puzzle pieces to be assembled. I remembered there were photo albums and old letters, because Momma had made a point of coming up here one cool, fall day and organizing things by type. She was like that. Very organized and efficient, always the one to be in touch with tour organizers, media, and events. She was the spokesperson of Spellbound Hearts, even though they rarely gave interviews. If there were photo albums or anything up in the attic regarding the twins, it would be easy to find.

At least, that's what I thought.

The attic was expansive. There were intimidating piles of old toys, some so lifelike, like they could wake up at any moment and move towards me, their beady, glassy eyes boring into my soul. There were teddy bears with one eye, so old they may have come from when Azalea House was first built, as well as other stuffed animals with the fur worn off, either by love or by creepy crawly critters that skittered all over the attic.

The air was stuffy. It was, perhaps, a horrible idea to come up here in the summer. I pushed sticky spiderwebs aside and opened a few windows. On such a stormy, windy day, it made all the difference. It even let in a bit of additional light, so I could set out on my task.

I searched through old sixties pulp paperbacks and piles of old income taxes, trying to ignore the sounds of shuffling rats or skittering insects. Distant, hushed nursery rhymes and ghostly laughter echoed just over my shoulder. Maybe the twins were antsy for me to find something, but perhaps they were just frisky. This was originally intended to be their playroom, after all.

In the back southeast corner, I finally located a large stack of photo albums, worn and ratty.

When I opened the first one, I had to choke back a sob. It was Momma and Daddy's wedding photos, and oh how beautiful they both looked. Daddy had inky black hair that curled at the ends like mine, and Momma's hair had been teased and coiffed into a beehive. There was the wedding dress she always talked about, the detailed crochet number she had made herself. She had always talked about it when I asked about her wedding day, and there it was, right before my eyes.

Julia was in the picture, too, and even though she was much younger, pretty even, but she still paled in comparison to Momma. Julia had a forced smile as she looked on at my beaming parents. Her skin was dull compared to Momma's radiance. The man who stood next to Julia could only be my Uncle Theo, who died before I was born. He was very tall and lean with dark, mysterious features. I could see a bit of Vivienne in his dark, piercing eyes and lean stature.

There was something else strange about the photo, too. Julia had her usual forced smile, whereas Theo's was something of admiration. There was warmth in his eyes, and when I followed his gaze, it was fixated directly on Momma.

Lots of people looked at Momma that way. It got to be that Daddy learned to ignore it. But if Julia saw what I could see in this photo, it must have been maddening for her to see her husband look at her sister this way.

It was the only picture in which Theo was making any sort of expression at all. In most other pictures, his gaze was stone-cold and unsmiling. I could see where Vivienne got it from. His icy stare sent a creepy shiver through my body, despite the stuffiness of the attic.

That wedding picture spoke to me. I needed to show it to Marcus. He always had good insight when it came to things like that. I pulled the photo out of the album and stuck it in my pocket.

I took my time looking through the albums until I discovered pictures of the twins as babies. As I thumbed through, they grew up. There they were at their first birthday party, covered in blue frosting and laughing. There they were with Daddy, him holding one on each shoulder.

There were pictures of them at the zoo, the park, and everywhere in between.

There were a few pictures of the twins with the other band members, cute pictures of them banging on Drew's drums or trying to hold Mike's bass guitar, a couple of Mike's wife, Monica, holding them and talking to Momma. Monica sometimes sang backup or played the tambourine, but she mostly helped Momma with booking tours and press related stuff. I had met Mike and Monica a few times, and they were always so nice to us. Monica made us cinnamon rolls, and Mike let me sit on his shoulders when we went to Mardi Gras parades. They lived in California and I wished Marcus and I could go live with them. We could be the family of M names. It had been years since I had seen them, at least five. They didn't come to Momma and Daddy's funeral; they wrote us a letter, saying it was too hard and to call if we needed anything.

Maybe I would call them. It would be nice to hear a friendly voice or two.

There were even a couple of pictures of Aunt Julia with a young, bubbly-looking Vivienne. Seeing the pure smile on Julia's face, the way the corners of her eyes crinkled, and her thin lips stretched across her face—it made me smile, too, despite my hatred of both of them. I was glad to see that at some point, she was happy. There was a caring, glittery look in her eyes, something that conveyed she really cared about Vivienne.

In one picture, she had her arms around Theo and at their feet was a puppy, probably one of Uncle Theo's German Shepherds. I had a vague memory of Momma saying he worked as some sort of artisan, someone who mined crystals and turned them into polished works of art, but I wasn't sure if it was a false memory. Was he the one who made the bracelets for the twins?

It seemed like happier times when the twins were alive. Why couldn't I have been the firstborn? When I came along, there was already a shadow of grief hanging heavy as a storm cloud. Maybe that's why I had such a hard time talking.

Looking at the pictures made me wonder more about Theo, the uncle I had never met. I remembered asking Momma about how Uncle Theo had died, and she just said it was natural causes. Whatever that meant. When she answered, she sucked in a big breath of air and drew back her shoulders. I remembered that well.

Something urged me to close my eyes and I fought it. The thought of being blind in the attic filled me with a hot ball of dread. The noises intensified. Every faint scratch and squeak jarred me. The musty smell of the attic made me dizzy. If I kept my eyes open, I could hang on to this dusty, memory-filled reality.

The push to close my eyes came on again like a tsunami, my eyelids pulling down under some magnetic force. I shut my eyes, my hands still on the sticky surface of the photo album.

Uncle Theo's tan face appeared in my mind's eye, his dark eyes the color of Tiger's Eye gemstones. The eyes drew me in like a portal with their variations and intricacies, like his soul was trying to pull me into his mind. I resisted, but felt a pull so strong I had to give up and dive in. There was a reason this was happening, I told myself.

At first, there was a sense of contentment, the same feeling I always got when I wrote in my journal or painted on a canvas. A feeling of completion. Dry, dusty earth trickled from my fingers, and the distinct smells of sand and the sage filled my senses as hands pulled something sparkling and jagged out from the dirt. Then, there was a drop in my stomach. I remembered a time when Daddy took us to a park in Baton Rouge, and we rode the roller coaster. When it dropped off from that climb, I felt like my stomach had been left behind. I felt it sometimes when Momma drove over the bridge leading out of town. She'd speed up and make the car go faster to go over the bump and say "Wee! It's like a roller coaster!" and it would always make Marcus and me laugh hysterically.

After the dropping sensation in my stomach, the marvelous gemstone appeared to shrink until there was a feeling I'd hit the ground. It was not much different from a falling dream I kept having after Momma and Daddy died.

I opened my eyes, still shaken from the weird daydream. The attic was much darker. The sun had shifted, casting long shadows throughout the attic. How long had I been up here? I had only been looking at the photo albums for a couple of hours or so, but looking outside, it seemed like several more had passed.

What a strange experience. Had Theo really died from natural causes? Had he committed suicide? Maybe his death was no accident. Either way, I was determined to find out.

9

I was in the attic so long, the dust had seeped into my nostrils and tickled the back of my throat. I could stay there for hours digging through its secrets. Still, the heat of late afternoon was settling in, and sweat formed under my arms and the wire of my bra. I rubbed at it, grimacing at the sensation of the wire wrapping around my chest like a boa constrictor. I'd have to get new underthings soon. My breasts were already spilling over the bras Momma had bought for me back in the spring.

Theo's image was seared into my mind. Those dark brown eyes haunted me. Every time I looked at that photo, I desperately wanted to know what was going through his mind. I went back downstairs and cleaned off, then sat in my room and stared at the bracelets.

There were little blue stones set behind each name. Birthstones? I was afraid to clean them, because I didn't want to damage them any more than the pond had.

I dialed the number on the card Mike and Monica sent, then promptly hit the hang-up button. Moments like these unnerved me. I could feel my throat closing. They were so nice to us. I really didn't have anything to worry about, but the anxiety was always there.

I brought the phone into Marcus's room.

"Can you please call Monica and Mike?" I asked him. "Just tell them about the bracelets and see what they say?"

To my relief, he nodded, expressionless. If Marcus was upset with me or disappointed I couldn't call myself, he didn't show it. He dialed the number and put it on speakerphone and typed something that resembled green hieroglyphics into his computer while the phone rang.

"Hello?" a female voice said.

"Monica? This is Marcus and Marianne. How are you?" I marveled at how cool Marcus sounded on the phone for someone his age. He was always very well-spoken and sharp.

"Marcus! How wonderful to hear from you! Mike! It's Janelle and Abel's kids. Pick up the other line."

A click.

"Hi, kids," Mike's familiar voice bellowed. "We're so sorry about the funeral. You both holding up okay?"

"It's been tough. And to be honest, we're not crazy about Aunt Julia living here, but we're okay." They both laughed. I didn't understand what was so funny. Marcus and I frowned at each other. "Actually, we called because Marianne found something really weird in our pond. Do you remember the twins wearing little gold bracelets?" he asked. I admired him for getting to the point.

There was a long pause, so long that Marcus and I glanced at each other, both of us thinking the connection had gone bad.

"I don't remember," Monica said with hesitation. "They wore them all the time. Marianne, where did you find them again?"

"Marianne found them in our pond," Marcus said.

My heart throbbed in my ears. I wanted to say more, but that stone came back and caught in my throat.

There was a silence on the phone that seemed to last forever. "Hang on to them, okay my man? And keep it a secret for now, will you?" Mike's voice was forced chipper, almost like a sales-like.

"Give us some time to make a few phone calls and call you back soon. And hey, look—we're glad you trusted us enough to call us. Really."

"We'll call you back soon, okay? Just stay by the phone," Monica said. Her voice sounded a little shrill, but I wasn't sure if it was the ringing in my ears.

We hung up. I sat on Marcus's bed and hugged my knees to my chest and Marcus looked at me. An unspoken sense of dread passed between us. Clearly, the bracelets being in the pond meant something to them, but my teenage brain couldn't grapple with what it was.

Two hours later, they called back.

"Wish your parents knew those bracelets were in there," Mike said, his voice cracking on the speakerphone. "It was one hell of a mystery."

"What'd you do?" Marcus asked.

"We called Leblanc's attorney. Never thought he was responsible."

"Why?"

"Carter was a little odd, but he doted over those boys. He'd never done anything remotely illegal before. At least, not to my knowledge. He was, different—which is enough in a small town like yours. But since they found the bodies, um, well, based on what they found in his car, he went to prison. Monica and I always thought it never added up."

I finally got up the courage to speak. "What happened that day? Do you know?"

I always appreciated the fact that neither Mike nor Monica made a show about when I did talk. Everyone else said something stupid, like, "she speaks!"

"It was Memorial Day. We were all out at the house, all the band members, along with your Mom's family: her brother and sister. Theo was there. Your Uncle Joseph had this hippie girl with him. And your grandparents, Ed and Lily, were there too, but they weren't talking much to the rest of us. And the twins, of course."

I could imagine the scene already. Marcus and I glanced at each other.

"At some point, people started splitting up after we had all eaten. Julia went off with Theo and Joseph went off with his girlfriend. Me and Monica were helping your mom clean up. Your dad was outside, doing something. Ed and Lily were sitting out in the sun, reading paperbacks and drinking iced tea. It really was a beautiful day."

I had a hard time imagining Uncle Joseph with a girlfriend. He was always so wasted he could barely stand up, and when he could brace himself, it was usually with a hand down my pants.

"At some point, I don't know when, the twins disappeared. We looked everywhere."

"Were they ever out by the pond?"

Mike sighed into the phone. "I don't know. They were afraid there were alligators in there, so they didn't like to go near it. They were out there playing with some toy trucks. Though I guess it's possible. It had been raining a lot, and the flood waters were still receding."

"So they were found days later," I said. "How?"

Mike sighed again. When he told the story, I could picture it in my mind like a movie:

The evening the twins were found, the sun lingered low in the sky, fat and orange like a caution sign. Sometimes it didn't get dark until about nine o'clock, leaving endless hours to roam the woods or find some other trouble to get into.

Most people passed through our little fishing village on their way from Gonzales to their camps on the Amite River. From the right of the crossroads, there were cypress trees with Spanish moss hanging like a dead woman's hair. On the left are old Creole cottages, most of them raised up off the ground in case of flooding. A river snaked through the village, slicing it in half.

Alligators, snakes and other creatures lurked in the river's murky depths, but everyone who was anyone in this town skinny dipped in it at some point.

A couple of local teens, Jimmy and Kim went swimming there that night

Jimmy said it was like a rite of passage. You had to do it before you graduated from high school. Everyone did it.

Kim whined as she eased herself in the too-warm water. She made a face at Jimmy as she swam out. Jimmy chuckled, pot smoke coming out of his nose and mouth in small bursts.

"My feet are scraping up against something." She paused, perplexed. "It's like...metal."

Jimmy snickered. "You ready to get out already?"

"No, really. What the hell is it?"

Bubbles languidly rose to the surface of the dingy water and burst in somewhat of a slow motion.

"Jimmy!"

She almost asked him what sort of joke this was. Jimmy's pale, shocked face answered that question for her.

They had been looking for Leblanc's car for days now. He said it had been swept away by the flood water.

But Kim found it that day.

The detectives came and pulled it out of the water, opened the trunk, and that's when they found the twins' bodies. They immediately arrested Leblanc. He was quiet. Weird. Didn't socialize. Didn't fit in with the rest of the people in the village, though he did hunt and fish like many of them. When he talked, he stuttered. To them, it was an open and shut case.

"What's your theory on why they were found in *his* car, of all places?" Marcus asked. I could tell the visuals of that story were getting to him like they were getting to me. Mike was a good storyteller, despite the horror and sadness of the situation.

"He occasionally did landscape work at Azalea House. Your mom took care of most of it, but Carter would come in and help from time to time. And when he did, you'd see him now and again talking to the kids. He'd bring a present for them sometimes. To us, it seemed like a guy who didn't have kids but liked to be around them"

Marcus turned to me. "Did you know that?"

I shook my head. My bottom lip began to tremble. If he was the killer, he was getting out soon. If he wasn't, would he be seeking revenge?

"He's just—he was always hanging around those boys. Playing with them. He hardly ever interacted with any adults other than your mother."

Marcus and I glanced at each other. His eyes flicked with fear.

Mike cut back in and said, "I'm sure it'll be fine. It was a long time ago now. Trust me."

I did. But I was still afraid. The sentence Carter served was too long. What would come of Mike calling Leblanc's attorney? Would he be released sooner? There was no telling what sorts of things happened to him in prison.

Maybe my parents dying had been enough justice for him. Something good had to come from their deaths. At this point, I would take anything.

"Can I ask you one more thing, Mike?" Marcus asked.

"Sure, kid. Shoot."

"Who do you think did it?"

"Honestly, I'm not sure. There's a faint possibility Leblanc did it, but I don't think so. Maybe they drowned accidentally, and maybe he put them in his trunk to see if he could revive them. He was into all kinds of weird spiritual stuff. Maybe the river crested and swept the car away. I really don't know. But you finding those bracelets is monumental. Try to stay away from the press, okay?"

"We will," Marcus said.

"Call me if anything else happens. And hey, maybe we can get you out to California someday, huh?"

I was somewhat comforted after the call, but new worries swam in my head. Those were compounded with the fact that we had to return to school in a couple of weeks. I was not looking forward to it. I'd be starting my junior year, and so would Vivienne. She was already popular, from what I heard from Marcus's incessant internet stalking. That was going to make the school year even worse, I was sure.

Who would know about Theo in the meantime? Aunt Julia

was of course the best resource, but I didn't want to talk to her about anything, much less her dead husband.

Maybe Troy would know. Surely, Julia talked to him at some point about Theo.

The next day was Saturday. Julia and Vivienne always slept in until about eleven, but Troy was up early drinking his favorite juice by nine, so I had time to talk to him.

He was sitting in the kitchen as usual, eating chocolate chip pancakes and drinking juice while the news blared on the television. I wrinkled my nose and poured a cup of coffee.

"How are you able to consume so much sugar?" I asked. It was like seeing a ten-year-old eating a dream breakfast.

He shrugged. "Want some?"

I frowned and shook my head, then sat across from him at the counter. We both watched the news feed. There was a little headline at the bottom of the screen that noted Leblanc was going to be released on Monday. We looked at each other.

"Does Julia ever talk about that?"

He shook his head. "Not to me," he said with a mouthful of pancake.

"What about Theo?"

He swallowed, his Adam's apple bobbing up and down. For a second, I thought he'd choked.

"Why do you want to know about Theo?" he asked. He followed the question up with a large gulp of vodka and OJ.

"It's just very mysterious, that's all. Did she ever tell you how he died?"

"He was some sort of gem hunter. I think he fell while he was rock climbing. Julia found him."

My eyes practically bugged out of my head. "Julia was with him?"

He flashed a quick smile. "Yeah. She used to rock climb with him. I've been with her. She's pretty good."

The thought of my aunt ever doing a fun thing with her life besides shopping was really messing with my mind. I wasn't even sure if I believed Troy.

"He was an adrenaline junky, or so I've heard. Used to dive, travel a lot, all kinds of stuff. I think gems were their bread and butter. After he died, Julia became more involved in religion."

I eyed him with suspicion. I always wanted to ask him about religion, but there was never any way to transition into it.

"And what about you? How religious are you?"

He shrugged and polished off his drink. He was already looking a little tipsy. "Not much. I tell Julia I am because it makes her happy. But I don't know what I believe." He put his dishes in the sink and looked at me. "Do you?"

I shrugged. Momma and Daddy never made us go to church, even though we were the only kids from around the village who didn't attend. It outcasted us even more at school. "I don't know. I guess I'm comfortable with not knowing."

He looked me up and down again, that way he'd been looking at me for a while now. "You're wise beyond your years, Marianne. Some older boy is going to scoop you up. You better watch it."

I flushed and looked at my feet.

"Why are you asking me about Theo?"

"I found a picture of him in the attic." I didn't want to tell Troy about the baby bracelets. Not yet. I wasn't sure who to trust. "And Momma and Daddy didn't really talk about him."

"There's a reason for that," Troy said. He took the cup out of the sink and fixed himself another drink.

"Why are you drinking so much lately?"

"It sucks here. Do you want to hear about Theo or not?" He didn't look at me this time, just seemed to concentrate unnaturally hard on fixing his beverage.

"I want to hear about Theo."

"Julia was pissed because Theo had a crush on your mom, or some shit like that. I don't know if there was any sort of affair, but Julia drinks sometimes and bitches about it. Says it's probably a good thing he died."

"Jesus," I said. I took a few deep breaths as a strange thought occurred to me.

Would Mike or Monica have known if Momma had an affair? Would they even tell me? Probably not.

I shook my head. I was about to ask him again why the hell he married Julia, but I knew the answer. Troy was great for information, especially when he was drinking. I took my coffee cup and turned to go upstairs.

"Wait. Where are you going?"

I stopped and turned to him, confused. "To check on Marcus."

"Marcus is old enough to fend for himself, you know. Julia and Vivienne won't be up for another couple of hours. Stay here."

"What for?" I searched his eyes. He had some sort of faraway, lonely look in them that made me edgy for some reason.

"I don't know. We could talk more about them before they wake up."

"Okay," I said, uneasy in my voice. "For a few more minutes." I set my coffee cup back down and sat down, wondering what else he wanted to talk about.

"You must be thinking about what will happen on Monday," he said. "Word is that Leblanc plans to move back into his same old shitty trailer in the village."

I was surprised to hear that. Either he was stupid, or really brave to move back to a home everyone knew of. Maybe he didn't have anywhere else to go.

"I'm not afraid," I said, sitting up straighter. Troy laughed. "Where is his trailer?"

"Down Crack Alley."

Crack Alley was right along the river, a low-income stretch of trailers that were in a constant state of decay due to floods. It amazed me people still lived there. I had been once with Momma, exploring, and she stopped on the muddy, gravel road so we wouldn't hit a baby alligator. Momma got out of the car and picked it up and put it back in the river. I was amazed. She never seemed to be afraid of anything. She often encountered snakes while gardening, and she always picked them up and just moved them out of the way.

"Which trailer?" I asked. Something wicked was forming in my brain.

"Marianne," Troy said. He gave me a disapproving look.

"What?"

"Don't go down there," he said as he stood up. He went to the fridge and pulled out the stuff to make another drink. "You'll get murdered or raped or attacked by snakes."

"I told you. I'm not afraid."

He left his drink mixing stuff on the counter and walked up to me. "Show me."

I opened my mouth to say something, but he grabbed my hand. His skin was cool and dry against my hot, clammy hand. He put my hand on his neck, his fingers closed around mine, encouraging my grip. I squeezed.

We locked eyes and his pupils dilated. Then it was like all the pain from Joseph and my parents flowed out through my body and out through my hand, and Troy took it from me.

I pressed my fingers tighter into his neck, the flesh yielding. His hardness pressed against me and I swallowed back a lump in my throat.

"Do you like this?"

He strained a little and said, "It makes me feel…*something*." I let go. "It's tangible. Real. More than anything else."

I took a step back.

"You like it, too," he said. "You pretend that you don't, but I can tell you do. And you're not afraid. Not really."

His words stabbed me so hard they scraped against bone.

"Afraid of what?" Vivienne said from the doorway. "I can bet you're afraid of everything, Marianne. And I see you two are just chatting away like old friends."

I rolled my eyes and turned to leave, cursing her under my breath.

"She *speaks!*" she said as she blocked my way. I ducked underneath her arm and escaped the kitchen. "Make me some pancakes, little boy," she said to Troy, "or I'll tell Mommy you were drinking her vodka again."

"Jesus," Troy muttered as he swirled the drink around. "Marianne, are you sure you don't want anything?"

"I'm fine," I called back over my shoulder as I went up the stairs. My body seethed with hatred for Vivienne. I resented she had control over my movements throughout my own house. She knew I couldn't stand being in the same room with her and had taken to proving that point lately. I was almost ready for school to start. At least it would give her something else to do.

But in the meantime, *I* had something else to do. And I had until Monday to plan.

10

By some glorious twist of fate, Vivienne, Troy and Julia were out of the house when a detective and some attorney came by to investigate the bracelets. Marcus did most of the talking.

"We don't have to wait until Julia gets back, do we?" Marcus said as I let them in.

The attorney, an older tall man with a shock of gray hair, shrugged. "We can come back when your aunt is here if you want. But that's one of the reasons I came by with Detective Delaney here," he said, indicating the stocky guy standing next to him. "I knew your parents. I have your best interests in mind. Now, shall we see these bracelets?"

I went upstairs and retrieved them. We hadn't cleaned them. Mike and Monica said not to clean them.

"How did you find these again?"

"Our cousin pushed her in the pond," Marcus said for me. "She found them down there."

"What made her push you in the pond?" the detective asked.

"Marianne told Vivienne that she had no talent and had to show her ass to be famous," Marcus said.

The detective chuckled and rolled his eyes. "We'll want to

have some tests done," he said. As he sealed them up in an evidence bag, my heart hammered away. Would we get them back? Why were they taking them away for testing?

"So this means their case might be reopened?"

"It's too soon to tell. This could be new evidence. Let's see what the tests say."

New evidence. The turn of events made my head spin, but I took some sort of comfort in it. I imagined them down there in the depths of that dreary pond, holding each other's hands as they tried to suck in air. Maybe holding hands made it less scary for them.

And if Carter did it, why did he do it?

I needed to talk to him. It would take me a while to get to his trailer, maybe a half an hour by bike. But I was going, and I was going to get answers. I didn't want Marcus to come with me. He would be too scared.

That Monday, before anyone got up, I packed food for myself and set out on my bike to wait for Carter Leblanc to arrive.

It was mild in the shade. My skin burned in the sunny parts, like it was cracking in the hot Louisiana sun. Even though it was a quiet morning, gators fidgeted about in their swamp lairs, watching me with vacant, reptilian eyes. They hid in plain sight in the algae of the still waters, blending in too well. The swamp smelled musty, a rotten egg odor that made my nostrils flare.

Much like gators, Carter Leblanc blended in too well—hidden at the end of the dirt road. I reached his ramshackle trailer by the river. There was nothing special about it at first glance. It was like every other trailer on the short dirt road that ran parallel to the river. I stood there and stared, trying to glean anything I could from that tan trailer covered in algae, with bits and bobs surrounding it. I stepped in closer. There were things hanging in the trees, slowly succumbing to the wrath Spanish moss, things with ivory jagged shapes. Animal skulls. There were bizarre objects all over the place, things I recognized from occult books I read in secret at the library.

Things that were put to ward off curses.

Or people.

I remembered hearing some rumor that he and his mother practiced Voodoo. I didn't know anything about Voodoo, other than it was frowned upon.

A bizarre shiver passed through my body, almost like a fever chill. I stepped closer. The sides peeled off the trailer like they were trying to escape. The wooden stairs and porch sagged in places. All the trailers back down this alley were run down, but Carter's was in an alarming state of decay.

When I finally caught sight of him standing on the porch, I suppressed a scream. There he was, the accused killer of my twin brothers. My knees buckled.

I was not sure what I expected by coming here. I was hoping I could glean answers by standing in front of his house, without confrontation, without seeing anyone.

And he emerged from the shadows, smaller than I imagined, not much bigger than I. He had a cherub looking face and large pale eyes. There were horizontal worry wrinkles etched into his forehead. We stared at each other for some time before he spoke. He clasped his hands in front of his body and wrung them, like he was nervous.

"I-I-I know why you're here," he stuttered. "I know... I know who you are, and I d-d-didn't do it."

He pulled out a pack of cigarettes and lit one. When he exhaled, all the tension washed away from his face. When he spoke again, he didn't stutter at all.

"All I know is that when I got done fishin', I drove here. The water came up real fast and I lost my car. I was figurin' it was a total loss. Then the cops came and pulled it outta the water and they found those boys in there, drowned. But I didn't do nothin', I was justa fishin' is all. Don't talk to no one. Just wanted to catch a few bass is all. Felt real bad seeing them dead in there like that. Just little kids, they were. But they musta been in there when I drove off. Didn't hear nothin'. Just drove here. Didn't drive it into the water. Why would I do that? Didn't have no damn car after all that, not that I'da needed one in jail anyway."

I almost asked him how the hell the bodies got in his car, but he started talking again.

"I had the trunk open. Was puttin' stuff in there, my lures and whatnot. Went back to check to see if I cleared out okay, then when I walked back to the car, the trunk was closed. Didn't remember closin' it, didn't think much of it. But I wish I'da checked then. Wouldn'ta made no difference anyway." He hung his head.

There was something about the way he spoke that made me believe him. I couldn't pinpoint what it was, probably the way he met my eyes when he talked, like he was searching for something. His face scrunched up a bit, too, when he talked about the boys.

"I wouldn't do it, Miss. You know what they do to jailbirds who mess with kids?"

I lowered my head and stared at the mud. I knew.

"Not tryin' to make you feel bad. Hell, you wasn't even born yet. But me and you, we got a few things in common, now don't we?"

I met his eyes again, those mossy, pale eyes set in his tanned, weathered face. It wasn't just the speech thing he was talking about. My ears thrummed with a sudden understanding.

"They haunt me too, lookin' for answers," he said.

Something passed between the two of us when I really looked into his eyes, like he could easily see right through me and knew all my secrets.

You have it, too. So did your Momma. Someone who can see beyond this world. They only want answers. And you'll find the truth, miss.

I knew he said it. It was his voice. But I didn't see his lips move.

And here he was on the outskirts, isolated from the rest of the world, an outcast, kind of like I was. And I could tell eye contact was hard for him usually, but not with me. His eyes teared up a little, like he knew I was beginning to understand him.

"Why were you near Azalea House?"

"Good, deep bass ponds around there down by the road. Not on your property, but near it. Know 'em?"

I shook my head.

"You don't fish?"

I shook my head again. Daddy said he was going to teach me, but he died before he got the chance.

"I see," was all Carter said. A long moment of silence passed, but it wasn't uncomfortable.

More birds were waking up and chirping and flitting around the trailer to a little spot off to the side. When I peered through the dense foliage, there was a nice little oasis there with a fountain for birds to bathe in, and many sorts of plants I had never seen before. I must have walked closer without realizing it.

"Have you a l-l-look," Carter said. He lit another cigarette. "This one was your Momma's favorite." He pointed to the most exquisite, unusual looking plant I had ever seen in my life. It had a large fuchsia flower with petite violet-colored smaller flowers surrounding it like little dancers, their leaves forming tiny pools for morning dew. Its broad, deep green leaves unfolded a little to greet the morning light. "Curcuma ginger," Carter told me. He yanked up a root and handed it to me. "Its center is bold and beautiful with lots of little fans worshippin' it."

I laughed. I could tell he was not only referring to the flower, he was talking about Momma, too.

"How well did you know her?"

"Knew her alright. Talked about plants a lot. Nice lady. She called me once in a while when she needed a hand. Got another landscapin' job in town, so wasn't workin' there much once she was pregnant. Ancestors were slaves at Azalea House."

I gulped, and Carter chuckled. "Still didn't do it," he said. "Your Momma and Daddy were good people. Never forget it. The rest of your family..."

"Not so much," I finished for him.

"Not so much."

I inhaled the last of the morning air, satisfied. It had worked out better than I had hoped. I guessed he sensed I was more relaxed, so he held out his hand.

"Carter."

"Marianne," I said, shaking his hand. It was dry as an old root, but there was something warm and friendly there, too. "I'm really sorry you went to jail for all this, Mr. Carter."

"Not your fault, Ms. Marianne."

"Thanks for the ginger," I told him, not really knowing what else to say.

"Come by and get more when ya ready," he said, lighting another cigarette. He pulled up a chair and sat in his oasis, smoking and looking around like this was the best place to be, like it was a cafe in Paris or the best bar in New Orleans.

"Can I use your bathroom before I leave?"

He looked back at me as he sucked on his cigarette, his eyes blazing with something I didn't recognize. He nodded once and pointed me towards the trailer. I walked around the corner, somehow knowing he was studying me, analyzing my movements.

I didn't need to go. I wanted to see inside his world, to pull back his wrinkled skin and see all his secrets.

The inside of the trailer was as damp and humid as outside, that unmistakable, unattended smell of mildew, earthy and decaying. The shadows inside stretched long and thin in the dying light, almost as if they could take on human shapes and turn towards my presence.

The living room was an ode to all things boyish. There were toy trucks in all shapes and sizes, some rusty from the dampness inside the trailer. There were action figures lined up on the shelves, years of dust caked into their tiny crevices and plastic folds. Little farm animals and farm men with faded faces and bendable legs, some sticking out at odd angles like they were broken, lined other shelves.

I meandered through the trailer, found the bathroom, splashed water on my face and flushed the toilet. Something cold tightened in the pit of my stomach. Why did he have all those things? Something about it made me wonder if Carter understood little boys too well.

What had I expected? I expected to go there and see if there was any activity, and to be intimidated by it all and to hop on my bike, go home and dread the start of school. But he had opened the door like he was expecting me. And was understanding. Even friendly. I did not expect to relate to him. And I did not expect to have that foreign, psychic connection with him. He was the first outsider I had ever been acquainted with in my strange, isolated existence in the village. I looked back as I hopped on my bike and he waved over his shoulder, his back still to me, cigarette still wedged in between those gnarled fingers.

Something by Carter's shed stopped me.

The faded black and yellow colors swirled. Dizziness took over my body, and I held onto the handlebars to keep my balance.

Black and yellow. Two little black and yellow Tonka trucks. With plants growing out of them. Identical Tonka trucks.

Just like the ones in the newspaper article I'd seen.

But what was even worse than that was the two baby doll heads with plants growing out of them. The features were weathered, the plastic cracked and slimy with algae.

I stopped on my bike, staring at this strange little altar.

"Miss?"

I biked away from that place, mud caking my legs. I thought I heard Carter call out again. But I peddled until my legs burned.

They're only mementos, Miss.

I heard it in my mind. He told me.

Was that his confession?

He did it. He did it and kept those toys as mementos, just like serial killers did with jewelry and hair and all kinds of weird things. He built a memorial for them to shake off the guilt.

They were playing with them the day they died. Mike and Monica had said so.

It made so much sense. Why else would Carter be arrested?

But he couldn't be. He couldn't be a murderer. He had been so gentle with me. So understanding.

As I biked away from the river, I started to question myself. What if it was all a lie? Why was he fishing near our house if he lived near a river? Then again, Daddy did tell me bass liked still ponds, and there *were* quite a few down in the low points of the woods right off the road. If Carter worked out at Azalea House occasionally and all his family had worked there over the years, he would know the area like the back of his old hand.

I was home too soon. Vivienne and Julia were sitting in the living room when I returned. Every time I made the mistake of walking in through the front door and saw them there, hate and anguish coiled together in my body. I regretted not going in and out through my window instead.

"Well, *you* look like hell."

"Marianne..." My aunt rolled her eyes and sighed. "Did you even wipe your feet? I hate when you go traipsing around the woods and track stuff inside."

"I never track stuff inside," I said, avoiding her fierce gaze. "That's the three of you doing that."

She scowled at me and Vivienne gave me a look like she knew what was coming. "Get upstairs right now. How dare you talk back to me like that."

I shrugged. I wanted to be alone in my room anyway. I needed to brood over everything that happened that morning.

I trudged upstairs, took a shower and then collapsed on my bed. It was already almost noon. We'd be in school a week from today.

My heart pounded at that prospect. Vivienne would be going to school with us. She was already getting asked out on dates. I'd heard her on the phone the night before, bragging to her friends back in the city.

School was my worst nightmare. Every single teacher there knew how it was hard for me to talk, and they always singled me out and made me answer questions while the rest of the class was so quiet, you could damn near hear life stirring on other planets as they awaited my stupid answer.

Nausea rolled through my whole body. I put my hand on my stomach and tried to swallow it back.

I didn't have new clothes for school. Vivienne had been out shopping with Julia four or five times already and had designer everything. I couldn't work up the courage to ask her for new clothes. I needed new bras badly. How was I supposed to work up the nerve to ask her without embarrassing myself? I broke out my journal and wrote it all down, even a few sentences to say to her that wouldn't sound stupid. But everything sounded stupid.

I put on one of Spellbound Hearts' albums for the first time in a long time. I stretched out on my bed and closed my eyes. Momma and Daddy's songs lulled me into a deep sleep. I dreamed I saw Marcus walking steadily towards a beam of light and the sounds of music. I called out to him to stop, to turn around and look at me, but he didn't hear me. As the beam of light swallowed him up, he glanced back over his shoulder and saw me. He looked much older, wiser, almost like he didn't need me and pitied me.

It was late afternoon by the time I woke up. I slept the rest of the day away.

But hadn't I done something monumental this morning? Hadn't I confronted the accused killer of my brothers? I had to give myself credit for it. Not only that, I had a conversation with him and was able to get my words out.

I longed to tell Marcus about it. And I needed to show him the wedding photo. But something held me back. I envisioned the terror in his eyes, and that faraway look he got when I did something without him. I went to his room and see what he was up to.

I slipped into the cool, dark room to find his face shrouded in the blue light of his computer.

"What are you doing?" I asked him.

"Learning to code and build websites."

"Well, that's useful. But we don't start school for another week."

"Don't remind me. Where were you all day?"

"The woods."

He turned to me. "What are we going to do? If we stay here, they'll end up shipping us off to boarding school. *Christian* boarding schools. Or we could beg Mom and Dad's band mates to take us in. Or we can run away—let's do that."

"How?" I was a bit shocked by his proposal, but the desperation in his eyes twisted my heart. He did not want to stay here, did not want to go back to the hell that was school. I couldn't blame him. He had been bullied tremendously for his CP, and the fact that he had a mute sister didn't help things at all. We were freaks, outcasts, damned to be put down for the rest of our youth at school. I wanted to get out, too, but Azalea House was all we knew.

"I don't know. Maybe I'm catastrophizing. Maybe it won't be so bad. Maybe people will have more sympathy for us now that Mom and Dad are gone, and their songs are popular again."

"You know that won't happen."

He sighed and pushed his glasses back up. I noticed they were held together with tape. "It's all about Vivienne now. She's destined to succeed, and we're destined to be losers."

"I just don't understand how someone who is so self-absorbed can be so well-loved," I said.

"That doesn't matter in today's world. You should see some of the message boards online. It's ridiculous. As far as I can tell, the only reason people follow her is so they can see what she wears. Welcome to the 90s, I guess."

"Speaking of that, we need to get you new glasses and new clothes. I—need a few things, too," I said, stopping myself short. I didn't want to admit to Marcus I needed bras.

"Maybe Troy can bring us," Marcus said. "If he is ever in a sober state. I suppose you're right. I can't go to school with tape on my glasses. That'll make things worse."

I stood up and marched out of the room, straight into the living room. I stood in front of the television and crossed my arms over my chest.

"Get out of the way, you trash," Vivienne said. "Mom!"

Julia studied me with her dead, piercing eyes. "Marianne…"

"I need new bras and clothes for school, please. Nothing fits."

"Because you're fat," Vivienne chirped.

"Marcus needs new glasses."

Julia looked right through me.

"You don't have to take us. We just need the money."

"Then how will you get there, you dumbass?"

"Vivienne, classy girls do not curse," Julia said pausing for a moment.

"Vivienne can take you in her new car."

I blanched. "What?"

"What?" Vivienne mimicked. "Mommy, I will not."

Julia regarded her with pity. "Okay," she said. "Troy can take you."

"Vivienne has a car?" I asked.

"I'll give you my credit card. If I see any unnecessary charges, I'll send you both to boarding school early. You understand?"

I nodded.

The next day was Tuesday, and we were off to the mall with Troy. Before we left, I rooted around in the back of my closet and found the old birthday bag with the lingerie from Uncle Joseph. There was a receipt inside. I held up the bra and panties, disgusted. White, lacy, and already too small. They were the gift of a man who spent too much time with the bra photos in the Sears catalogue. I stuffed it back into the bag, swallowing back the embarrassment of that horrific day.

I wadded up the gift bag and crammed it into my purse.

A horn blared and I ran outside to see Troy out front in Julia's Mercedes. Marcus was in the back, arms crossed over his chest, a scowl on his face. I followed his eyes until I noticed it: a bright red BMW convertible.

"How come Vivienne gets a car, and we have to beg for basic necessities?" Marcus asked as I climbed in.

"I don't know," Troy said. "Get yourself some really nice glasses is all I can say." There were dark circles under his eyes. When he caught me looking, he slipped his shades back up the bridge of his nose.

"Troy," I said. "Are you okay?"

"Just a little tired." He pulled the car out of the driveway and gunned it down the highway.

"Are you okay to drive is more the question," Marcus said. I turned around and looked at him.

"What?" he asked. His arms were crossed over his chest.

"What is your deal? You need new glasses. You can't go to school with tape holding everything together."

"Yes, I can. I changed my mind."

"No, you can't. You'll be made fun of."

"I already am anyway! What difference does it make?"

God, he was really agitated this morning. "What's your deal?" I asked again.

"I just hate the mall."

I held on to the door handle as Troy whipped the Mercedes around another curve. He had also turned on the radio, and it was blasting Alice in Chains.

"Um..." I said, not sure what to say.

"Want me to teach you how to drive?" he asked with a strange little sneer on his face.

"Don't do it," Marcus cautioned. "Unless you also want to drive like your life is an empty mess."

Troy slammed on the brakes and turned around. We were stopped in the middle of the highway.

"My life," he said, slipping his shades down his nose, "is not empty."

"Yes, it is," Marcus snapped. "That's why you drink all day. Anyone would if they were married to Julia and had Vivienne as a stepdaughter."

I turned around and glared at him. He shrugged. I blasted the radio so the three of us wouldn't have to talk.

The mall was dizzying and people my own age stared as they slouched around and smoked cigarettes on the benches scattered throughout. Great. Everyone else my age had a car or smoked or hung out at the mall, and my only social interaction, other than my family, was with the notorious Carter Leblanc.

I slipped into the lingerie store and glanced around, the adult air of the shop weighing on me. There were racks of frilly pink and white things, delicate as cake frosting, things that Vivienne would probably wear to disguise her black heart. Perfect mannequins donned figure-hugging sets that reminded me of what women in phone sex commercials wore. Some of the lingerie looked like it was plucked right off the paperback romance novels Momma sometimes read, understated and elegant.

None of it resonated with me.

But in a back corner was a rack full of dark and powerful clothing, things that defied normal conventions, clothing that conveyed a sense of sureness and authority.

I picked out a black bustier. I'd seen someone wear something like it on House of Style. It didn't feel particularly comfortable, but as I adjusted it and looked in the mirror, I looked so much older in it. I couldn't help but think about Julia looming over Troy, his eyes drinking in her curves. It wasn't practical, but I exchanged it because of the way it made me feel, like it released a power from within me.

With that and a few more everyday bras, I paid at the register and wandered next door to find Marcus, who was digging through black clothing.

He still had a noticeable gait, but at least he wasn't using the crutches anymore. I stared at anyone who looked at him the wrong way, threatening to murder with my eyes.

"Stop it, Marianne," he mumbled as we were looking at clothes.

"But you don't have your crutches to defend yourself anymore."

His eyes blazed strangely, and he pulled something out of his pocket. A lump formed in my throat when I saw what it was. Brass knuckles.

"Where did you get those?"

"Shh. Dad kept them in his office."

"Why would Daddy have those?"

My words hung in the air. Since my parents died, there were more questions than answers.

11

I cried the night before school started and hugged my stomach. It churned and clenched, and I sobbed in agony. Sleep was scarce, and when my alarm went off, I wiped the tears from my cheeks and dragged myself to the bathroom to splash cold water on my face.

I didn't have makeup, and Momma never got around to showing me how to put it on anyway. Looking for anything to give me the confidence I needed to get through this day, I put on the bustier and looked in the mirror. I felt the same surge I felt in the store. But I wondered what the boys at school would think. Would they leer at me? So I compromised and covered it up with a white button-up blouse. Superpower intact. No creepy boys.

I thought it looked okay. I leafed through some of Vivienne's magazines when she wasn't looking, searching for clues on how to put outfits together. Everyone in those magazines was wearing little miniskirts, stockings and baby tees. I opted for baggy jeans and new combat boots with the white blouse. I brushed out my hair and pinned the sides back, so I'd look trendy enough without attracting attention.

When I went downstairs, Troy was the only one in the kitchen. He peered over his drink at me, his eyes devouring me.

"What?" I asked.

"Nothing," he said, shuffling closer to where I was standing. "It's just that you look—"

I scrunched my brows together. Was it that bad? I ignored him and poured coffee.

He put a hand on my shoulder. "I mean that you look more mature."

I faced him. Our eyes locked.

He ran a warm finger down my neck, my collarbone, leaving little vibrations of electricity.

"You got rid of that stupid birthday present. I saw you go in and exchange it."

I swallowed back a knot of fear and nodded.

"It's more you. What do you think?"

His index finger rested on my clavicle, like he was restraining himself in some way, doubting his actions. I pushed it away. He bit back a small grin. I shoved him off, only a little, not in a forceful way...more playful, allowing him a better look.

I undid the top button on my blouse.

"White lace is too simplistic for such a complex person." He watched me, his arms folded over his chest. I undid another button. And then another one.

"But black is more you. Strong and sophisticated."

"You two freaks are always in here," Vivienne bleated as she walked in the kitchen. She stopped and glared at me. My whole body burned with fleeting desire, but now it was replaced with horror. Vivienne rolled her eyes.

"You're supposed to wear it with the shirt completely open, or don't wear a shirt at all over it," she lectured. "You look like a dork with it half unbuttoned like that." She swiped a diet coke from the fridge, walked right up to me and unbuttoned the bottom three buttons of my shirt.

"Not half bad," Vivienne said. She was wearing a short plaid miniskirt with a skin tight white shirt and knee-high socks with

Mary Janes. It made my cheeks warm just to look at her. "You need foundation. Your face kind of looks like shit."

"Vivienne," Troy warned while stirring his cocktail. His eyes drifted back over to me and lingered on my breasts.

"What? Come on," she said to me. "We have the same complexion. Let me show you how to put some on. With that and some lip gloss, you'll look like a normal human being."

What the hell. I followed her to the bathroom, thinking she would make me up like an idiot, but when she was done, I could barely tell I'd been crying. Whatever concoction she put on my face made me look well-rested and fresh.

"You're going into eleventh grade and you're associated with me, so you need to look decent," she said. Even though she was being nice, her tone was still sassy. I decided to keep quiet as usual and when we exited the bathroom, Marcus was there. He shot me a quizzical look. He had given himself a crew cut and his blue eyes blazed behind his glasses. He wore head to toe black. He seemed taller somehow.

"Everyone is going to think you're a creep for wearing goth stuff. Are you a Marilyn Manson fan, too? Ugh," Vivienne said, rolling her eyes.

"No. But I don't mind being a creep. I just want everyone to leave me alone."

"Well, they *will*. They're going to think you're just another weird loner."

"Fuck off, Vivienne."

"You better be nice to me," she said, getting face to face with him. "Or you'll lose your chance to ride to school in my BMW."

"I wouldn't be caught dead in that flashy yuppie shit," he said. He pushed past her and went into the kitchen.

"Marcus," Troy said, "you and your sister ride with Vivienne. Julia wants it that way."

"Why?" I interjected. I didn't actually want to ride in the Bimmer, either.

"It'll be good for you. You need to all start getting along."

"Christ," Marcus muttered in between bites of toast.

"Speaking *of*," Vivienne said, "let's go. We're going to be late."

Oh God. My stomach rolled again. Marcus seemed to sense my anxiety and made me eat a banana and a piece of toast on the way, but I was still so tense my shoulders and neck ached.

Troy must have taught Vivienne to drive, because we went at warp speed and were at school in seconds, despite the horrific music Vivienne blasted from the stereo.

"What the hell is this crap?" Marcus asked.

"It's the Spice Girls," she snapped. "Everyone listens to it. Grunge is dead."

"Marianne and I both listen to more industrial stuff," Marcus smarted. "Not that you'd know what that is."

I had to bite my lip to keep from laughing. I didn't know if he was tearing into Vivienne to lift my spirits or not, but it worked.

"I know what that is. Like Nine Inch Nails. Trent Reznor would be hot if he weren't so *brooding* all the time."

"Admit it, you do like men who wear black."

"Not you, cousin. You're a fag anyway," she said.

Marcus kicked the back seat, and she sneered at him in the rear-view mirror like she'd won. What a great way to start off the school year. We parked and everyone turned their heads to see the cherry red BMW convertible that pulled into the student lot. I could hear people talking as soon as Vivienne cut off the engine.

"It's Vivienne Easton, the model," someone said.

"Who is that with her?"

Were they talking about me? Or Marcus? I glanced over at Marcus as we exited the car. His cerebral palsy seemed like a distant memory now, the only noticeable remnant the stiffness in his left leg. But he was biting his lip, like he was putting in effort to walk normally. My heart dropped for him.

"Quit looking at me like that," he said to me.

"Sorry," I mouthed silently.

"You dorks can walk in with me," Vivienne said. But she walked too fast for Marcus to keep up. Soon we were trailing behind her like her court. Several people swarmed her and asked her questions about modeling and about her aunt and uncle.

"You don't have to walk with me," Marcus said. But I did anyway, and he dropped his shoulders and even quit neurotically adjusting his glasses as we neared the building.

The first bell rang.

"Find you at lunch," I said. He nodded and gave me a little wave.

Walking with him lessened my anxiety a bit. I found my homeroom and sat in the front. I always sat near the front so the teacher could hear me if I absolutely had to speak.

I was beyond relieved to see Chloe in gym class later that morning. I ran over to her and gave her a hug.

"I missed you!" she said, holding me tight. It was an awkward hug, as always, with Chloe's gangly limbs and tall stature, me with my face nearly buried in her breasts. But it was the best hug I'd had in a long time.

"Lesbians," some girl hissed, and Chloe flipped her off.

The gym teacher was an old lady with a disheveled wig. She took roll, made us do jumping jacks, and then let us sit on the bleachers for the rest of the period. Chloe and I bought Pepsis and sat off to the side, catching up.

"So, there's this rumor going around that you went over to Carter Leblanc's trailer," she said.

My brain swirled with anxiety. How did they know? *Think of something quick*, I told myself.

"I was just bored and ended up out that way. I kind of wanted to see if he was there."

"Was he?"

I shook my head no, and she seemed satisfied. Good. If Chloe heard any more rumors, she'd set them straight.

We were sitting close, leaning forward when something cold slid down the back of my pants. When I turned around, three guys burst out laughing. I didn't even know they were sitting behind us.

"What the hell are you doing?" Chloe said, standing up tall.

"We were just playing," one of them said. They were all dressed like preps and that made the lump in my throat come back. I stood up and shook out my jeans and pennies fell out through my pants leg.

"Are you three slow or something?"

"Like Marcus Easton? Nope, I'm afraid not. We just saw a slot and wanted to know how much it took to get her going," said the one in the middle. "Your pants are so baggy that there's a huge gap in the back when you sit down."

"Yeah," one of them said. "Blake wants to see more."

"How many pennies would that take?" the one who I guess was Blake asked.

I swallowed and fought back tears. He was clearly the leader, the best looking. I recognized him from every sports team our school had, but I couldn't remember his name.

Chloe picked up the pennies and chucked them at the group, grabbed my hand and led me into the girls' bathroom. I cried while Chloe hugged me and wiped my face off.

"It's okay. If you show them it doesn't bother you, maybe they'll leave you alone," she told me. The bell rang and I jumped and sniffled. "Come on," she said. "Let's go to lunch and find Marcus."

He acknowledged us with a vague nod and then headed to a spot off to the side in the lunchroom. We sat and ate peacefully, Marcus and Chloe catching up while I stayed quiet, until the jock showed up again. He had a half-smile on his face. Before he got to our table, he looked over his shoulder at Vivienne, the rest of the jocks in his group, and a bunch of girls I recognized as cheerleaders.

"Hey Marianne, you know I was just messing with you, right?"

"Hey Blake," Marcus said. "Fuck off."

"Or what, faggot?" Blake got right in his face and a tiny whimper escaped my throat. My face warmed. But Marcus stood up before anyone could say anything else and popped him in the face. When Blake staggered backwards, a geyser of blood rushed from his nose. Marcus stood there, his face totally deadpan, with the brass knuckles in his fist.

It all happened so fast. A couple of teachers hauled them both away, as Chloe and I sat there in shock, looking at the blood on the lunchroom table and floor. Some of it had even landed on my wilted salad. Everyone in the lunchroom was silent. Then, as if on cue, the bell rang.

I tried to concentrate on stuff the teachers were saying for the rest of the day, but I couldn't—everyone had eyes on me. Their stares bored into my soul. It was my fault their beloved Blake got punched out. Marcus did it, but he did it because of me. And Marcus was my brother.

Sweat drenched the underarms and underneath my breasts, soaking the blouse I was wearing. I walked from fifth to sixth period with my arms folded over my chest, my shoulders hunched. And as soon as the tardy bell rang for sixth period, a voice came over the speaker.

"Marianne Easton to the office, please."

Everyone turned around and looked at me. That teacher assigned seats, and I was forced to the very back where I was subjected to blatant stares and jeers that I didn't talk loud enough. I unfolded myself from my chair and sulked to the principal's office.

The principal was a stocky, tall man with a booming voice and a soft spot for jocks and cheerleaders. I had never been to the office for anything other than check-outs for doctors' appointments and other random administrative things.

"Tell me what happened."

"That Blake guy was putting pennies down the back of my pants. When my brother told him to leave me alone, Blake called him a faggot."

"Did you know your brother was carrying around brass knuckles? To school?" His voice was rising, and my heart was pounding so hard it travelled up to my temples. I shook my head.

"I understand you two have had a rough year. But encouraging your brother to sucker punch one of our best students is unacceptable."

I looked up and locked eyes with him. "What about what

Blake did?" I asked. There was some defiance in my voice and instantly regretted it.

He stared at me for a long time before he spoke again. "Go back to class," he said.

I got up to leave and took my time walking back towards class, hoping enough time had elapsed and the bell to go home would be ringing soon. I stopped off in the bathroom to splash cold water on my face before I went back to sixth period. Eyes all shuffled back to me when I walked in, but luckily, the teacher was in the middle of some speech about history, and everyone was forced to keep their eyes front. I was relieved.

This class was going to be the worst of them all. I knew it. I had this teacher last year, and she wanted to be best friends with all her students. All the students swooned every time this teacher walked into the room. I supposed she seemed like a caring, sweet woman to everyone else, but to me, she was nosy and overly concerned, with eyes that were too close together and features that were a disaster and somewhat disguised with her heavy makeup. Tall, whitish hair, high-pitched voice, and some sort of perfume that made my head spin.

I took my seat. She said she wanted to see me after class.

"Marianne, why are you so quiet?" she asked as people filed out. I stayed silent and looked down at her shoes instead. They were very high-heeled, not unlike the shoes Julia wore in the bedroom with Troy.

She sighed with a dramatic emphasis and shuffled some papers around. "You scored perfectly on all your tests last year. Are you going to answer me when I call on you this year?"

All I could think about was running out of the room. I studied the door instead of answering.

"You can talk to me about your parents' death, you know."

I wanted to open my mouth to tell her to fuck off, to never mention my parents again, and that she would be the last person I'd approach with any sort of problem.

"You can go, I guess."

But when the bell rang again, that sense of dread didn't leave me. Vivienne's car wasn't in the student lot. Which meant I'd have to either run to catch the bus or walk several miles home.

I opted for the walk.

It took an hour. I cut through the woods and swampy patches, and my clothes were filthy by the time I got home.

"And where the hell have you been?" Julia screamed.

"Vivienne left me at school, and I missed the bus. Thanks for asking about my day."

"I did not leave her," Vivienne yelled.

Everyone was sitting around the kitchen table. Marcus had that same deadpan look on his face. Troy leaned back in his chair, eyes closed, probably drunk out of his skull. Vivienne wore a satisfied grin. Julia's eyebrows were drawn together in a scorn. Her hair was wild, and she had on an extra layer of makeup today, making her look like some enraged clown.

"Your car wasn't there when I went to the lot," I said. I went to the fridge to look for something to drink. "So I had to walk. Thanks for waiting. And thank you, Marcus, for standing up for me."

"At least someone appreciates me."

"Jules, you're being hard on them. Leave them alone," Troy slurred.

"Shut up, Troy. And you," she said, sneering at Marcus. "I want every corner of this house spic and span. You're suspended for three days. That should give you plenty of time."

Marcus didn't appear to hear her. Either way, I was shocked Marcus only got three days' suspension. From the way the principal sounded, I was afraid he would be expelled. I grabbed a bunch of stuff out of the fridge and followed Marcus to his room. We pigged out on cheese, turkey, Nutella, and olives while we talked.

"How did it feel?" I asked.

"Pretty good," Marcus said in between bites of Nutella. "I could actually hear his bone breaking."

"Why did you do it?"

Marcus frowned. "Blake's been getting on my nerves for years.

He calls me fag constantly, and I just got tired of it. I ignored him for so long. You know what they say, homophobes always do stuff like that for a reason. He's probably flaming. But then it seems he turned his attention to you. I would have done it anyway to make everyone afraid of me."

It was getting late. I glanced over at the clock and noticed it was already after nine o'clock. The house was winding down, creaking and groaning in its old house way as the foundation settled.

"I've always hated the way this house sounds at night," Marcus said.

As if it heard him, it quieted down.

That's when the freezing sensation hit me. My skin broke out in goose flesh. I shivered.

"What?" Marcus asked. I must have had a look on my face that made him uncomfortable. I could tell by the way he shifted his body and adjusted his glasses.

"You don't feel…"

The dead quiet was broken by murmuring emanating from my room. It was shrill murmuring, as if it was coming from a small female child. It went on and on nonstop, only pausing to take a break for a breath before beginning again. It sounded almost like the voice was reading something.

Marcus mouthed 'what the fuck' silently, and I couldn't answer. It wasn't Vivienne, Troy, or Julia speaking. It didn't sound like anyone I knew, but it was clearly coming from the other side of the wall, next to Marcus's room. My room. It had to be.

Just as suddenly as it started, it stopped. Marcus and I looked at each other. I stared at the door, waiting for it to be knocked down by whatever force was torturing us.

A blast of arctic air blew in from underneath the door.

A giggle cut through the silence, clear as a bell. It came from outside the room. It was a girl's voice.

"Go away," I said, and footsteps clunked away from the door and down the hall. As the steps faded, so did the chill.

"That wasn't Vivienne," Marcus said.

"I know. Come with me," I told him.

I opened the door and looked around. Nothing. Marcus was holding on to the back of my shirt for dear life. I crept down the hall towards my room. The door was ajar. I could have sworn I shut it earlier. I pushed it open, and it creaked.

I didn't see anything off in the room.

"That doll," Marcus said.

"What?" I whispered. I didn't know what he was talking about. Then I followed his pointed finger and saw what he was talking about.

The doll that usually sat in the rocking chair was gone.

"What'd you do with that stupid thing?" Marcus asked. I shrugged. Surely, that could not have been what was making all that noise. "Well? Where the hell is it?" he continued to pester.

"I-I don't know," I said, and really meant it. The doll was such a part of my room that it blended in with everything else, a fixture. "It was there this morning, though. I'm sure of it."

There it was again. That giggle. This time, it came from further down the hall, closer to Vivienne's room.

"That's right. Torment her instead," Marcus said. He yanked my shirt and pulled me back into his room. "Just sleep in here if you want."

Sleep? There was no way I could, not with everything that happened at school and this horrifying experience. But Marcus put out a really comfortable mat on the floor and gave me one of his best blankets, and I was off in another world within minutes. To hell with the doll. If she wanted back in my room, she knew the way.

I awoke early. When I went back to my room, there was no doll. I went about my day with a tense ball of nerves, albeit more rested. I hated thinking about a three-foot Raggedy Ann doll stalking the halls and going in and out of my room. I almost told Chloe about it but decided against it. The worst thing was, I had no idea why Momma chose to put that doll in my room or what the history was behind it. She was very insistent I keep it.

"It has to stay in here," she had said as she situated it carefully in the rocking chair.

"I hate that thing."

She whirled around and glared at me, a wild look in her eyes. "Don't say that," she snapped. I gasped. I was shocked at her reaction. "I'm sorry, honey," she said, her voice sweet again. "It just needs to stay in this room. It's just a Raggedy Ann doll, that's all. It can't hurt you."

It can't hurt you. It can't hurt you. It can't hurt you.

The next day, Momma's words were still chanting during P.E. when one of the guys in the jock trio approached me and Chloe. I had seen Rob leering over Vivienne the day before in the student parking lot. He had thick black hair and the steeliest blue eyes I'd ever seen. They were inhuman, with no hint of empathy whatsoever.

"What?" Chloe barked at him as she stood up to get eye level with him.

"Nothing!" the guy said with a laugh. He stepped back and put his hands up in mock surrender. "I just wanted to talk to Marianne."

Chloe gave me a look and I nodded. She didn't move out of his way, though. Rob hesitated.

"Anything you have to say to her, you can say in front of me," Chloe said, her arms crossed over her chest.

"You know, one day, you're not going to have anyone around to protect you," Rob said to me with a hint of anger in his voice.

"Okay, you can fuck off, too." Chloe pushed him back.

"Blake only did that because he thinks you're pretty. You should stop being such a snob and talk to other people."

"That's his excuse for being an immature douchebag? We're done here. Bye." Chloe waved him away, and he took his time retreating, eyeing me with suspicion and shaking his head. "Blake 'wants to fuck you," she said to me. Her tone was thick with sarcasm, but I shrugged. It was a setup in the making, some way for him to get back at me for my brother breaking his nose.

I didn't have the brain space to worry about Blake. I was more concerned about that damned doll. There was so much I didn't know about that house and the kinds of people who passed through it. Like Theo. And the twins.

But there was one person who did know. Carter. If he was the killer, would he kill me if I visited him again?

I had to know. I had to work up the courage to talk to him again. If I was going to die, at least I would die with the truth.

12

The house sparkled so much, it reminded me of when Momma and Daddy were alive. It was nice to come home to it. The floors gleamed and when I dusted my fingers across the banister, they came away clean.

I trod carefully when I walked through the foyer. It was like the cleaning had chased the evil spirits away. I had taken the bus to school that day because I didn't want to be alone in the car with Vivienne, and the walk through the woods from the bus stop to the house was actually pleasant. I ran upstairs to check on Marcus. He was sprawled out on his bed, headphones covering his ears.

"You finished the whole house today," I said.

"Troy helped me."

"Well, that was nice. He's not so bad all the time, is he?"

Marcus gave me a look and shrugged, then put his headphones away. "Want to see something cute?" he asked me. His face lit up in a way I didn't see often. I nodded, and he reached underneath his bed and pulled out a kitten so small, I thought it was a stuffed animal at first until it meowed. It was a pure white ball of fluff with gigantic green eyes that took up most of its face. I squealed in delight.

"I named him Ghost," Marcus said.

"Where did you find him?" The kitten tottered towards me, his eyes wide with curiosity.

"Out by the road."

"Speaking of the road..." I didn't know how to bring up the fact that I had gone to see Carter Leblanc.

Marcus shifted his glasses and stared at me. "Marianne. What?"

"I took my bike down to The Alley a week before school—"

"You *what*?"

"It was no big deal. I just wanted to see if Carter was living in that same place, and he was. It was like he was out there...I don't know. Waiting for me, or something." I paused. Marcus's expression didn't change. A tiny thread of worry cut through me. I could never tell exactly what he was thinking these days. Ghost curled up in my lap and I stroked his head, which calmed me a little.

"He was nice. But there was—I don't know. Like an altar or something. With toy trucks. And doll heads."

"I heard he's into voodoo and all kinds of weird shit. Maybe it was nothing. But that doesn't matter as much as someone seeing you go over there. You shouldn't do that again."

"I want to go back and ask him about the history of this place."

"Are you worried about that dumb doll again?"

"Yes," I admitted. "And other things. Look, we don't even know whose doll it is. And why Momma was so insistent I keep it in my room. Aren't you curious?"

"Ignorance is bliss," he said. "What we really ought to do is burn this place down."

"I want to know what happened here. I feel like if I find out, I'll sleep better."

He looked at me for a long time before he answered. "Is that really true, you think? Or do you just need more time to accept that Mom and Dad are gone?"

That hit me like a dart. He was right in some way, I supposed. I still hadn't come to terms with their deaths. When I did sleep, I would have dreams they were alive, or that we were called to the hospital and told it was someone else's Town Car that was involved in the accident and our parents were fine. They were just in the hospital, getting checked over.

But there were too many unsolved mysteries fueling my anxiety. The twins talked about a puzzle. My intuition was screaming that Carter had some of the pieces to this puzzle. I had that same psychic thing with Marcus, but not to the extent I had with Carter. The thought of it filled me with nervous energy, but I had to know more about it. Who else could I ask? I knew of no one else who experienced those things and talked openly about it. Marcus always questioned things or was too afraid to step that far into the darkness with me. Chloe was the same way. Yet both had been so brave lately...

"Why don't you come with me?" But I already knew his answer before he opened his mouth. Momma and I communicated like that all the time, wordlessly, using only our minds, transferring thoughts back and forth to each other like Chloe and I passed notes at school.

"Hell no," he said. "Nope. And I don't want you to go, either."

"Oh, come on."

"Marianne, if someone sees you, they'll leak it to the media. You know how the media has been lately."

He paused and studied me for a moment. "You're not worried he might be...I don't know. Creepy? And you're an attractive girl. You know what I mean."

I shook my head. I didn't want to know.

I also didn't want to see Momma and Daddy on television or on magazines or anything. I could barely stand to look at pictures of them. I missed them terribly, I really did. Maybe Carter could tell me more about my parents back in the day.

"I'll cut through the woods," I said. "No one will see me." I handed Ghost over to Marcus and slipped out through the window. If I left right then, maybe I could make it back before bedtime.

I navigated through the bushes and the tangled underbrush, through the trees and muck to The Alley. It was almost sunset when I got there, and the shadows were long. Again, I could see Carter sitting outside like he was waiting for me in his plant oasis, his cigarette smoke curling in the air like ghostly fingers. He waved me over.

"That memorial, I didn't mean harm. I gave those as gifts. Found 'em later, after they died, out in the trash." His eyes were wet with emotion, like I had really hurt him by thinking he was guilty. Maybe he really wasn't. I looked at the ground, ashamed.

"You wanna talk about the doll first? Or Theo?"

"Theo." I searched for some sign of someone spying on us or the media, but it was quiet.

"No one will come here." I wasn't sure if he said it aloud or not. And I wasn't sure if he said the rest aloud, either.

"Theo was an adventurous man. Used to really get off on that kinda thing. He did things for the thrill, and he did them all the time. Drinkin', gamblin'..."

Chasing women, I thought.

"Yes," he confirmed.

This telepathic thing I had with Carter put me at ease. It was familiar, like communicating with Momma. Still, he spoke, as if he didn't want to make me nervous.

"Your momma was a pretty lady, and I don't know what happened, really," he said. "But people talked in this town. They always do."

"Were the twins his?"

He shrugged. "Sorry to say I don't know that, either. Something you have to figure out."

My mind tracked back to the baby bracelets. They had stones set into them. Had Theo done that for his kids? How would I know for sure?

"How did Theo die?"

"A fall, I heard. Right after the twins died."

I would have to look up the dates. "How soon after?"

"Oh, a few weeks, I think. A terrible time for everyone. Especially Theo." He gave me a strange look.

Oh, I didn't like what he was getting at. I couldn't think of Momma doing something like that to Daddy. What if Theo killed them? What if he found out they weren't his and got mad and killed them? What if it was my aunt, jealous of her husband's attraction to Momma? Or what if my Dad killed the twins because they weren't his? Maybe that's why he sat in that spot to look over the pond.

Oh, how my head spun with so many wretched possibilities, almost like they were going around in my brain like a deranged carousel.

"I know one thing, though," he said, lighting another cigarette, "it's something with that pond. With that land. It brings out the worst in the wrong kinda people."

That scared me even more. He confirmed my anxiety around the house, why I was always watching for something in the woods or heard whispers tingling my brain.

"There was a child left there at some point, back when that old place was a boarding house. Used to carry around that doll. Betty let her stay there. She never really grew up. She was thirty when she drowned in that pond, they say by suicide. And your Momma saw it. I think that's why she kept that doll. She thought kindly of that young lady."

I wasn't sure if I liked story time with Carter all that much anymore. The thought of some childlike grown woman carrying a three-foot-tall Raggedy Ann doll around was very unsettling to me.

"The girl—woman, whatever. Ann was her name. Like the doll. And very attached to that thing, she was. Said the doll told her things about the house."

"What should I do? I mean, Momma insisted I keep it in my room."

Carter looked at me like I should know the answer. "Well, suppose you should keep it in there. And listen to her. I told ya." And then he stood up and went inside the trailer.

I sat there, still a bit shell-shocked, and blinked stupidly before deciding to go back home, too.

It was dark by the time I was half-way home, but a strange light seemed to dance in front of me, just enough for me to see the way. I felt like I was being guided safely.

When I got home, the doll was back in the rocking chair. I stretched out onto the bed and stared into the doll's black eyes, silently willing it to tell me more about this house and everyone who passed through here, even the good stories. But those eyes remained soulless and bleak. I turned off the light.

"*Leave this place*." A muffled, childlike whisper. I turned the light back on. The doll was still.

But was it advice, a warning or a command? The next day, I went back to school, and I was surprised when Blake was there. He seemed unfazed by everything that had happened. I caught him sneaking glances at me occasionally, but he never said anything to me or to Marcus.

Marcus got what he wished for. Everyone was afraid of him. To me, his changes were so subtle every day, but to the kids at school, they could see he had gone through puberty over the summer. He was taller, walking almost normally, and his voice changed sounded more mature. We were both changing so quickly, wanting more for ourselves and each other. With Momma and Daddy gone, the future never seemed so present and so far away.

13

"From here on out, you three are going to get along," Julia said, her fists balled up on the dining room table.

"Mom!" Vivienne protested. She pushed her plate across the table and crossed her arms over her chest.

Marcus said, "Fuck that. Vivienne is crazy."

"I'm not the one who assaulted someone at school."

"Vivienne," Julia warned. "Take Marianne with you to that party later."

"I'm not going," Marcus said. He piled peas on top of his mashed potatoes.

"That's right, you're not. You're grounded. You're to stay in your room for what you did."

Marcus flashed a quick smirk at his pea-topped mountain. I knew staying in his room was what he wanted. Troy rolled his eyes and downed his juice.

"Marianne, go out and socialize. It'll be good for you."

My stomach dropped. Vivienne glared at me across the table, her eyes glassy and cruel.

I went to bed thinking about last year's Labor Day, when we

all went to Gulf Shores. My parents would have never forced me to go to a party.

I wanted to dream of gentle waves and the soft calls of gulls, but my head was full of nightmares, of opening my mouth and vomiting pond water instead of words.

"Marcus!" Julia screamed from the kitchen the next day. "Get off the Internet! I'm expecting a call from Vivienne's agent! Marianne, go upstairs and tell your brother to get off the Internet."

I trudged upstairs. Anything to delay going to this Labor Day party with Vivienne.

I banged on Marcus's door.

"What?" His voice sounded irritated, deeper.

"Aunt Julia says to get off the Internet."

"Aunt Julia can fuck off." Something with a loud tattoo of a beat and shredding guitars followed. I tried the doorknob. It was locked. "Just go on to the party with Vivienne," he said. Something in the mockery of his tone made my stomach queasy.

I went to my room without any idea what to wear to this party. I hated parties. It was hard enough to talk to people I did want to speak to, let alone people I hardly knew. After trying on a few things, I settled on a t-shirt, same as always. But while waiting for Vivienne to get ready, I took it off and put the bustier on.

Wearing it made me feel like I had a superpower. It cinched in my waist and showcased the tops of my breasts. I could see the look in Troy's eyes when he saw me in it. Like he was weakened by it. I decided to keep it on and put the t-shirt over it so no one could see it underneath. Wearing it under my t-shirt, feeling it hug my body, it made me feel that for once, I had some power in this world, even if it was my little secret.

I went into Vivienne's room to see if she was ready. The blinds were open, letting in a little light. There was a poster of Kate Moss on the wall, a minimalist black and white portrait with the word "Obsession" printed across the top. I stared at it, and Kate stared back with eyes that saw through me, black, dead eyes that did not display any sort of obsession or strong emotion whatsoever. They resembled the dead ducks' eyes. Kate's clavicle was sharp and prominent.

"Vivienne?"

"I'm ready," she said from behind me. When I turned around, she was wearing a black tank top much like the one Kate Moss was wearing in the photo, with jeans with holes in them. And like Kate, her clavicles could chip ice. She looked up again. There were dark hollows under her eyes.

"Are you okay?" I asked her.

She stuffed something deep inside of her purse. Something strange flashed across her eyes, something alive, but it only lasted a split second. Her eyes went cold again, and she said, "I'm fine. Let's go."

I kept my eyes away from the speedometer and focused on the black of night outside the window instead. I turned my head at the click of the lighter and the sudden offensive odor. Vivienne was lighting a cigarette.

"It keeps me from eating too much."

"Okay," I said.

"Don't tell Mom."

"Okay."

There were lots of other cars parked around the house, mostly BMWs and Mercedes, probably mom or dad's borrowed cars to arrive in something classier than their own Civics.

We walked around the back. I kept my arms crossed over my chest and shadowed Vivienne.

"Hi, babe," said a blonde girl in an outfit like Vivienne was wearing. "Did you get that Calvin Klein shoot?"

Vivienne gulped. "Not yet."

"It's been a little while since House of Style, huh?" the blonde said, pursing her lips as if suppressing a grin. Vivienne rolled her eyes and took a long drag off her cigarette, sucking on it until it burned well into the filter.

"You're definitely thin enough," the girl said, not looking at Vivienne but at me. "Who's this?"

"This is my cousin, Marianne," Vivienne said, and lit another cigarette. "This is Carina."

Carina shook my hand softly, her eyes darting back and forth between me and Vivienne. I folded my arms across my chest again.

"Well, maybe you just need to be thinner," Carina said, and glanced back at me. Her eyes were very green, almost technicolor like spring leaves. "I can get some ice for you."

"Yeah, okay," Vivienne said. Carina glanced at me again and flipped her hair over her shoulder. "Nice meeting you," she said before turning away. I opened my mouth to say something, but my voice caught in my throat.

"Why is she getting ice for you if you don't have a drink?" I asked.

Vivienne scoffed. "Jesus, Marianne." She took a long drag off her cigarette. I stood there with my hands across my chest, already sweating.

"I didn't know you tried out for a Calvin Klein thing," I said, trying to change the subject.

A pause. She took another long drag and blew out the smoke in a long, languid breath. "I didn't." She looked at me, her eyes still glassy. "I just wanted Mom to think I did. Troy took me to the mall instead."

I didn't know what to say. She seemed very tiny all the sudden, slouched over, smoking a cigarette, staring out at the pool. There was a long pause as she finished her cigarette. She dropped it to the ground and stepped on it, then wandered off. I stood there, not knowing what to do with my hands. No wonder people smoked. It gave them something to do, something to fidget with.

Carina came back. "I have Vivienne's ice. Where is she?"

I shrugged.

"Do you model, too?"

I shook my head.

"I've seen you at school. You're friends with Chloe."

"Yes," I managed to say. My voice sounded strained.

"Chloe is very straight edged," Carina said, frowning. "What about you?"

I didn't exactly know what she meant. "No," I said, hoping it was the right answer. Carina smiled. She took my hand and led me past a group of guys. One guy with a chain wallet and blond spiked hair stepped in front of us. They were smoking something that smelled slightly sweet and chemical.

"Carina. Got something for me?"

She reached in her purse and held out a clasped palm. Spike reached for it and she put out her other hand, palm up. "Money first."

"Of course. You know I'm good for it." He tugged on the chain and fished out some cash, and Carina dropped something in his palm. She tugged at my sleeve and I followed her.

Inside, the bass thumped, and Beck sang about someone being alone in a new pollution. It echoed in my head. Still, I followed Carina, hoping she wasn't going to lead me into something worse. The darkness of the stair top beckoned. It was much cooler up there, almost like a tomb. She went inside a room and I stood at the entrance, mesmerized.

This was her bedroom. Had to be. The walls were white and there were black-and-white photographs pinned up everywhere. Mostly photos of fallen trees, cemeteries, and old broken toys. Her bed had black and white pillows and a plain down comforter.

"What are all these?" I wasn't sure why I felt so comfortable here. Pure curiosity coursed through me. I inched up closer to a picture of a dead tree, its limbs like old, gnarled fingers.

"I took them," she said. She looked very different all the sudden, sitting on her bed, surrounded by all that contrast, an almost perfect representation of a high school Barbie type in a world of strange, stark decay. She reached over and pulled out something from the nightstand, something that smelled strangely musky and enticing. "They remind me that things can be forgotten. But there's beauty in that." She paused and rolled a joint. I closed the door and sat down. "Do you smoke?"

I would have accepted anything from her then. She lit it and puffed, passed it to me. "Inhale slowly, otherwise you'll cough a lot."

The sensation was a bit like the first burn of soda, something pleasantly glowing and tangy. When I blew the smoke out, a warm sense of relaxation passed through me. My throat even relaxed, and I sighed, relieved.

"If you like that, you'll like these, too," she said, and handed me a small pill. "It helps with anxiety." She took one and I followed her lead, swallowing back embarrassment.

"Vivienne told me about your parents," she said. "It sucks."

I nodded. There was a shot of downtown Baton Rouge, a row of abandoned buildings with paint peeling off the buildings. I knew the area. My parents took us through there, explaining they played a few shows around there back in the day. But like a lot of places in Baton Rouge, it was left to rot. I almost asked Carina why she took that picture.

"My mom lives in Dallas," she said. "Or she did. She's in jail again. My dad is homeless. This is my grandparents' house. They leave me here to go to Florida a lot, though."

"My grandparents are in Florida too, I think," I said.

"Yeah."

I looked at her profile. Her hair was a blonder replication of Jennifer Aniston's. Her nails were painted blue. And I couldn't believe I was sitting here with a cheerleader, who was sharing the intimate, not always sunny details of her life.

"Here," she said. "Breathe in." She blew smoke in my face. "It's called shot gunning. You blow it back and forth to conserve the smoke. And guys practically cum in their pants when they watch you do it."

I laughed. She turned and met my eyes and laughed, too. I forced myself to look into her eyes. They were very green, even in the dim light of the room. And then her lips were on me, warm and plush and comforting like the pot.

"Did you like that? Carina asked.

I nodded.

"Can you feel the pill kicking in?"

"I think so. What is it supposed to feel like?"

"It makes you feel relaxed. Uninhibited. It lets you be yourself. Do you feel relaxed?

"Definitely."

"Can I see what you're wearing beneath your shirt? It looks really cool."

"Do you think so?" I said. Feeling buzzed, I grabbed the bottom of my t-shirt and lifted it over my head and off my body."

"Whoa. Where did you get that?"

"At the mall."

"I bet guys cum in their pants when they see you in that, too."

That really made me laugh.

"I like to take the pill to relax, and then with the air conditioning blasting, I like to take my clothes off and wrap myself in the comforter. The cold air and the warmth of the blanket feels amazing. Wanna try with me?"

My mind was fuzzy, the sounds of the party beyond the door just static noise as our bodies intertwined in the quiet bubble of the down comforter. The sheets were cool, her body was warm as we pressed against each other, the pot making our movements languid and fluid.

"It feels even better with you here," Carina said.

She rolled on top of me, and all that existed was the present moment, wrapping around me, pulling me further down into the cocoon of Carina's bed. The sensations of the drugs and her touch were a symphony that I yearned to hear and feel. After the crescendo, my eyes closed, and we plunged into the darkness of the room.

A few hours later, I woke up alone in the bed, and it was quiet. I walked out of the house past the last remaining guests. All the houses were typical suburban mansions in this area, but they looked nearly identical, like the adjoining cemetery, all the same too, even in death. But I had slept with a popular cheerleader, who sold drugs and who also had a dysfunctional family.

Vivienne was sitting on the Bimmer's hood, cross-legged, smoking a cigarette. She turned a little when I walked up behind her.

"Did you have fun?"

I shrugged. I thought I saw a small smile on her face. We rode back home with the top down, the early morning mist refreshing us on what would be a humid day. She blasted something loud and upbeat on the radio, something I didn't recognize.

Why did I want to bond with her? Maybe we had finally shared something together, more than smoking and doing drugs at parties.

"Vivienne?" I glanced down at my shirt, which was damp with mist and slightly see-through. The lace edges of the bustier poked through the shirt.

She ignored me and reached over to blare the radio. I reached over and turned it down.

"What?" She didn't try to hide the irritation in her voice.

"Did Joseph ever…do anything inappropriate around you?"

"Joseph is always inappropriate." She turned the radio back up.

"No, I mean—"

She glanced at me. "I know what you mean."

"He gives me money after. It makes me feel worse." I had never told anyone that before. Saying it out loud took the tension out of my neck and shoulders.

She punched the gas and the BMW lurched forward.

"Vivienne…"

Her hands gripped the wheel, her knuckles white. She whipped the car into our driveway.

"I can't believe it. I can't believe he *pays* you for it."

When we pulled up, she removed a small bottle of perfume from her purse. "Here," she said. "You smell like pot. And pussy." I flushed, but she said it so nonchalantly I took her advice.

When we walked in, Troy was asleep on the couch. I stopped when I saw the headline running across the screen on television. Princess Diana had died in Paris in a car accident. The news anchor mentioned something about the paparazzi chasing her.

Vivienne walked upstairs without saying a word.

Julia babbled on, her voice terse, and then Vivienne said, "No. I'm not going. I don't care how much it pays."

"Get dressed this instant! It's an important job. I know you didn't get Calvin Klein…"

A door slammed.

I took the cup from Troy's hand, pulled the quilt over him and turned off the television. I went upstairs and that Beck song played in my head in a loop, and I thought about being alone in a new pollution.

All of us were.

School seemed even stranger that Tuesday after the holiday. I saw Carina in the hall, her blonde hair bouncing like she was in a hair commercial and tried to meet her eyes. She looked right through me, as though without the bustier, I was invisible.

After lunch in English class, I eavesdropped on a few of the popular girls talking. I pretended to write a note to Chloe, but instead I transcribed what they said.

"Blake is sleeping with Vivienne." It was from one of the girls on the cheerleading squad. She was wearing a pink silk halter top with a choker and looked like Reese Witherspoon. Her nipples were outlined by the material of her top and three guys, one of them the guy from the party with spiked hair, were staring at her.

"No he's not," some vaguely familiar looking girl with shoulder-length black hair said. She looked like Cordelia from Buffy the Vampire Slayer. "He's sleeping with Carina."

"Blake is sleeping with a guy from another school, I heard." That was the student body president, another blonde. She leaned over, turned towards the Cordelia look alike and took a vial of coke out of her bag.

And Carina is sleeping with Marianne, I expected them to say next.

"No," said the first girl. "Blake and Vivienne are together. I'm telling you. It happened at Carina's party over the weekend."

The Cordelia look alike took the vial of coke, snorted some

and said, "Where did you get that top? Is that Versace? It looks like Versace."

"Of course it is. RIP. I saw Vivienne wearing Versace over the summer and it's so chic. It's *so* tragic. Poor Gianni."

"I know your mother didn't give you the money for that," Cordelia said. "How'd you get it?"

"I take her car down to New Orleans on the weekends and see a few guys. She thinks I'm studying. I usually make around eight hundred dollars."

"Shit! Hook a girl up."

"How do you find them?"

"Online. I use the library's computers."

Just then the Reese Witherspoon look alike glanced over at me. We locked eyes and the other two girls turned around. One of them said something and they all laughed.

I thought I heard her say she paid Marcus Easton to get around the parental controls, but I wasn't sure if she said Marcus's name or if she said mine. I almost said something, but my throat closed up again.

Maybe I could leave a note for Carina to sell me more of those pills and more pot. They didn't really help with talking, but they made me not care. And I was tired of caring. I remembered Vivienne that morning after the party, when she walked up the stairs while Princess Diana's death was on the news.

Maybe they did know about me and Carina. I suddenly wondered how much money I had stashed away from Uncle Joseph. I had never really counted it before. Then I wondered if Joseph was one of the guys she was talking about. I thought he had a condo down there, but I couldn't remember. Uncle Joseph seemed to have a condo everywhere.

I expected Vivienne to run her mouth about what she knew, though, but I heard nothing at school that day.

When I got home that afternoon, she was watching House of Style on MTV and didn't acknowledge my presence. It was like the whole incident with the weed and sex with a popular girl, the whole Labor Day weekend was just a figment of my imagination.

Marcus was locked in his room, Mr. Self-Destruct by Nine Inch Nails blaring on the other side of the door. I knocked. He didn't answer. I tried the door. It was locked.

I had never felt more alone.

Bored, I went into the attic. Tiny things scurried away as I shined my light around.

I escaped down through the passageway, following the voices of Janice and Troy, hoping they would distract me from those disturbing images.

Troy said, "I cannot believe you got Vivienne a fucking cell phone."

"What, Troy? You have to spend money to make money. I keep trying to tell you that. If you would listen to the gospel, it says prosperity is the will of God! And stop cursing."

I looked through the hole. My aunt was in the far corner of the room, doing some sort of strange massage on her neck. Troy was on his back with his hand over his eyes, the other on his chest. He was in tight black boxer briefs. He took his hand away from his eyes and started fiddling with an earring I hadn't noticed before.

"What did you expect, Jules? You found me on Bourbon Street."

"Stop that."

"Did you intend to pimp me out? Make me dance for your friends?"

"Troy, if you don't shut up..."

"You won't divorce me. That would look bad to the church, wouldn't it?"

Just then, Troy sat up a little. He looked right in the direction of the peephole and opened his mouth like he was about to say something. It stunned me so much it knocked the wind out of me. We stayed like that for a moment, locked in a secret. Then, he smiled a little and my aunt went over to the bed and turned off the light.

I was hoping I wouldn't run into him the next morning, but it was like he was waiting for me in the kitchen, dancing around to

Around the World by Daft Punk. I tried to ignore him, but he turned up the radio.

"I used to be a go-go dancer," he told me as I poured coffee. "Did you know that?"

"Stop that." He was close, so close I wanted to lean into his warmth, but didn't want to see what he was doing.

The beat wore on and he kept doing this hip swaying thing, trying to make me laugh. He stopped and leaned up against the counter next to me as I fixed my coffee.

"Want something to put in that before you go to school?"

"What do we have?"

He reached into the pantry and pulled out something amber colored, poured a little into my coffee. There was a bite of something there, but since it surprised me, I kept drinking it.

"The women used to grab my crotch a lot," Troy was saying. "They were worse than the gay guys. You know, Jules liked it. You would too if you just gave it a chance."

"Stop that," I said again, but the whole thing was too funny to ignore: Troy very tanned, dancing in a red jockstrap in the French Quarter, letting the ladies reach up and stuff money in there, let them have a feel, shaking his finger...bad girl. My aunt getting all hot and bothered, out on the town, drinking. It was enough to make me erupt with laughter, which weirdly embarrassed me at the same time.

"I can't imagine her there," I finally managed to say.

"Bachelorette party for some church friends. They go crazy during those parties."

"And you were saved after that?"

"Not exactly. I just play along."

It somehow made me feel like I had more leverage against my aunt. Oh, drunk partying Julia—it was so hard to imagine her ever having a good time without the expense of someone else, but I supposed it was possible. How she'd changed after that, how severe she'd become after she found Jesus. No wonder Troy drank all the time.

"Do you ever think about going back?"

"Dancing in the French Quarter? Ha," he said, playing with his earring as if remembering. "I don't know. I could dance for you, though."

"Troy!"

He laughed and walked away. Had he seen me spying? Did he know about the passageway? There was no way. All he did was drink and lounge on the couch.

The liquor burned in my stomach, easing thoughts of the past weekend, those horrifying images of the twins, and the possibility of Troy finding out about my spying.

But as soon as the bus pulled up at school, I already made a plan to find Carina. I needed something that lasted a lot longer than alcohol. I waited until after school until her crowd of admirers were gone. I followed her to the bathroom.

"Carina," I said. I kept the wad of bills wound up in my hand. I had all this money from Joseph. Why not spend it?

"Look," she said, a little smug smile forming on her face. "I don't want to..."

"That's not why I wanted to talk to you," I said. I opened my palm to show her the money. "I want more of what you gave me at the party."

"Oh," she said. Her shoulders slumped. She reached around into her backpack and pulled some out. I handed her the money and she put the pills in my hand, making sure her skin touched mine.

"You know, the other night, that was no big deal..."

"Sure," I said, and shrugged.

Her mouth opened to say something, but she closed it. It might have been my first experience, and I was okay with that. I had a good time, and now I had someone who could hook me up with pills and pot whenever I wanted.

But what did she get out of it?

I said no more. I put one of the pills in my mouth and left school on a cloud, the dwindling chatter of high schoolers fading behind me. Everything sounded like gentle background television noise.

14

By this time at school, Chloe and I were left in peace, and so was Marcus, but we still hung out as a trio during breaks and lunches. Marcus even got pleas from a few girls to go out with them, but he coolly refused. We continued to take the bus together instead of riding with Vivienne, which pleased her.

Then one day, I was at my locker when Blake materialized out of nowhere. "You have a homecoming date?" he asked.

I shook my head.

"Go with me, then," he said, and put a hand on my locker so I couldn't close it.

"No," I said, and he laughed and let me shut my locker. His hand caused the door to resist, and when it shut, it banged and echoed throughout the halls. I had drawn attention to myself without even trying.

They're trying to trick me again, I thought. I pushed my way through the crowds, my face hot, my palms sweaty.

The days zipped by, the same roundabout way of life each day: wake up, wake Marcus up, get to decent mode, and then get out of the house before Troy woke up. Since that night in the closet, he seemed to be getting bolder. Almost all of our conversation was fueled by his innuendo. He continued staring at my breasts, but unlike the time with the bustier, I didn't feel powerful. I liked that we were friends, and I needed him as an ally in the house. I decided it was too much for me to deal with, so I started spending more time at school.

I joined the library club and the art club to keep me out of the house as much as possible, but that subjected Marcus to sticking around school, because he sure as hell wasn't going to go home without me. Eventually, he figured out he could hang out in the school library and use the computers there. The librarians liked him and gave him treats, so he seemed content.

We both dreaded the Thanksgiving break coming up. A week at the house with Vivienne, Julia, and Troy seemed like hell on earth. And if you added Joseph and our grandparents to the mix, it sounded even worse.

On the Thursday night before Thanksgiving break, we sat around the dinner table as Julia chattered on about the meal plan, what everyone was to wear, and how she wanted us all to behave. This was a practice run. Marcus and I were finally allowed to eat at the table with everyone else. I had forgotten to take a pill beforehand, and I daydreamed about the floor opening up and diving down into it.

"And Marcus, I want you to bow your head during prayer."

"God's not real," Marcus said as he plunged his knife straight into his chicken breast like it was a murder victim. "It's like believing in Santa Claus."

"Marcus!" Julia roared, her eyes bulging. "Don't say another word about God, do you hear me?"

"You brought him up," he said, rolling his eyes, then carved up his chicken with the precision of a surgeon.

I stayed quiet and concentrated on my food like I'd be quizzed on it later. Chicken, mashed potatoes, peas, fork, knife. Drown out their voices.

"Marianne, why are you so quiet?" Troy asked me. I glanced up, not meeting his eyes. He should have known the answer by now.

"Who's coming?" Marcus asked. I detected a faint vein of contempt in his tone.

"Your Grandparents and Uncle Joseph."

Marcus's eyes studied me for a moment.

"Why does Uncle Joseph have to come?"

"Yeah, Julia," Troy said, "All he does is drink up all the alcohol."

"He's my brother, Troy, and it's Thanksgiving." There were those bulging eyes again.

"Yeah, let's let him come so he and Marianne can play grab ass," Vivienne said.

"Shut up, both of you. Marianne, I want you to wear something appropriate and modest. Do you understand? And Marcus, no black clothing."

I flushed.

"She wears baggy guy clothes," Marcus said. "How much more modest can she be??"

Troy spoke up again. "Jules, that guy is bad news. Why are you always covering for him?"

Julia got up from the table and slammed the dishes into the sink. Her plate shattered and she left it there for me to clean up later.

"Troy, I will lock you out with those two heathens if you don't shut up. I want to have a nice holiday."

"Good," Marcus said. "I'd rather be locked outside."

Marcus and I did the dishes in silence, a web of apprehension connecting us as we worked.

What did Troy mean by Julia covering up for Joseph all the time?

A memory of something Momma once said came bubbling up.

"Has Joseph ever touched you?"

"No, Momma," I said because I had never seen that look in her eyes before.

"Because if he did, you need to say something."

Images of Joseph came to mind, him knocking the twins into

the pond, watching them flail around as he swigged his drink, uncaring and passive, that slimy smile of his playing on his lips.

What if that was a trait passed down through Momma's side? I'd seen flashes of blazing anger in Momma's eyes that time with the Ouija Board. That same feral, maniacal look was in Julia's eyes, and Vivienne's, too. What if that was an Easton trait?

Oh God, what if I had it too? What if Marcus had it?

I nicked my finger on a shard from the plate Julia smashed. I sucked air through my teeth and popped my finger in my mouth.

"You're overthinking," Marcus said, reading my thoughts. "We'll deal with Thanksgiving when it comes."

When we finished the dishes, I climbed the stairs to the sanctuary of my room and stopped before I reached my door.

Glossy photographs of naked men and women in lewd positions were pinned to the walls. I touched the corner of one of the pictures, one closest to the naked lady on her hands and knees, and my finger came away tacky. Then, to my dismay, the tattoo of Julia's high heels came click-clacking up the stairs. And right behind her, unsurprisingly, was Vivienne with a terrible grin on her face.

"What is this garbage?" Julia screamed.

I shook my head, swallowing back tears. *I didn't do it*, I wanted to say. *Why would I do this?*

"You clean this up right now! You little slut! If Joseph did anything to you, it's because you've got a dirty little mind and you're flaunting your body in front of him. You sit here and clean all this up, right now."

I used my fingernails to scrap, but the glue was already drying. Julia shoved me aside and ripped gobs of glossy nude bits and pieces off the door. She took a hold of my hair and held it to my face.

"You're going to wear it," she screamed, and her nails jabbed at my lips, prying them apart. She packed gob after gob of tacky paper into my mouth. When she was out of room there, she stuck the gluey papers to my body as Vivienne stifled a giggle.

"Julia! Stop it!" It was Troy, leaning against the wall in the foyer down below.

"Do you see what she did? She glued pictures from porn magazines to her door to taunt me!"

I sat there crying, pulling wads of newspaper off my skin. Julia stormed down the stairs and Troy followed her, leaving me alone with Vivienne. I stood up, shaking the last bits of print off, and started down the stairs. Vivienne moved past me and I turned to face her. Maybe, I thought, if I faced her, she would retreat to her room or at the very least, it would stop her from pushing me down the stairs. But she faced me now, unrelenting. I backed down. I knew that look in her eyes now, reptilian, cold, devoid of empathy.

"Why?" I asked. I didn't even try to stop crying. I was broken down and didn't try to hide it from her.

"Carina said you put the moves on her. And Blake asked you out, too. *And* you're a whore. Joseph pays you like one. Isn't that what you told me? I thought you could use a little education about what normal heterosexual sex looks like." She reached out and grabbed a fistful of my flannel and pushed me, throwing me off balance. My heart skipped a beat as I felt my feet begin to slide out from under me as my body fell towards the staircase. She grabbed my shirt, pulling me back and grinned. Her eyes blazed.

She had the same soulless look in her eyes that Theo had in some of his photos. The Theo that may have killed my brothers.

She let loose and gave my shirt a little more slack for me to stumble again, so I was hanging on to the top of the stairs by a tiny shred of luck and balance. She was going to let me fall down the stairs and break my neck. Right in my own house, with Marcus right there in the next room, oblivious.

I screamed until I ran out of breath and my throat was raw, and when I was out of breath, I screamed again.

Finally, thankfully, Marcus opened his door. He darted forward and grabbed me by the arm just as Vivienne let go. I slipped down one step before he pulled me back up

"What the hell were you doing?" I regained my balance to see

Marcus towering over her. Had he really grown that much over the past couple of months? His voice seemed deep, booming even.

"You two deserve every ounce of torture the world brings on you," Vivienne said, jabbing a finger at Marcus's chest. He swiped her hand away and put his index finger on her forehead.

"You," he said, pushing her with one finger. She was so thin she lost her balance and staggered backward. "Go to your room."

She turned to me, a faint glimmer of amusement playing on her lips, and said, "We're not done. We'll never be done."

She slammed the door.

"We have to get out of here," I said to Marcus. "I can't take much more of this. Why is she doing this to me?" The last sentence came out strained as I struggled to choke back a sob.

"You know why. She's jealous."

"Of what? *She's* the model, the one with the BMW, the one with everything. And her mother's still alive."

Marcus shrugged. "Some people don't have a reason. They just are."

He went back to his room.

I wandered downstairs to get a glass of water to clear the last remnants of glue out of my mouth. Julia was nowhere to be seen, but Troy was stretched out on the couch, watching MTV. I followed the strange synth sounds coming from the television, towards Troy's calm presence. Some guy with spiky black hair was singing something about someone watching as he fell down the stairs, so I stood there and watched.

"What is this?" I asked.

He looked back at me from the couch, his face upside-down. "Ministry."

"It doesn't sound like Ministry."

"Well, it is. I'm surprised you haven't heard this. Your parents' music was kind of synth-like."

I pictured Momma's fingers flying over her keyboard, her face in a meditative state, the synth as natural as a heartbeat. Something must have shown in my face, because Troy got up and put a hand on my shoulder.

"Come on. I have the cassette in Julia's car."

I just stood there. He shut off the television and motioned for me to follow him. It was clear outside, a tiny thread of cool weather weaving through the air. I didn't want to be alone with him.

"C'mon, I'm not going to bite you."

We slid over the leather seats and Troy started the car. He inserted the tape and I squinted at the tape deck at the first few notes of the first track.

Troy laughed. "Just listen."

The lyrics were oddly relatable, and something strange passed between Troy and I at that moment. He listened to the same things, was more mature, willing to let me into his past and open my eyes to things, things that were familiar to him, but new to me. I watched his profile as he tapped on the steering wheel.

"It's pretty good. Not industrial, but I kind of like it."

"Al Jourgensen would be very angry with you." He put the car in reverse.

"Troy," I said, moving to exit the car.

"I'm sober. Let's get out of here for a few minutes."

I protested with my eyes. He ignored me, blasted the volume, and sang along with the lyrics as we peeled out of the driveway, Al Jourgensen growling about walking around a small town, suffocating on the surroundings, about not wanting to be an effigy.

Something about letting go, riding in the car and just listening to music pushed a sigh of relief from my body. I sank back in the seat and let the music wash over me, the village just an inky blur out the car window, Azalea House's feverish red madness far behind us.

"I knew you'd like this."

"How did you know?"

He took a deep breath in. "You're an old soul," he said. "Like me."

"Did you know," Marcus said to me the Wednesday before Thanksgiving as we were walking in the woods, "that ethylene glycol has a sweet taste?"

I stopped and searched for meaning in his face. It was the first cool, crisp day, and Marcus was shrouded in a backdrop of red, orange and yellow leaves. "What is ethylene glycol?"

"Antifreeze."

Something about the stony tone of his voice unsettled me. I decided not to engage in this conversation. What was going on with Marcus? On one side of the coin, he cared for all these sickly animals like he was some sort of angelic veterinarian, but lately, him punching out Blake and all his carefree insults towards Vivienne and Julia were starting to worry me.

"It's nice out, isn't it?" I chirped. Marcus didn't respond. He appeared deep in thought. I presumed he was fantasizing about various poisons.

Julia seemed intent on making everything perfect for Thanksgiving. She started shopping the week before, gathering fresh ingredients in order to make everything from scratch, I knew, to impress my grandparents. She had everything now. My parents' house, the money, the fame, the younger husband—everything except her parents' approval.

The night before Thanksgiving, I ventured up to the attic, down the musty passageway, and peered into Julia and Troy's bedroom. They were talking, and Julia was very animated.

"They are going next semester. I don't care," she was saying.

"This is their home, Jules," Troy said.

"They both brood and just go around looking forlorn all the time. I can't stand it anymore. Marcus with his *black* clothing, and Marianne barely says anything. They both worship Satan. I know they do."

"Sending them away doesn't solve anything. When Marianne turns eighteen—"

"I don't give a damn about that, either. Damnit!" She flailed her arms around again and stalked back and forth in front of the bed. What were they talking about?

My grandparents arrived the next day, early, it seemed, because Julia still had curlers stuffed into her hair, and she screamed at the sound of gravel crunching under the Cadillac's tires.

"They always do this!" Julia hollered. Troy rolled his eyes and walked past me and Marcus as we were sitting in the kitchen. He answered the door. To my surprise, he appeared poised and sober.

Marcus was pouring something into little two-ounce cups.

"What are you doing?" I asked. I was still sipping coffee. I had slept in late, but Marcus got up early to work on whatever he was doing.

He smiled slightly at me. I didn't like the look on his face. I hadn't seen him smile like that before.

"I'm helping Aunt Julia make Jell-O shots."

I reached for one, and he swatted my hand away without looking up.

"They've got to go in the fridge first," he said.

I meant to question him about what the hell his problem was, but Granddaddy and Grandmere Lily burst in through the front door.

"Oh, you look like such a ragamuffin," Grandmere whined. Her skin was pulled tight, and she and Granddaddy were both tan and smelled like coconuts. She approached me with her arms open wide, as if she expected me to run to her. I backed away instead. Marcus quickly stuffed the shots in the back of the refrigerator and went to Grandmere to hug her. I knew it was an automatic response to keep her away from me, and I appreciated it. I crept through the back of the kitchen, through the dining room, and across the foyer. Before I could cross the threshold, the door opened. It was Joseph.

"Hiya, darling," he said as he staggered to stand up straight. He sized me up. I forced a grin and set off quickly. I decided on the attic as a decent hiding place. It was cool and dark up there now, so it would be half-way pleasant.

Once upstairs, I sat on the floor and went through the photo albums again to distract myself as the rest of the family kissed each other's asses. I'd go down once Marcus came and told me Thanksgiving was served, and I'd go down quietly and during one of their heated discussions, just so they wouldn't notice me.

But I would not have Momma to defend me anymore. It was just me and Marcus. The tension was almost tangible, even from up in the attic.

The house belonged to my parents. They didn't inherit it. They bought it with their own money. Momma took great pride in the house and painstakingly kept up the gardens as if her ancestors were watching from the shadows. But with my parents dead, would the house go to Julia and Joseph? I couldn't bear that. Not unless by some good fortune, Julia, Joseph, and Vivienne all died.

I fantasized about it, and I know Marcus did, too. Sometimes I wasn't sure if they were fantasies from my own mind, or if they were put there by the little whispering voices of the twins. Sometimes, the urge to see the three of them dead was so strong, the warm breath of the twins danced in my ear as they told me how to do it.

Lure Joseph and stab him.

Push Vivienne down the stairs.

Poison Julia.

Ridiculous notions, they were. Just fantasies. I didn't want to let go of that sweet nostalgia, didn't want to let go of those fond memories of walking with Momma through the woods, winding through those labyrinths Daddy created for us back there. I didn't want to struggle to remember Daddy's laughing face as he found me hiding up in the treetops. It terrified me to think there was a possibility Marcus and I would never see the house again.

It held bittersweet memories, some so haunting they scared me, and some so saccharine sweet they made me tear up. Besides, the twins were buried here. We couldn't leave them, could we?

Something bound me to Azalea House. I didn't know what.

Awful retching noises came from the kitchen, then clattering and yelling.

"Forget it!" I heard Uncle Joseph yell. "I'm off."

My aunt protested, then the front door slammed. I got up and tip-toed over to the attic door and poked my head out.

"Nothing I could do, Mom! He said he didn't feel well. What do you want me to do, run after him and drag him back?"

I heard Grandmere Lily say something that sounded like, "Well, you could have..."

With Uncle Joseph gone, that might make the day more tolerable.

When I got downstairs and we all decided to eat Thanksgiving dinner, it wasn't too bad. Granddaddy took over the conversation talking about his time in the war, and I was happy to sit back and listen.

Marcus and I walked in the woods after we ate, the fall leaves crunching under our feet. The trees had changed and were now a dizzying array of warm fall colors. The air was dry and crisp and lifted my spirits. I inhaled and gazed at the clear sky, which appeared even richer blue with the chilly November air. Had we finally had a decent family day since Momma and Daddy died?

As the sky darkened, I was really beginning to think so. We headed back towards the house and had dessert. When it was well past nightfall, I went outside to the patio. Granddaddy was there.

Granddaddy was a short, stocky man with a crew cut and crisp blue eyes, almost like Marcus's. Granddaddy's were lighter and Marcus's were so dark, they appeared black. But they had the same shaped eyes. And there was something piercing in them, cold and perceiving.

I got closer so he could see me, but I was sure he'd heard me come outside, even though he seemed utterly transfixed on the night sky. Granddaddy was always very perceptive. He was a Colonel in the Air Force and knew all the constellations by name.

"Marianne, come here," he said while still looking up. I did as he said quickly. Granddaddy wouldn't have it if I was too slow to follow his commands.

"Look," he said, pointing at the sky. "You can see Jupiter tonight."

It was beautiful, clearly visible as something different from the rest of the silvery stars in the sky, standing out in a bold, bright orb. I marveled for a minute, relishing the quiet of the night, a faint chorus of crickets and frogs way off in the distance towards the pond.

"Granddaddy," I finally said. "Momma and Daddy never told us what happened to the twins."

"That's because it hurt them."

"I know, Granddaddy. But I'd like to know."

He finally looked at me. "It's a terrible thing," he said. "They were found in the trunk of a car. The car got swept away by the river, but some kids found it while they were out there swimming."

I didn't know what to say, so I kept quiet.

"Who would do that? Well, I'll tell you who." He stopped and took out a handkerchief and blew his nose. He always blew his nose, but something about the way his eyes got all teared up and red, it made me uneasy. It was hard to swallow.

"They were five. They were out here playing in the yard, and your Momma was tending to the azaleas like she always loved to do. And then they were gone. It was that damn Carter Leblanc! He was always doting over them. Sometimes he'd give them things. They got used to him being all nice to them. Then he lured them into his car and took them down to that trashy river shack and hurt them, strangled them and locked them in the trunk. The river got high and washed the car down a little before he could hide them, but the police found them. He should have rot in that jail."

I felt hot, even though it was cold outside. Granddaddy put his hands on my shoulders.

"I don't want you or Marcus going near that man," he said. I had to look away from his wet, red eyes. It was too much to bear. I had never seen Granddaddy get emotional, never in my life. Not even when Momma and Daddy died. And I knew Momma was his favorite. Maybe the twins were, too.

"They drowned in the car?" I asked.

Granddaddy nodded. He took his hands off my shoulders and looked back up at the sky. I glanced in the direction of the pond.

"Granddaddy," I said, still uneasy, "were there other people here? I mean, at the house when it happened?"

"It was Memorial Day," he said. "We were having a barbecue."

"And you were here? And Grandmere and Aunt Julia, Uncle Joseph?"

"Yes," he said, still looking sad. "And your mom and dad, and Julia's husband at the time, Theo. And Joseph had some girlfriend with him."

Theo. I hadn't heard many people say his name.

"And they just..." he shrugged as his voice cracked. "Disappeared. Everyone was hysterical. And you know the rest," he finished up quickly. "Let's go back inside."

I glanced up once more. The stars twinkled like tiny diamonds, and Granddaddy ushered me back into Azalea House, his hand on my back.

A tolerable day, for sure. But that evening turned much darker. As we walked inside, my aunt stood there clutching the phone, her knuckles white, her jaw slack, her eyes wide. And she was looking right at me.

15

"He's dead."

"Honey, who are you talking about?" My grandfather's voice shook behind me. I hadn't realized his hand was on my shoulder until it formed into some sort of vice. I winced and pulled away.

"Joseph," Julia said. "Joseph's dead." She put the phone back on its cradle, never taking her eyes off me. She was looking at me strangely. I had never seen her look like that before. It was almost the same look I noticed in Marcus's eyes lately. No expression, that same strange deadpan look. Maybe it was a trait he got from Aunt Julia.

"How? Wasn't he drinking today?" The question came from Troy, who was splayed out at the kitchen table with Grandmere Lily and Vivienne, their dessert plates still spread out. Marcus wasn't around.

"I…don't know." She looked away from me and at Troy. "The neighbor heard him retching and sort of like...these...these *choking* sounds...and went to check on him and...oh, God. Daddy," she said. Her expression finally changed. She scrunched her face up and pushed past me and into Granddaddy's arms.

Just then, I saw Marcus, lingering in the shadows of the stairwell, listening to everything. When we made eye contact, he pivoted and walked up the stairs. I was in awe at how quickly he ascended them. He used to have so much trouble, but he took them two at a time, silently.

I weaved out of the dining room, towards the stairwell, and after Marcus. His door was shut. And locked. I knocked quietly.

"Marcus. Let me in."

"I'm busy."

"It'll only take a second." I stood there for too long—long enough to shift from foot to foot, before he unlocked the door. I waited a beat, then opened it with trepidation—but I didn't quite understand.

He was spreading himself out on his bed. He crossed his legs and put his hands behind his head. "What is it?" he asked. I couldn't decipher his tone, but it was different.

"Did you hear?" I asked.

"Hear what?"

The room was dim, and I could not make out his emotions. He had gotten good at hiding whatever feelings he had left. Usually, if he was thinking or had some sort of notion, or even if he was nervous, he would adjust his glasses. It was like a tick of his. But I hadn't seen him do it in a while.

"About Joseph," I said. I looked around the room. He had taken down all his band posters. The walls were completely blank. "Are you alright?"

"I'm fine. I did hear about Joseph. You saw me standing in the stairwell when Julia was on the phone. It was only a matter of time for him anyway. Right?"

I nodded.

"Is that all? I'm kind of tired."

I nodded again. I turned to leave, but something stopped me.

"What was in those Jell-O shots?"

"Jell-O. Marianne, I really am tired…"

"Can I have one?"

"They're all gone. Joseph seemed to really like them."

He shifted on his bed and smiled at me.

"Goodnight," I said.

But Marcus didn't say anything back. My heart pulsed in my ears. What had he done?

As I walked to my room, I could hear my grandmother sobbing, or maybe it was Julia. Numbness fogged my brain, with little jolts of confusion and worry concerning Marcus.

And why was my aunt looking at me like that? Like I had done something? I had wished Joseph dead many times, I admit, but did that mean my wishes had come true? I wanted to slap her and Grandmere across the face and tell them both he had touched me. I knew that they knew. But I wanted to hear them admit it. All the expensive clothes, his BMW, his perfectly manicured hair and persona, it was all a lie, crafted so they could pretend he wasn't a snake underneath that flashy veneer.

I sat on my bed and retrieved the box where I'd kept the money he'd given me. I counted almost two thousand dollars. It wasn't worth all his vile actions. The compliments, his hands all over me, the first hands to touch me that way, none of it was worth what he gave me in cash. I still hated him, even though he lusted after me like they all lusted after Vivienne at school.

Unlike Vivienne, I couldn't stand the torture of being desired like that. None of them knew my mind; none of them understood me. I wanted that white hot bloom of acceptance I sometimes got when people understood me, like I had with Marcus—but I wanted that with someone before I got into the ever-intimidating phase of romance.

There was a knock at my door. I didn't say anything. I turned off my lamp and tucked the box away.

"Marianne?" It was Troy.

Did Troy understand me? Sometimes it seemed as though he did. He stuck up for me, which was like digging his own grave. But I didn't think he really understood me. He pretended to understand me the way men do before they ask for what they really want. If they even ask.

"I'm fine," I said. His shadow remained by the door. *Go away*, I thought. But the twin shadows of his shoes remained at the door until I finally opened it.

His face was ashen. "I know you didn't like him."

"It doesn't mean I wanted him dead." But did I? Hadn't I hoped and prayed he would drink himself to death?

"Come on," he said. "Help me with the dishes."

What a Thanksgiving. I didn't know what to think or feel. We stood there in silence, washing and loading the dishwasher until the giant heap of dishes disappeared.

"Funny," Troy said, wiping his hands on his jeans. He pulled out the top dishwasher tray and counted on his fingers. "I thought we had eight of these glasses."

"Maybe one of them is broken," I said. "I'm going to bed."

With the lights out and the house settling, the voices of those long gone from Azalea House started chattering again.

It's good he's gone, good, good, good...

The house makes people do those things...

The house, the house, the house...

I slapped my hands over my ears. I wasn't so sure I wanted to hear what they had to say tonight. Something caught my eye. Did the doll move? The room was so dark and there was a new moon tonight, so I could barely make out her threadbare features.

I stared at her, my focus never wavering. I had to see if she moved again. The grandfather clock ticked off in the background. My eyelids grew heavy, and I closed them down, just for a second, then snapped them open.

There. The doll uncrossed and recrossed her legs.

I dug my knuckles into my closed eyes and rubbed vigorously. I looked again. Her legs were still crossed. A girl's voice whispered from within the walls. I pulled the covers over my head and sobbed until my nose ran and my pillow was wet. I wanted to get up, to run to Marcus, or to anyone. Hell, even Vivienne would be better than being alone. Terror gripped me first at the heart, then at my trachea, squeezing and squeezing.

I wondered if Marcus could hear the house speak to him the

way I could, urging him to do it. Would he tell me if could hear it speak?

I woke up several hours later, my hair wrapped around my neck, strangling me. When I pulled it off, it felt like I was removing alien tentacles. I had been sweating, and my hair was matted, wet and sticky. I winced as I pulled it off. Several strands stuck to my fingers like they were dipped in glue.

I went straight into the bathroom Marcus and I shared. Momma kept shears in there, tucked into the back of the cabinet. I grabbed them, grasped one side of my hair, and chopped. My hands were shaking, but I got it off. Then I moved on to the next side and cut all that off as well. I now had hair just past my chin. I marveled at the two chestnut-colored locks. They seemed like live wires, the way they curled and twisted. I threw them in the trash and cleaned up haphazardly before I went back to bed.

When I finally slept, I dreamed the hair slithered back to bed and wrapped around my neck again. I woke up, the light shining brightly through the window, with my own hands wrapped around my neck, pulling at imaginary hair.

But there was no hair to be found. I ran my hands up my neck, but that part had been real. The hair was gone.

I went to the bathroom and checked my work in the mirror. I hadn't done a terrible job. I looked a bit like the actress in that French movie, but it would need some work. Maybe Marcus could help me with it after breakfast. He had a steady hand.

I took a quick shower because I had had terrible night sweats and evened up my hair before heading downstairs.

"Mother!" Vivienne yelled as soon as she saw me. "You better get in here!"

"Cool," Marcus said. He was sitting at the table, his arms crossed over his chest.

Julia buzzed in and looked at me like I had blood all over my face. Her hand flew to her chest like she was ready to clutch some non-existent pearls. She was in her bathrobe still, mascara still staining her face in angry streaks, her hair jutting at wild angles.

She narrowed her eyes and said, "You had something to do with Junior's death. I know you did."

"No. I didn't. I had bad dreams that my hair…"

"Joseph was a bad person anyway. You know he was." It was my brother.

"God forgives all," Julia said. She put her hands in a prayer position before going over to the coffee pot. "God forgives all. But you two are an exception. I don't know what went wrong with you two. Momma was right. You are both going to boarding school next semester." She blew on her coffee. Her hands were shaking.

Vivienne sneered at me. "Dyke," she whispered. "Mom, I want to cut my hair, too. I want layered hair and highlights like Jennifer Aniston from Friends."

"You can't do that," Julia said. "Your agency won't let you change your hair."

Vivienne screamed and shoved her bowl of grapefruit across the table.

I ignored them both and found mother's old blue coffee cup. It was bigger than all the others and I always felt like I was channeling her sense of peace when I drank out of it.

"Can you help me with the back of this?" I asked Marcus, pointing to my hair. Marcus nodded. I finished pouring the coffee, then he followed me upstairs. Vivienne and Julia glared at us the entire time. I thought their gazes might bore a hole into the back of my t-shirt.

"Why did you do that?" Marcus asked.

"I really did have a nightmare it was strangling me."

"Want me to check the trash can so it doesn't come back to get you?" That old sardonic tone was threaded through his voice again. It was out of place with all the melancholy hanging around in the house, but it made me smile.

I sat in front of the mirror in my room and watched Marcus as he snipped. I could tell by his furrowed brows he was concentrating hard on what he was doing.

"So, why did you do it?" he asked again.

"Why did *you?*" I asked without really thinking first. God, I was doing that more often.

"What?" he asked. He looked at me in the reflection for the first time since he started.

"Marcus," I said. I tried to keep my inflection serious, like Momma used to do. I cradled her coffee cup in my hands. "You know what I mean."

"If you're suggesting I did something to Joseph, no. He was bound to get sick anyway. You know that." He shook his head as he talked. Another knot of worry burned in my stomach.

"Anyway?"

"You know what I mean." He looked me in the eyes and fidgeted with his glasses.

"You hated him too," I said.

"Yes. I mean, he's worthless. Remember how much grief he would give Momma?" He glanced at me one more time, his expression unreadable, before he dove back into the task of fixing my hair.

"Yes," I said. I was surprised Marcus remembered. I was surprised he was talking about Joseph in the present tense still, too.

Momma got collect calls all the time from Joseph, from jail. She always paid his bail. She never complained. But I guessed Marcus heard or picked up on something I didn't. One of those calls must have upset her, right? I needed more reason he would do something like this. I knew he did it.

"I'm not going to ask what was in those Jell-O shots," I finally said.

"You already did," said Marcus with a slight shrug. "Jell-O."

I met his eyes. He let the scissors clatter to the floor and glared at me.

"Marianne. I'm about to scalp you. I swear to God."

I raised my eyebrows at him.

"I did not put anything other than Jell-O in those. I had two. Troy had about ten. So did Joseph. It made the day more tolerable. I don't know why he left here gagging and carrying on. It's probably alcohol poisoning."

I didn't know if I should believe him. He picked up the scissors.

"If I did do something, why trust me with these scissors? I could cram them in your neck right now." He flipped them around in his hand and held them like a weapon. I flinched.

"The only thing I'm guilty of is thinking about it. I mentioned antifreeze as a joke after seeing it in the garage. There were new bottles of it in the garage."

"So?"

He rolled his eyes. "You think Julia and Troy know anything about what makes cars tick? Antifreeze is used for extreme temperatures. Why would either one of them go out and buy bottles of antifreeze? They probably don't even know where the gas tank is on the car."

After a few minutes, he had me turn around and hold a mirror so I could see the back. He had done an excellent job. It was short. Really short. But I didn't care. It made me look less feminine, but I liked it. I wanted to be invisible, to be left alone.

That night, I ventured outside, the autumn evening clenching me in a chilly embrace. There was no moon. I tucked my arms inward, a flashlight wedged under my left arm as I explored the garage.

I squinted as the flashlight's beam highlighted Daddy's old tools, ice chests, and Momma's gardening concoctions.

There was no antifreeze.

I walked, suppressing the urge to run, gravel crunching under my shoes.

I wanted to do this when Momma threw out the Ouija Board. I should have. Just to see if it was still there.

I opened the garbage can at the end of the driveway and withdrew when the stench of ripe leftovers hit me. I tore open the bag on top, not really sure about what I was looking for.

Something clinked. When I shined the flashlight towards the sound, it reflected neon-green and transparent like a prism. I picked it up. It was a glass from the kitchen, part of a set Momma had and that was used at Thanksgiving. The odor coming from it was pungent and fruity.

I used a coffee filter to pick it out of the trash, flicking coffee grounds and scraps of Thanksgiving dinner from it. I carried it back with me and tucked it underneath my bed.

That Monday, I wore baggy clothing instead of the trendy crap I got at the mall. I kept my head down. It worked somehow. I caught a few glances, but then they shifted away. I faded into the crowds in the hallways and became just another number.

There was something so strange about having shorter hair. A new sense of control flowed through my body. I never wanted another man to stare at my breasts ever again, never wanted to be touched like that again. I figured even with Joseph dead, someone would eventually take his place. But for the time being, I relished the control I had over my hair and my body.

Aside from that, a sense of numbness worked its way into my brain. Was Marcus a killer? If someone figured out what he did, what would happen to him? What would happen to us both?

When I saw Marcus in the hallways, he cast me a brief glance. At lunch, he was nowhere to be found.

"What's gotten into you two?" Chloe asked.

I just shrugged. I never told Chloe about what Joseph did to me. She knew I liked to avoid him, but I was sure she thought it was because he was an alcoholic. The only person who knew about that secret was Marcus. No one truly knows your secrets, not even your best friend. Especially if those secrets make you feel shame. I felt like things would completely change between us if she knew. I didn't know why.

At home, Marcus was locked in his room. I didn't know what he was up to, only that his light was off, and he didn't answer the door.

The funeral for Joseph was on a Wednesday. We weren't allowed to attend. Instead, we were forced to go to school. I didn't want to go anyway, and I knew Marcus didn't, either.

Suddenly, the mystery of the twins went to the wayside, and I needed answers about why my brother was acting so strange. Maybe he felt guilty about what he did?

After school that day, I continued through the woods past my house. It was a clear, crisp day, and though the sky was crystal blue, the sun would be down soon. There was frost on the ground in the places the sun didn't reach, and it cracked underneath my boots as I walked. It was hardly ever this cold in Louisiana, but I relished the biting sensation on my skin. It felt good to feel something, even if it was a physical sensation. Inside my head, I fought against the numbness.

The shadows were long by the time I reached Carter's trailer. He was outside smoking on his porch, his movements very languid.

"Hi, Carter."

"Hello, Ms. Marianne."

"What'd you mean by the house getting to people, Carter?" I asked him as I got closer to the porch. He looked at me, then at the fading blue sky, as if it held answers.

"It just does. Years and years of bad things built up all in one place there, I 'spose. You know how you get a bad vibe from people?"

I nodded.

"Same thing kind of lives in that house. Only it gets inside people."

"I think…" I hesitated. I wasn't sure I wanted to tell him about my brother, and about Joseph.

"Doesn't make your brother a bad person," Carter said. Once again, he had read my mind. "But he's gotta leave that place. And soon."

My heart leapt. All we had left was each other. And as much as I felt I needed to take care of Marcus, part of me felt like I needed him there to look after me.

Then again, he wasn't relying on me so much anymore. That was what brought us together for so many years: me opening doors for him, me helping him out of the car or carrying things for him. What was I going to do if he didn't need me anymore? I suddenly had the urge to stretch out on top of the twins' graves and stare at the sky. It always helped clear my head.

"What happened at Azalea House?" I asked.

Carter pulled up a plastic chair and I walked up the porch stairs. Algae covered everything. Part of me thought Carter might be growing it, but it seemed like he cared for one part of the property, and that was the little oasis. Even in the chilly weather, that area seemed to thrum with life. There were late afternoon birds flitting about in the fading light.

He lit another cigarette and began.

"It was originally built as a getaway mansion for a wealthy Portuguese man, a slave trader. Some say he got his wealth by running with pirates back in the day. He did business in New Orleans and would take a pirogue up the river to get to that place. Lots of his pals would take the pirogue with him off the boats in the village, and they did some bad things back there, story goes..."

He paused, like he didn't want to tell me.

"Lots of enslaved women were raped. The rest set up a revolt. But somehow, they got trapped in their quarters and burned. And then the house was passed down through that man's family, until your family bought it. And your Aunt Betty planted all those azalea bushes where the slave quarters used to be. But there were still stories."

He sucked the rest of his cigarette down quickly. I tried to swallow but couldn't. I never imagined Azalea House's history was that bad. And all those beautiful azalea bushes were covering up centuries of dirty secrets.

"It's the house. Something about it draws these things out in people. The Portuguese man supposedly tore up an old Native American village and lots of acreage to build that place. A lot of folks say it's cursed."

My stomach felt weird, and I put my hands over it, somehow thinking it might comfort me. I stood up.

"Can't let you walk back through them woods, Miss," he said. Night was creeping in. Soon, I'd just be able to make out Carter's cigarette tip.

"I'll be fine," I told him, but there was quavering in my voice.

He reached to his side and tools clinked together. Then there was a cold metal flashlight in my hand. I thanked him and told him I was sorry about what happened. He waved me away, unbothered. I appreciated his time, but sometimes I worried if I annoyed him. On the other hand, I always got a sense he was waiting for me. He always knew the underlying reasons for my visits. He waved me away again, as if he understood, like it was no big thing.

I set out through the woods again, maneuvering around roots and limbs and bramble like something was guiding me. It wasn't just the flashlight.

The more I peeled back the history of the house, the more tragedy and sadness released into the air, fighting the flowers for ownership of the land.

There was so much tragedy.

I wasn't so sure I should stay at Azalea House anymore. As I approached it, it really did feel like it was watching me. All around me in the dark woods, there were whispers, voices of a crowded past talking over one another, and I couldn't understand anything. The constant chatter got louder and louder as I neared to the house. I stopped, dropped the flashlight on the ground, and covered my ears. That didn't help, though. No matter what I did, they all wanted to tell me their stories.

I couldn't take it much longer. I walked in the front door, the voices trailing after me. They would never leave me alone.

16

"She's back!" It was Vivienne, sitting at the kitchen table again with Troy.

Julia walked straight up to me and slapped me across the face. The impact was so intense it nearly knocked me off my feet. I staggered to the side and put my hand over my face. It felt like my teeth moved. Vivienne suppressed a giggle.

"Jesus Christ, Jules!" That was Troy. His chair raked across the floor.

"You," Julia said to Troy. "Don't let me ever hear you take the Lord's name in vain ever again!" She turned to me. "And you."

I didn't dare look up at her. I knew her Medusa-like gaze would make me shrivel. I stared at the floor instead. I could see her hands clasped into fists in my peripheral vision.

She spoke through clenched teeth. "Someone called and saw you walking down The Alley. What were you doing down there?"

"Mother, you should have her empty her pockets. She's probably on drugs. Or maybe she's prostituting herself," Vivienne suggested. I didn't dare look at her, either. I knew it would make me want to leap across the table and kill her.

I turned my pockets inside out and produced bobby pins. Change. Nothing else.

"I was just walking," I lied.

"You and that rotten brother of yours are going off to boarding school after Christmas. That is, if I don't have Marcus sent to jail for poisoning Joseph," she said.

"You seem to know an awful lot about what exactly happened to him," I said.

Her eyes narrowed. "Go to your room."

Now I did meet her eyes. "I found something interesting in the trash after Thanksgiving dinner. It was a glass."

She blinked.

"It wasn't broken or anything. Why did you throw it away?"

She squeezed her fists into tight balls and shrieked, her teeth gnashed like an animal. "I said go to your room!" she brayed.

I did. It was where I wanted to go anyway. I put my headphones on and listened to music so the voices wouldn't bother me.

Maybe boarding school would be best. Maybe it would give me a chance to be away from this place, to get a break from my aunt and cousin. And maybe it would be good for Marcus, too.

The next morning, I headed down to the kitchen to find more of Troy's alcohol.

Vivienne's door opened.

"Hey there, Xana-Banana," Vivienne said, giggling and swaying.

"Don't call me that."

"What? It's just a joke. Carina told me all about your new pill habit. It's helping you talk like a normal human being, right?"

I tried to step past her, but she blocked my path.

"Going to flirt with Troy? He's passed out drunk on the couch again. He gave me some vodka. Want some? It's really good with Xanax!" She said the last sentence in a too-loud voice, loud enough for Julia to hear.

"Why are you like this?" I asked her in a shushed voice.

She laughed, a wicked laugh that rattled me. "Hmm. I think I get it from my father, you know."

"And Julia?"

She laughed again, this time piercing me with those cruel, cold eyes of hers. "No. Mother's not so bad. My father, though, was a psycho, you know. Maybe he killed your precious little brothers because they were…*different.* Just like you. And Marcus."

I blinked. She giggled again.

"I know you've been trying to solve your stupid little mystery, Scooby Doo, but the damage has been done. Marianne the detective. You're so pathetic. Grow the fuck up. They're *dead.* My father did everyone a favor."

"And now what?" I managed to choke out. "You'll take care of me too? And Marcus?"

She turned and threw me a nasty grin over her shoulder. "We'll see." And with that, she slammed the door in my face.

Troy was snoozing on the couch, arms crossed over his chest like a dead pharaoh. MTV was on, Tupac rapping about so many tears.

I nudged Troy. "Troy. Are you sober?"

"Mostly."

"I need a ride to the library."

"Aw, Christ. Why? You have enough books here."

"Come on, Troy. If you help me with a project I'm working on...I'll…"

His eyes popped open. "You'll what?"

I ran my finger down his chest and stopped at his belt. "I don't know," I said. "I'll think of something."

He looked me up and down. In the background, Tupac said he wasn't living in the past. I really wanted to do that, too. But first I needed to know more about Theo.

I stood up straight and let Troy look at me.

"It's not like that with you," he finally said.

"Whatever. Can you give me a ride or not?"

He peeled himself off the couch.

Despite going over the centerline a couple of times, we made it to the library.

"Can you pick me up in an hour?"

"An hour? I thought you were just going to check out a few books." Troy curled his lip and adjusted his sunglasses.

"There's a bar across the street. I'll be quick." Before he could say anything else, I bolted inside.

I was almost at my hour limit when I found an article about Theo on microfilm. I thought for a second my eyes were playing tricks on me, but when I focused on the headline, there it was. Clear as day. Man arrested for grave robbing. Theodore Daly. Julia changed her last name back to Easton after Theo died.

My stomach churned and my palms were sticky with sweat. If he was doing this, how much of a leap would it be for him to kill someone? He certainly had experience handling corpses.

I printed the article, hands shaking, and went out to the parking lot.

Troy was fast asleep at the wheel.

"Scoot over," I told him.

"You don't have a license," he slurred.

I shoved him over and drove home, sitting on the edge of the seat because I couldn't figure out how to move the seat up. Troy snored away in the passenger seat.

When we got home, I left Troy in the car. He needed to learn a lesson anyway, and maybe Julia would find him there and yell at him for letting me drive. I'd get blamed for it anyway.

I carried the printout to Marcus's room and banged on the door. After breaking through the heavy bass playing on his stereo, he finally opened the door. He had The Downward Spiral by Nine Inch Nails on again. It felt like Trent Reznor was living in the house lately.

"What?" His face was expressionless.

I handed him the printout.

"Ha," he said, skimming the newspaper printout. "What a con. Christians always are."

I kept looking at him, hoping he would get it without me having to delve into my theory.

"What, Marianne? I'm trying to finish doing this webpage. The dude's gonna pay me for it."

"Marcus," I said.

He raised his eyebrows and reached for the volume on the stereo again. I swatted his hand away.

"Okay, Sherlock. Go on."

"Vivienne told me the other day she thought her father killed the twins. Did you read the article?" I jabbed my finger at the bit about him robbing graves for jewelry. "If he was capable of that, he could have drowned our brothers."

"And then what? Not gone into the water for their bracelets? That sounds stupid."

I looked around the room. He had a point.

"Look, Marianne, you need to give this up. Even if Theo drowned them, it's over. There's nothing we can do about it."

"That's not true. There's a reason I've been seeing them. They're trying to tell me something, maybe even trying to help us out of this hell..."

"Not us. I'm not in hell. I can handle myself. You on the other hand..." He rolled his eyes and turned back to the computer. "Besides, I don't even think it was Theo. I think it was probably Joseph."

A dull ache of shock bloomed in my chest. "What makes you think that?"

"He was a pervert. You draw your own conclusions."

I didn't ask him what he meant. I knew.

Not us.

He thought I was crazy. I left the room and Nine Inch Nails started blaring again.

He was building websites and making extra money. I, on the other hand, was trying to solve some mystery that didn't even matter to anyone anymore, for brothers I had never even met.

But they told me where Momma's ring was. They told us about the hidden stairway that led to Momma and Daddy's room.

There had to be a reason for that. It was a warning. And I had a feeling if I started putting the pieces together, I *would* get out of this hell.

Joseph. He certainly got wasted enough, enough to impair his reasoning. Something unsettling uncoiled in my stomach at the way Marcus said Joseph was a pervert. What if something happened to Marcus at some point and he kept it a secret? I wouldn't be able to bear it. How could Momma's brother do something like that?

I couldn't bear this much more. Marcus and Chloe were slipping away from me, and I was stuck on the edge of a cliff, and all that awaited was a sharp decline of destruction.

I went to my room and put my hands over my ears, curled up in a ball, and tried to let exhaustion wash over me. With all the walking and stressing I had done, I hoped sleep would come soon. But the more exhausted I was, the harder it was to sleep.

The voices began again in the dark, whispering their death sonnets to me, swirling around, interrupting one another. The whispering crescendoed until I snapped my eyelids open or sat up and looked around. Then, the cycle would repeat itself. My eyelids drooped, my brain trying to ignore the sound, then the drop off to sleep, and then the loud whispering. It went on and on until I cried in frustration, my tears soaking my pillow.

Maybe the voices had sympathy for me, for they finally let me drop off to sleep around three in the morning.

But it was like that the next night, too. And the next.

It wasn't long before I could barely keep my head up in class. My eyes felt dry, cracked, like they were as brittle as sandcastles. If only I could keep them shut for any amount of time...

I would have to go back to Carter's if I needed more information. I knew I would get in trouble for it again, though. Would it be worth it? Carter always had answers for things. But I never liked what I heard.

I did something I hadn't done in a while instead. I went to the twins' graves. Maybe it was because they were the strongest voices and could overcome all the others. Maybe I'd restore some semblance of sanity by asking for their help. After all, they had told us about the passageway and Momma's ring.

The ground crunched under my feet on the way to their little resting place. There were spiderwebs of frost covering the ground, otherworldly under the beam of the flashlight Carter had loaned me. The woods were always alive, no matter when I visited. A deer, unperturbed by my presence, nibbled at leaves off to the side of the path. Night things fluttered and scurried in the thick brush. There was the call of an owl, the hum of insects all around the path.

I sat between the grave markers and turned off the flashlight.

"Tell me something. Anything."

I waited. There was the owl again, but this time, much closer. Something else fluttered overhead. I stayed still, closed my eyes, and let the night overtake me.

There was crunching behind me, like an animal walking. Adrenaline tickled my veins. I knelt on the ground. If it was big enough, it could easily overtake me. I froze, hoping the cold ground would absorb me somehow.

It stopped. I turned around.

There were words there, stamped into the frost.

Be patient. It will come.

Fear froze me.

What would come? What did I have to be patient for? Frustration rattled my brain.

The next day was the first of December. That meant next semester was approaching. I'd have to think of something to avoid boarding school.

It was around ten o'clock when I returned from the woods, and the heat of the house was so intense I started peeling off my clothing as soon as I walked in. Julia blasted the heat in the winter and the air conditioning was always on full tilt in the summer, like she was intentionally trying to run up the bill. I was sweating by the time I pulled my coat and sweater off, and then I noticed Troy standing there, leaning up against the refrigerator.

"Hi," he said. He was drinking out of his usual plastic cup.

"Shouldn't you be entertaining Julia?" I said, wiping sweat from my forehead.

"Probably."

I was surprised he didn't get offended. I never knew what to expect out of Troy.

"I wanted to catch you because I have some good news," he said. "I convinced her to let you stay in the same school." He grinned before taking another big swig of his drink.

I didn't know whether to hug him or to tell him to fuck off, that I wanted to get away from here. Did I? It seemed any situation in the future was just as depressing as the past. I missed my parents terribly. They always knew what to do.

"Why?" I asked instead.

His lips parted. He hesitated. "I thought you wanted to stay here," he said.

"I do. I mean, I don't. I don't know. What happens after I graduate, Troy? Are they going to continue to make our lives hell?"

"No," he said a little too loudly. He stepped towards me. I stepped back. "Why don't you trust me?" He sounded sad and lost, like a little boy. He stepped towards me again and I let him. Another step and he had his hands on my shoulders. "I won't let anything happen to you."

"But what about Marcus?"

"I won't let anything happen to Marcus, either."

"But what is the plan with Marcus after I graduate, Troy? You must know that. Julia must have told you." I knew she told him. All that spying through the peephole told me they talked about us all the time.

"I-I don't..." Troy ran his hand through his hair, and then put it back on my shoulder.

"Tell me." I put a hand on his chest to push him away, but he must have taken it as a sign I was welcoming him into an embrace. He pulled me in, his breath on my ear.

"He'll finish the last two years at boarding school," Troy said. "It's all in the will."

"There's a will?"

"Of course there is. I'm surprised your parents' bandmates haven't said anything to you about it. You get the house when you turn eighteen, and custody of Marcus."

I hugged my arms to my chest at the mention of my parents, trying to put anything between my body and Troy's. Some days I just pretended my parents were away, practicing in another room, or Momma in the garden or Daddy out on some errand.

"It's a good thing. We can be together. I can stay with you and help keep up the house."

I tried to push him away again, but he held tight.

That is, until Vivienne walked in.

"Well, well, well!" she cried, hand on her hip. There was an amused look on her face. "What do we have here? A little love scene between the destructive niece and her young step-uncle. Wouldn't this be an interesting story for the media?" She pranced around us and went to the fridge to pour herself some vodka and topped it off with cranberry juice.

"Mother will be pleased to hear about *this*," she said as she glared at Troy.

"She was upset, and I hugged her. You and your mother are always so nasty…"

"Oh, shut it, Troy. I should shove this bottle of vodka up your ass for lusting after Marianne all the time." I stepped away from Troy, my face hot. "Don't pretend you don't notice it, slut," she said to me.

I fled upstairs. But there *was* something I had been keeping a secret. It had been happening since just before Thanksgiving.

Some nights, Troy would drive me around in the Mercedes while everyone was asleep, just like we did that night when we rode around listening to Ministry. There were many sleepless nights, cutting through the chill of autumn, hugging the twisting black roads by some special force. We did not go the way my parents went when they died, towards town. We always went deeper into the swamps where the edge of the road barely kissed the water, where the road cut through the wilderness like black licorice tar.

I would look at the clock and do my best to imprint it into my memory and think, it's half past eleven on a Tuesday night, and I am riding with a handsome older man. I shall never forget this moment. I will bottle it up like a vial of perfume and dab it on my wrists to relive it in my older years.

I had fleeting thoughts about how weird it was. But I felt safe. He never tried anything on me. We just drove and listened to music. It kept the voices away, even for a few hours.

I do not know if I felt a strong pull of attraction to Troy because I felt sorry for him, or because he took care of me, or because I hated Julia. I couldn't decide if I hated Julia because of her vile attitude, or because I cared for Troy. But each time we went on these secret late-night drives, I felt closer and closer to him, like I was giving him some secret part of myself only reserved for people very close to me. But in that silence, there was a mutual respect, a comfortable quiet that passed between us, barely noticeable, carried away by the dwindling fall.

I was happy in the silence, yet eager for him to speak and tell stories, even if they were negative ones about his childhood. I took comfort either way, the wind in my hair, my hands in my lap, the music playing on the stereo. Sometimes he would chatter on about music, about being in college and seeing bands, about his life before Julia.

How odd it must have been for him to meet an older woman and to be carried away from his youth, to some strange house high on a hill with a thin shade of a girl and her crippled younger brother, thrust rather suddenly into an adult life to care for two teen girls. No wonder he drank. But on those nights, he stayed sober for me, stayed locked in reality because he got a sense I enjoyed these evenings away from the prison of Azalea House and its haunting memories, its slaughterous red façade.

Time crept along. December was so cold and dreary, spiders took residence in every corner of the house. The ground was soggy and miserable, so I stayed inside a lot. So did Marcus, who was right next door in his room, yet worlds away. He never answered the door anymore when I knocked. I barely saw him in the house or at school. He seemed to fade away.

Christmas came and went, and no one bothered to wake us up. I ate leftovers once everyone cleared out of the kitchen. Julia got a new Mercedes, and Vivienne got a newer model BMW, but this time, it was a darker shade of red because apparently cherry red didn't suit her.

I cried silently that night as I listened to the sleet tapping on my window. I was almost lulled to sleep by it when I heard knocking on my door. I leapt up, hoping it was Marcus, but it was Troy. He presented me with a little black box.

"What's this?" I asked. I hoped he couldn't tell I had been crying. I opened it. It was an evil eye necklace, nothing extravagant, but seeing it made tears run down my cheeks.

"I hope you like it," he said. "Marcus said he didn't want anything, so I took Ghost to the vet and got him all his shots..."

I threw my arms around Troy. "Thank you," I said. "I love it." He squeezed me back, pressing me closer for a few seconds longer.

He went back to his room, to his strange world with Julia, and I tried once again to knock on my brother's door. "Marcus, it's me," I said. This time, I heard him turn the lock. It startled me until I tried the handle and felt it give. I walked in.

He was getting resituated on the bed again. Ghost jumped up and sat on his stomach. I sat on the edge of the bed. Marcus said nothing. The only sound in the room was Ghost's purring.

"I wish you would talk to me more," I said after a moment.

"About what?" he asked. His voice was much deeper than I'd ever remembered.

"Anything," I said, and shrugged. A stream of awkwardness flowed through the room.

"Okay. I hate school, I hate this house, I hate our family, and I wish we would have gone off to boarding school. Is that what you want to hear, Marianne?"

I just sat there. I didn't know what I expected him to say.

"You really want to leave here?"

"Yes, I really do. But you don't. I can't make you."

"Part of me does. But part of me feels like I need to figure out what happened to our brothers. And do something with this house. I don't want Julia to have it. She doesn't deserve it. It seems so unfair our parents put so much work into it, and now it's barely recognizable."

"You know they only did that to impress Ed and Lily," he said. He had been calling everyone in our family by their first names lately. He didn't use aunt or uncle or anything anymore. "Janelle just didn't want her parents to call her a hippie anymore."

I sighed, resigned. There was nothing we could do about it at this point, anyway. It was late, so I let Marcus rest, but I wasn't tired at all. I decided to sneak down the passageway to see if Troy and Julia were talking about anything interesting.

I could hear them as soon as I was about half-way down the stairs. They were arguing.

"If what she's telling me is true, I'll cut your dick off."

"Come on. I'm just trying to be a good step-uncle. Vivienne is dramatic. You know that."

"I will not let another man cheat on me. Do you hear me?" Julia was doing that thing she always did when she was angry, pacing back and forth with her fists clenched. "My sister had everything, and she had to take my husband, too."

Julia began sobbing, her chest heaving involuntarily.

"Yeah, babe, I hear you," Troy said, pulling her into him, the way he just did to me earlier.

"How about I put that thing on you gave me?" he said.

Maybe he really didn't think of me that way anymore. His eyes still seemed to, but his actions didn't reveal him.

A rage filled my body, not just at how casually Troy seemed to move between me and Julia, but by Julia accusing Momma of stealing her husband.

There was no way. She was an innocent and beautiful songstress who loved music and gardening and being with her band. Why would she cheat on my father? He was so handsome. She was so pretty, she could have had any man she wanted. Why would she ever choose Theo?

I trekked back to my room, away from the dust and mold and long-dead voices in that attic. They would follow me, I knew. Every time I went into the attic, they were always strong when I came back down to reality. There were many secrets there, and the voices were afraid I'd spill them out once I got into the real world, I supposed.

I put a pillow over my head to drown them out, but they persisted.

I thought about what Carter had said about the voices.

Listen to them, Miss. It's the only way out sometimes.

I pulled the pillow away. Listened. There was nothing but silence.

But when I strained my ears, there was something. A trickle of water. Then, a rush. When I sat up in bed, I could see the water churning and splashing, the moon's silver slice in the sky barely illuminating it. But it danced in swirls and waves and pooled around my bed. My heart thrummed in my chest like a war drum. I put my hand on my chest to calm it, but the water was moving in fast. And there was that eerie croaking again. It was coming from underneath the bed.

I opened my mouth to scream and the only thing that emerged was the same croak I'd heard. I couldn't breathe. I peered around the edge of my bed and searched for the noise. Just as I was about to sit up again or wade through the flooding in a frenzy, two small bodies floated out from under the bed. The twins. Their identical bodies were bloated, their eyes plucked out by hungry fish or other creatures of the depths.

The water kept rising, swirling around my room like a

tsunami, and soon my comforter was soaked. The water felt slimy, muddy, and smelled of decay and dead fish. And the twins' bodies were getting closer to me. I pushed them away, but they kept floating back over to me like magnets.

The torrid waters rose over the bed, and soon, I was flailing, attempting to tread water. But before I knew it, the sludgy substance infiltrated my mouth, my nose, my ears. I tasted fish and decay, heard the muffled liquid noises as it plugged up my ears. When I opened my eyes, fragments of my room floating around wildly: my pillows, my dresser, that goddamned Raggedy Anne doll. And the twins. They opened their mouths and out poured sediment and muck and live minnows from the pond.

The pond.

I screamed. When the door opened and the light flicked on, the flood was gone. And so were the twins.

17

It was Troy who heard me and came in.

"Do you think Julia did it?" I asked him.

"Did what?" He had his hands on my shoulders. I shrugged them to get him to let go, but he didn't. "Marianne, what did Julia do?" He kept his voice down. I appreciated that.

"She pushed the twins into the pond. She killed her husband. Killed Uncle Joseph." My voice was still shaky, but I was sure of it. Troy let go of my shoulders.

"You remember that missing glass at Thanksgiving? I found it in the trash, Troy. When I confronted her about it, the look on her face..."

Troy sat still as a mannequin, staring at my comforter as if it had answers.

"Tell me what you know," I said. "She told you she caught Theo and my mom, didn't she?"

Troy looked at the comforter. "She did."

"We have to tell someone."

"Tell someone what?" Troy said. "Leblanc served his time for that. You don't have any proof of anything else, Marianne. Let it go."

"It's not, it's not over…"

Troy put his hands back on my shoulders and said, "Marianne. Stop this." I swiped his hands away. He grasped my hands in his and looked at me. "You turn eighteen soon. There will be a hearing. You need to prove you can provide for Marcus. And to prove you're sane. Do you understand? Do you really want to be telling these people that you've been seeing ghosts and voices told you that your aunt was a murderer? What if they really start looking into Uncle Joseph and arrest Marcus?"

He was right. I'd have to pull it together. Get a job. Prove I could do it. Troy's face was a mixture of sadness and seriousness.

"I understand."

"You have to stop all this talk about ghosts, about things in the past. Promise me that and I'll help you. Don't you want us to be together? We could have a life here."

"I want to call Monica in the morning, though. Troy, I found their baby bracelets in the pond. Granddaddy told me they were wearing them the day they disappeared. They always wore them. But when they were found in Carter's car, the bracelets weren't there. Something happened out there…"

Troy held up a hand and said, "I'll take care of it. Rest."

I finally did.

He came in early to wake me up. We went out to the pond. The sun rose behind us, offering only a glimmer of warmth. I pulled my knees up to my chest and hugged them.

"You cannot have her put away right now. It lands both you and Marcus in foster care. Do you understand?"

"You just love her," I said. I looked out at the pond, at the orange glints of light from the sun. It smelled cleaner today. The sky was clear, and the air was thick with the headiness of pine needles and sap.

"I don't. I don't love her." He had that same look in his eyes: misty, worried, longing. He opened his mouth to say something else. I waited. He stayed quiet and looked out at the water. I watched his profile as birds ruffled their feathers and woke up with their tentative morning chirping.

He put a hand on my knee. It burned there, but eventually, it was as warm and inviting as the sun on our backs.

And then he leaned in and kissed me. At first, it was a kiss on my cheek. Then I turned my head towards him to ask what he was doing, and his lips closed over mine. He pulled me close and sucked on my tongue and I moaned. It was brief. He pulled away, his eyes wild, and we stared at each other. Then I looked back out at the pond. He put an arm around me, and I cuddled in closer. We stayed like that for a while before it was time to go in.

The house hummed with noise as I entered, but I grit my teeth and told them to all settle down. I needed to stay sane for a little longer, needed to prove I was an adult. And not crazy. That I didn't hear voices. That I wasn't obsessed with death.

But to do that, I had to put the issue with the twins to rest. I knew they would never leave me alone if I didn't settle this.

Troy put a hand on my shoulder and whispered, "You're not alone. Okay? Don't forget about what I said." I practically purred at his touch and the warmth of his breath. *Stop it*, I told myself.

I went up to my room to think. It thundered outside. The birds from earlier went quiet.

Twisted storm clouds formed, creating a prismatic shock of color behind the sun. Then came another jolt of lightning and thunder. The wind picked up and the torrent of rain came down in sheets. It gave me time to think about Troy, and about what I really wanted.

I knew the main reason I was so compelled by him was that he gave me attention, something I was lacking in my life, something I craved so badly. But when he was gone or behaving himself, like now, a sense of emptiness filled me.

I would just have to wait it out in my room. I writhed on the bed and looked over at my nightstand. There was a picture of Momma, Daddy, me, and Marcus there. She looked so angelic in that photo, her chestnut curls framing her face, her eyes deep and green, her smile so white and wide, like nothing had ever happened at all. I picked up the photo and put it in a drawer. I didn't want to think about the facade she'd been leading, or whatever double life she'd had with Theo.

But Troy said he'd help me. I would have to believe that. What else could I do? I couldn't trust anyone else.

It was like something started in the pit of my stomach and scratched me there, then as time dragged on, it howled to get out.

Weeks passed. My birthday was uneventful, but Troy and Marcus remembered. I got cards and a cake, and the three of us sat around the kitchen and ate, talking awkwardly about school. Marcus studied me through his glasses, his gaze cold.

I dressed hurriedly the next day. Troy was now a reminder of both the past and the future and I didn't want to face him at breakfast any longer than I had to, so I grabbed a banana and headed out early. The trail to the bus stop was still wet with dew, and the cuffs of my jeans were damp.

I paused when I heard running behind me.

"What the hell?" Marcus stopped beside me, panting.

"I had bad dreams and just needed to get out of there early," I said. We started walking again, this time, much slower.

"I thought you were mad at me. We haven't been talking and I..."

His eyes were red. Was he up late last night? Did he know what was going on with Troy?

"No. Of course not. Why would I be mad at you?" I asked.

"Marianne," he said. His voice sounded strange. Strained. "I feel disconnected from you lately."

I stopped and looked at him. When he kept walking, I put my hand on his shoulder and pulled him back, then faced him squarely.

"What are you talking about?" I knew it was more than not talking as much. Something else was going on.

He bit his lip and looked down at the ground. "Something's going on. At school."

"I know you're having a hard time. It'll be over soon," I told him. I wasn't convinced of that myself, and I could tell he knew it.

"Sure," he said. He shrugged my hands away from his

shoulders. The pain from that one little move sent jagged knives through my heart.

"Marcus!" I called out, startled at how loud my own voice sounded. But he was already at the edge of the trail. He seemed so small off in the distance.

Oddly enough, I didn't see him at school all day. A keen worry grew in my stomach like a wound-up knot, like the world knew something I didn't. The weather seemed to change with my mood. The early morning dew gave way to a sharp increase in temperature, and by mid-morning, it was so balmy and humid it was hard to breathe. Clouds formed in dark masses above the sky and rumbled with the threat of rain. Spring was making its presence known with a dramatic entrance.

Chloe was at her locker. But I stopped in the hallway, letting the crowds part around me.

A dizzying sense of betrayal blurred my vision. But it didn't make sense.

Why would I feel betrayed to see her standing there, laughing with Blake?

Was it because Blake made fun of me? Or called Marcus names? Or that he asked me to homecoming, and now Chloe was twirling her hair and smiling and batting her lashes and…

"Oh. Marianne. I didn't see you there," she said, her tone a little more high-pitched and musical than I remembered.

She was wearing a short pleated white skirt with an argyle plaid sweater vest. Her hair was cut in heavy layers and highlighted. She was wearing makeup and hoop earrings, too. She must have noticed me analyzing her, because she curled her lip and looked me up and down. I pulled my flannel over my chest and crossed my arms.

Blake gave me a look I couldn't quite comprehend, something between spite and amusement.

"Blake and I are going out this Friday night. You should bring a date."

Blake laughed. Chloe glanced over at him and joined in, too. She slammed her locker and walked away.

I barely caught it. "As if," she said to Blake.

By the time school let out, it was pouring. Marcus was nowhere to be seen. I ran home, my boots crashing into deeply trenched puddles, the rain stinging my face.

My suspicions were confirmed when I opened the door.

"Your brother is a fag!" Vivienne jeered.

I looked at Troy. "Where is he?" But I knew. The look on Troy's face told me. I went back out the door and dashed through the woods. Marcus was sitting next to the graves. He'd spread out a raincoat to sit on. His face was ashen.

"I'm gay," he said. I had to strain my ears to hear him.

"I know," I said.

He finally looked up at me and that familiar sibling recognition flashed across his face. I sat down next to him on the raincoat, and we both looked up at the sky. It was finally slacking off and it was misting. Vapors floated through the trees like ghosts.

"I took some pills this morning. Julia had to come get me. The whole way home, she kept talking about putting me away for poisoning Joseph. They just let me out of the clinic an hour ago. I passed out and they called an ambulance."

I looked at his profile, shocked. Why didn't anyone come get me?

"Why did you do it?" But I knew why. It was a stupid question. He knew it, too. He didn't answer. He shook his head.

"I taught myself how to make web pages. I'm leaving, Marianne. I'm taking the money I've been making and going somewhere else."

"Leaving?" I yelled. "You can't leave."

There was something different in his eyes now. It was the same look I saw that morning. His eyes didn't look blue anymore. They were shadowed with dark gray, like thunder clouds. The look scared me, made me draw my body back away from him.

"I'm gay. We live in a village in Louisiana. Everyone at school hates me. And Julia keeps threatening to have me arrested for something I didn't do."

"But you could skip..."

"I can't take it anymore. You could come with me. But you're in love with Troy."

My heart dropped into my stomach. How did he know that?

"I'm not..."

"You are. Even if you don't realize you are, I do. I'm leaving tonight."

"I have to finish high school, Marcus. We're so close. The house will be ours, and we can kick them out."

He looked at me and shook his head. "I can't wait for you. I can contact you when I figure out where I land and you could come, but I won't wait for you. Troy is a lot older than you are. It may not seem like a big difference, but it just is. Just ask yourself, would he be this interested if you weren't getting the house? Right now, he gets it either way."

I looked down at the ground. He was right.

The sky darkened and I followed Marcus back to the house. His movements were very stiff and controlled, never faltering as he rummaged through his stuff and packed a small bag.

"You're really serious," I said. I sat on his bed and with Ghost in my lap. *He'll come back*, I thought, but I wasn't so sure I believed that.

"I told you, I'm leaving. I'm getting a ride from someone in my chat group, and they're bringing me down to New Orleans, and then I'm getting on a Greyhound."

"Marcus, don't do this. Troy says I get custody of you once I turn eighteen. That's less than a year and..."

"I can't wait that long," he said without looking at me. He was stuffing things into his backpack with too much force. The nylon screeched as he crammed things inside.

I tried to choke back a sob, but it escaped. Ghost meowed in response.

"Take care of him," Marcus said. He slung the pack over his shoulder, crossed the room in one step, and hugged me. I clung to him and wouldn't let him go. He said, "Marianne." It was in a way I'd never heard before. I dropped my arms back to my lap, stroked Ghost instead, let a fresh batch of tears disappear into his white fur. Then Marcus was out the window in a flash, his all-black clothing blending in with the dead of night.

I howled with tears. Ghost stayed in my lap and looked up at me, his eyes quirked up in an almost human-like, worried expression. I looked around the room. Marcus had left everything: his CD collection, family pictures, a quilt Momma had crocheted for him.

How could he just leave like that? When was he coming back?

I should have seen it coming. But I didn't. I had been too wrapped up in Troy, in my own problems, and in figuring out what had happened to my long-dead twin brothers. They were only half-brothers anyway if my suspicions were correct. My only full sibling was now wandering through the trees, towards strange new cities and unfamiliar people.

Julia quizzed me about Marcus the next morning, but I said I didn't know where he went. It was true. He told me he'd tell me when he found someplace to stay, but what if he didn't?

"Just let it go, Mom. Marcus is a hoodlum anyway," Vivienne said. She was picking at a grapefruit for breakfast, the same thing she ate every morning. I had never seen her eat anything else. She was as thin as a rail lately but getting tons of local modeling work.

I wanted to protest, to smack Vivienne across the face and send that grapefruit sailing across the room. I even imagined the little pink juice kernels flying from her mouth. It would be so satisfying. But I glared at my feet instead and tried to keep my anger contained.

"One less mouth to feed," Julia said and shrugged. Troy shook his head. *Help me*, I pleaded with my eyes. *Help me like you said you would*. But his silence felt like a betrayal.

Spring came on like it had something against the cold winter we'd faced. Green leaves exploded everywhere, and the ginger Carter gave me finally bloomed and spread like wildfire. Birds rustled in the trees and bushes and insects leapt and scurried, almost like they were full of glee. The world was technicolor again, the skies bright blue, and everything so full of life. But I felt dead inside. I should have been able to keep Marcus from leaving, or to make him happy again in some way so he never wanted to leave in the first place.

I yearned for some sign of him. I checked the mailbox every day. Every time the phone rang, my heart galloped. But spring became summer, the days grew tormentingly longer and hotter, and I did not hear one word from Marcus.

I was alone once again.

There was Troy, but it seemed like he was avoiding me. I didn't catch him alone anymore. Julia was always around him. I did catch little glances from him occasionally; he'd peek over at me at breakfast sometimes or look at me curiously when I walked in the door, as if he wanted to ask me how my day was, but he never got around to it.

I was coming back from the twins' graves one morning when I saw Vivienne digging around in the mailbox. I ran towards her.

"Anything from Marcus?"

She hid something behind her back and said, "No. Fuck off."

I studied her gaunt, pale face. "Vivienne," I said.

"I said fuck off!" she screamed. She pushed past me, but I channeled Marcus's energy and stopped her. She had something behind her back. It was the day's mail. I ripped it from her hands. She swiped at me a couple of times, but I managed to keep her off. I probably had at least twenty pounds on her now and fending her off was simple.

There was a postcard. From Florida. The front had a picture of a beach at sunset. On the back was Marcus's carefully scripted words, his handwriting as neat and clean as calligraphy.

M,
I'm in the Keys now. Will send an address once I'm settled.
Love you,
M.

"Your thug brother is sucking dick down in Florida, probably living with a john," Vivienne mocked. She was over my shoulder now, reading the postcard. I swatted her away and ran towards the house. Who knew how many postcards Marcus had sent? Vivienne had probably been tearing them up. I went straight up to her room and sure enough, there were dozens of postcards from all over. New Orleans. Biloxi. Gulf Shores. Pensacola. Jacksonville. Miami. He did as he promised. He wrote. It's just that Vivienne got to them before I did.

I sensed someone behind me, staring at me from the door frame. Vivienne.

"Why'd you do this?" I asked.

"Marcus is a sociopath. I'm just looking out for this family. And you."

I stood up and faced her.

"If you ever take one of these from me again, I will kill you myself." Then I put my hand on her throat and pushed her out of the way, enjoying the flash of fear in her eyes.

It was the first and last time I saw any sort of humanity in them.

I went out in the garden to restrain myself from killing Vivienne right there. She was so damn greedy. She couldn't stand that I had a brother who cared about me, and Troy loved me more than her or her mother. I walked around and took in all the surroundings as a distraction. I liked to sit on the bench and imagine the twins there in the fragrant garden, playing games with each other and enjoying the prismatic colors. How happy they must have been. Sometimes, when I sat there, I thought I heard them chanting some strange song, or laughter as they played hide-and-seek and zig-zagged through the rainbow-like plantings.

Momma was obsessed with gardening. On clear days, she spent hours out there, pulling weeds and inspecting her plantings with much detail. It looked like something out of a garden magazine. Now, vines crept up the house and snaked up to the windows like they would invade it at any given moment. Moss grew on the statues, creating a weathered cemetery look, which reminded me of the old mausoleums down in New Orleans. Azalea House had an overgrown, wild look about it, almost like it was some creepy abandoned house kids would talk about.

The kudzu and other weeds stank as I pulled them up, and soon I was covered in small, snaky vines as though they had grown all over me. They proved difficult to pull up, too; soon, my hands were covered in light pink scratches and I itched all over. When my nose stuffed up and I began sneezing, I gave up as the sun went down.

At night, the gardens resembled something out of an English folktale and the weeds and overgrowth weren't as visible. After Momma and Daddy died, I walked around a few times to avoid the heat of the summer, but the statues turned their heads to follow my movements, the moss crackling, their eyes hollowing into my body like they didn't want to be disturbed.

Before I went back into the house, something from the window caught my eye. It was Vivienne, watching me from her bedroom.

18

The next morning, I pulled open the curtain to the window facing the gardens. The carnage of damaged flowers was everywhere. Vivienne had gotten up early and destroyed everything I had done the day before.

I pulled my robe on and ran out into the garden. It seemed so dead, so violated. I held back a fresh batch of tears.

Roses lay in scattered disarray. What she could dig up easily was thrown off into the weeds. It would take days to replant what I could. Some of the plants were so damaged, they wouldn't likely grow back.

But the ginger had survived. Somehow, she had missed it. I said a silent thank you to Momma and Carter and went inside to take a shower.

Vivienne had stolen my body wash again, and I walked in to reclaim it.

I pushed the door open and immediately heard the creaking of the rope.

Vivienne's lifeless body swayed back and forth from the rope. She hanged herself from one of the shower rod holders that had been screwed firmly into the wall. Had she been any heavier, it might not have worked, but she was just a wisp of a girl. Her limp and stringy hair hung in her face. I reached up and smoothed it back. She was bloated and purple, and a trickle of vomit had run out of her mouth and onto her white nightgown.

I stood looking at her for a long time, listening to the rope creak as she swayed. She reeked of freshly cut grass and urine.

A sense of numbness welled inside me. Well, I'd get Marcus's postcards from now on, at least. But the numbness gave way to sickness, quick as a punch to the gut. I retched, and out came something that smelled sickly sweet, like decaying flowers. I screamed until my throat was sore.

After I stood staring at her for a while, Julia came in and screamed for hours until her voice was raw. When found the note on Vivienne's bed, she wouldn't let me read it

My grandparents came to stay with us. Again, when they arrived, they smelled like cocoa butter and piña coladas. It was almost comforting, to take in that smell and think about Marcus somewhere in the Keys, basking in the warm sun, looking out over the clear blue horizon and the ocean. But there was something sickly sweet about that smell on my grandparents. I resented them more than ever.

Julia wouldn't speak to me. But Troy finally did, asking if I was okay, did I need anything, and how did I feel about finding Vivienne? Julia barricaded herself in her room. Grandmere Lily was the only one allowed in there. Granddaddy spent most of his time crying in Vivienne's room, hugging her pillows. At one point, I peeked in through the crack in the door. He had all her clothes piled on the floor. He was face-down in the middle of the pile, sobbing.

I tried to miss her. I really did. But I just couldn't get my eyes to form tears. It was nothing like I felt when my parents died.

I was on the phone like a bored secretary every time it rang.

Finally, Marcus called. When I told him what happened, I thought the line went dead.

"Are you there?" I said as I clutched the wire and wrapped it around my fingers obsessively.

He cleared his throat. "I'm here. I just…"

"I know," I finished for him.

"Her selfishness followed her until the end," he said. I never quite thought of it that way. But when school started back up again, I did.

The news came to school the very first day, and they interviewed people about Vivienne. It was sickening. She was made into a cult status figure on television. Kids from school talking about how she was going to be the next Calvin Klein model. The next Kate Moss. They had no idea. The celebrity culture machine creating a new martyr. They held a vigil for her outside of the school. Hundreds of people were there, lighting candles around black and white modeling portraits of her, back before she'd become emaciated.

"It's so awful," wailed one of her friends. Her mascara ran down her face in angry black streaks, and it looked trendy, staged. "Being beautiful killed her! All she wanted to do was be popular and have everyone like her!" The girl buried her head in her hands and ran off camera.

Dramatic.

I watched all this play out, with the living room all to myself. It was the first time since before my parents died I'd hung out in that room. It was totally different now. Julia had ripped down all the family photos and replaced them with the ugliest paintings I'd ever laid eyes on.

I watched with detached fascination as more reports came in, and weeks after that, people started questioning the modeling industry. They blamed fashion for Vivienne's anorexia. She was just a young girl trying to break into greener pastures and look what it did to her. Look what society is doing to young women. Young, bright, beautiful women who have so much hope.

I scoffed at the screen.

"Why do you keep watching this?" Troy asked from the kitchen. He was drinking coffee more instead of alcohol lately.

I shrugged. "Sick fascination." I smiled.

"Marianne," he said. He wrapped both hands around his cup.

"What?" I answered. I didn't look at him. I kept staring at the television.

"It's getting to you, too. You need to watch yourself."

Then I finally did tear my eyes away from the television. He had dark hollows under his eyes and his face was a pale mask of grief.

I stood up.

"Look, you can't deny that she was an evil person..."

He held up a hand and said, "I get it. But everyone is the way they are for a reason."

I stepped closer. Was he really defending her? I wanted to punch him. "Troy," I said, clenching my fists.

"Think about it for a second. Marcus got violent because he was pushed. Julia had a rough past. Everyone in this house did."

"It does not excuse what she did to us, Troy. And you know it." I tried to push past him, but he caught me by the waist.

"Don't be like that," he said. His eyes glittered with emotion. He pulled me closer. I could smell the coffee on his breath. He pulled me into him, and I opened my mouth to speak, but he kissed me.

It lasted longer than I intended, but it felt good: his embrace, his warm hands on my back. But this was wrong. It didn't matter he was younger, and it didn't matter that my aunt was an asshole. I pulled away.

"Things are going to change around here when I turn eighteen," I told him. "This will be *my* house, not Julia's. You'll both have to find a new place to live."

"Marianne, I told you. I don't care about Julia. I care about *you*. But if you hate Vivienne so much, don't be like her. It's not like you to delight in other people's misery." He turned and went back to the kitchen, and I went up to my room.

He was right. I shouldn't have taken any sort of glee in

Vivienne's death. But it was so difficult. I finally felt like things were looking up, even though morbid things happened to get me to that point. Joseph died, Vivienne killed herself. Now it was a waiting game until I turned eighteen.

It seemed to take forever, though. The entire school year was wrought with memories of Vivienne. Even though she was dead, she continued to haunt me. She was everywhere: on the news, in magazines, and her pictures were plastered all around school.

On a Friday, with an hour left of school, I retreated to the bathroom for some reprieve from it all.

Retching noises. They were coming from the stall at the end of the bathroom.

I couldn't help but peek. Chloe. Those were her Filas. But they could have been anyone's shoes. Everyone wore the same shoes except for a few freaks with Converse or Docs.

"Chloe?"

More retching. "What?"

It *was* her.

"You okay?"

A flush. She emerged, mascara smudged around her red-rimmed eyes, her face puffy.

"I'm pregnant."

I recoiled. It was Blake's. It had to be. Why she would let a boy put his penis in her and impregnate her, I had no idea. I took another step back.

"God, Marianne. You can't catch pregnancy, you know."

I looked at the floor. "I know that." *Especially if you only have sex with women,* I thought to myself. The closest I had come to being with any sort of man was my own uncle, but he never put it in me. Just grabbed me. An image of Troy flitted across my brain, but I stuffed it away.

Chloe splashed water on her face and blew her nose.

"What are you going to do?"

She shrugged. "I don't know. Stay here and have his baby, I guess. His mom can get me a job at the mall."

"You're going to stay in school?"

"Are you kidding? Look," she said, and smoothed out her shirt. "I'm showing already. I need to tell my parents. And then I'm quitting school. I can't go around looking like this."

"What? You haven't told your parents? And why can't you just stay in school?"

"Blake doesn't want it getting around," she sniffled. She wiped her face with tissues, blew her nose again, smoothed her hair and walked towards the door.

"See you," she said. "And I'm sorry about your cousin. I know you two didn't get along, but…" She shrugged and left.

And that was it. I was alone in the bathroom. And Chloe, my only friend, was quitting school to have a baby.

I sank to the floor and stared at the white wall, thinking about penises, babies, pregnancy, sex...and then that scene in the movie Alien where the creature pops out of someone's stomach. It seemed so invasive, letting a guy put something in you, and then there was this...this *creature* that lived in there, draining your energy, eating, drinking...and then like a full circle, it would come out of your vagina.

I scurried to the bathroom and vomited up what felt like weeks of food.

Other than a phone call from Marcus, the day of my eighteenth birthday was almost like any other day, except for a new awareness of my own power over Azalea House. I was an adult now, ready to wield power over my aunt and regain control. But really, the day didn't feel any different.

That is, until I went to bed that night.

Troy came into my room, just a shadow figure in the doorway. I barely heard the click of the door as he turned the handle, but I saw him. I could smell him, musk and sweat and that soap he always used that had a hint of spice and sandalwood. I pulled the covers up over me. He approached the bed and pulled them back gently, then sat on the edge. I opened my mouth to talk but all that emerged was a squeak. He put his hands over my mouth and leaned in close. "Shh," he said, and then he kissed my neck. One hand was over my mouth and the other was drifting down to the waistband of my pajamas. I squirmed a little and moaned underneath his fingers.

"Shh," Troy said again. "Don't you want this to be a secret?"

I nodded. He released his hand from my mouth and kissed me. Now, both hands were up underneath my shirt and on the sides of my waist. He was rubbing up and down my waist, stopping at the peak of my breasts and then at the top of my waistband. I moved my hips a little, almost involuntarily, and he climbed in bed behind me and spooned me. His hardness pressed against my lower back and my body tingled with excitement, fear, and a desire to restrain him. He put his hand on my hip and caressed me from there, all the way up to my nipple. I shivered at his touch, but his big hands squeezing my tits felt so good. He pinched my nipple, and it grew into a tiny, tight rosebud.

"You're a good girl," he whispered in my ear. His warm breath on my neck made me shiver again, but this time, I pushed up against his hardness. "You've always been a good girl."

He pushed my shorts down and I let him. This wasn't so bad, was it? How could it be, the way he murmured those sweet words into the sensitive flesh of my neck, the crickets singing in the woods beyond, the moonlight casting a soft glow in the room? It all seemed perfect. I wanted someone else to love me.

His hand drifted in between my thighs and stroked me there. "You're soaked. You want this too, don't you?" I moaned. What he was doing felt too good, and it was winding up some red-hot center in the core of my being, something almost demonic. It unfurled like a new leaf, wanting to be released.

If I moaned too loudly, he would stop his movements and put a hand over my mouth and shush me. This felt just as good as his hand in between my legs. "I want to be inside you," he whispered, and I squirmed a little in his hands. Tiny little thoughts popped into my mind, such as what if my aunt were to walk in, and what would she think? But the demon took over. I backed up against

Troy's hardness again, and he carefully slipped it in. I gasped at the way it filled me up. At first, it hurt, but with his hand in between my legs, stroking that secret spot, something else took over and sweet ecstasy filled me. He began to thrust.

I writhed against him, overwhelmed by the juxtaposition of pleasure and pain, and the strange sensation uncoiling within me. Troy flipped me over on my back and mounted me, then bent over so his face was close to mine. "I have always wanted you like this," he said. I didn't know what to say. Part of me wanted to run, part of me wanted to scream his name, and part of me wanted to regain control, to put my hands on his neck and squeeze and watch while he struggled to breath.

I could tell he was somewhat holding back, not wanting to hurt me, but something was about to uncoil within him, too. He had my arms pinned into place to keep me from thrashing around, but I twisted away and put my hands on his shoulders. I pulled him in, digging my nails into his skin, and he thrust deeper. Soon he was driving into me so forcefully the bed squeaked under our combined weight. I cried out as something foreign and terrifying wracked through my body. It started under my navel and wound around Troy and then up through my entire body. Troy's outburst was more of a repressed growl.

After it was over, he lay on top of me, kissing my neck and lips and whispering more of those comforting words into my ear. I wrapped my arms around his neck and let him.

Was this what love was supposed to be? Sneaking around and all these secrets, whispers in the dark? I had what I only guessed was an orgasm. Holding Troy in my arms felt good, but I knew this was wrong. It was shameful, even though I was probably helping him escape all the crazy things about Azalea House, too. Still, what kind of person slept with their step-uncle, even if he was incredibly attractive and every girl in the village lusted after him?

"You have to go back to your room," I said. Troy kissed me on the lips, three lingering kisses, then he pushed himself off the bed and pulled on his boxers. Then, just like that, he disappeared into the shadows and I knew he was gone when I heard the soft click of the door.

I eventually fell asleep, but my dreams were fraught with fitful tossing and turning. Each time I woke, I had to pull back the covers and let my sweat cool me down.

I had to do it. I had to see if they were awake.

I trod carefully on the stairs leading to the peephole. The stairs had been creaking a lot, probably because they were about to cave in, so I had to proceed with caution. It had only been an hour since Troy had left my room. When I got close to the hole, I noticed a light was on in Julia and Troy's room. I heard soft talking.

"Doing what?" I heard my aunt say.

"Just sitting in the kitchen. Thinking."

That was a lie. I could tell by the look on his face they were talking about where he had been.

"Thinking about *what*, Troy? Tell me." My aunt's voice was getting louder, angrier. I could tell by the way she held her jaw she was on the verge of yelling at him.

"Marianne is eighteen now, technically..." he said. *And I want to be with her*, I finished for him in my mind. But deep down, I had a feeling that would never happen. Julia would never let him go. He would never find a way to help me hold her responsible for the twins' deaths. He was too comfortable with her.

"And?" my aunt asked. The muscles in her jaw tensed.

"And we're going to have to find a place to stay. Technically, it's her house now."

"She hasn't seen the will," replied Julia. "That little sleaze has ten more weeks of school," she added. "I'm not ready to leave, and she'll probably become a raging slut once we move. I need to at least stay and make sure she finishes school. And I'm not ready to leave yet. My only daughter is *dead*, Troy. Marianne needs to stay in school and face all those reminders of *my daughter.*"

No, I really didn't. I'd finish school if it was the last thing I did, reminders of Vivienne be damned. Marcus would kill me if I didn't finish school. Momma would probably haunt me, too. Ten weeks did seem like years away, though. I couldn't wait to finish.

Julia would kill for the house. That much she had proven to me. Was I next? The way she analyzed me with those steely eyes of her told me I was next.

I had to confront them first thing in the morning.

When Julia banged on the door, I jumped awake. My hair was wet with sweat. I had been dreaming again.

"Get up and get your ass to school," she yelled. I yanked back the covers and stalked to the door, opened it and looked her right in the eyes.

"I want to see the will."

She held her gaze steady, her eyes icy and dead. "There *is* no will."

I put my finger on her chest. "You're lying." There was a brief flash of panic on her face. "You're lying," I said again. "It doesn't matter what you did with your copy. Momma and Daddy's lawyer will have the real copy."

Troy walked up behind her; his face flushed. He could barely meet my eyes.

"What happened to the will, Troy?"

. Troy disappeared down the hall and Julia ran after him.

"Troy!" she screamed. He walked into their bedroom and unlocked the black box on their bedside table. "Stop it right now!"

"What? You heard her. She knows."

I followed them into the room. Troy held up the will. Julia made a grab for it, but he held it out of reach. "You're acting like a child right now, honey. She has the right to see it."

I snatched it out of his hands and glanced through it, but it was evident: the house was mine and Marcus's the day I turned eighteen.

"Pack up your things and leave," I said. I took the will and left the room.

I didn't go to school that day. I roamed through the woods behind Azalea House, visited the twins' graves, the pond, the spot Daddy used to sit in, and all my favorite trees on the property. I planned to write an excuse for myself and sign it with Julia's name.

I didn't know how I felt. Angry, mostly. I was talking more, at least, and standing up for myself. I supposed my parents would be proud, but would they really? Marcus had taken off and was doing God knows what with his life. I felt partly responsible for that. Why couldn't he just tough it out?

He didn't know about the will. If he did, maybe he would come back. But there was the issue of school, too. I couldn't make him return, not after everything that happened to him. It would be cruel.

He was better off in Florida. He was in a new environment, totally different from our dreary little swamp village, looking out into the expanse of the water, taking in new sights, and not dwelling on the past like I had been doing. I needed something to look forward to, something that would take me out of Azalea House, lift me up and help me carve out some kind of future.

I sat on a downed tree and fantasized about Florida. Could he see the ocean from where he lived? Who was he meeting, and did he live with anyone? Did he have a pet? When I closed my eyes and let the warm breeze caress my body, I didn't think about Troy or Julia or Vivienne becoming some kind of cult icon at school. I didn't even think about my parents or Marcus leaving. I fantasized about sitting on the beach in a comfortable chair, writing and sipping a drink, and listening to Marcus talk about anything. I swore to myself I would never tune out again if he went on some long spiel about computers or science or math.

I had to get there. I had to make a plan. But first, Julia needed to be out of the way. I would never be safe while she was in the picture.

19

When I got back to the house, it was quiet again, save for the chimes tinkling. There were several boxes lined up by the door. Julia strolled into the foyer, her heels clicking on the tiles. It seemed so ludicrous she would be wearing heels to pack, but that was Julia. She studied me, her eyes narrowed, and her spidery lashes fluttered with disgust.

"We'll be out soon, dear. Trust me. I don't want to stay here any longer than I have to."

I nodded. "Good." I walked past her and bumped into her shoulder, just for good measure.

"By the way," she called after me, her voice a little too perky and sing-songy, "I look forward to your reaction when you go back to school. I'll be happy to write you a note for today."

What the hell did that mean? I ignored her. She probably meant she thought I was going to have parties left and right once word got around she and Troy left, but that wasn't the case. I was only really friends with Chloe. I didn't want to have anyone else over to the house. Everyone would look at me weird because my parents were dead, just like they did at school.

"Nothing has changed, Julia," I said, trying to keep my voice level and adult-like. "I'm going to school, and I'm going to finish."

She had a smug look on her face, her too-red lips pursed in amusement. "And do what, exactly?"

"Does it matter?" I asked her. "I'd like to do something with writing," I finished, knowing any answer I offered would never satisfy her.

She laughed.

"What?"

"Oh, nothing," she said, that sing-songy quality of her voice returning. "It's just cute that you think you'll make it. Let me say this, though: it's good you're planning on staying in school, at least. For now." With that, she turned and went back into the living room.

I left for school the next morning, her smug face still burned into my mind.

When I arrived, my stomach knotted up. I wasn't just imagining it. All eyes were on me. The halls were so quiet I could hear my own heart beating in my ears.

But when I reached my locker, I knew why. Vivienne's familiar bubbly handwriting was plastered all over it. It was all over everything.

"Marianne has been having an affair with my stepfather. Yes, technically her uncle. The slut disrespected Momma by taking her husband away from her. She takes everything away from everyone. And she prostitutes herself."

Oh, it went on. But those were the sentences that rang in my head the loudest. My face burned. Sweat pooled under my breasts, under my arms, in places I didn't even know I could sweat.

"Slut," someone whispered, and the beginnings of tears pricked the corners of my eyes. I ran until I reached the bathroom and then blissfully, the tardy bell rang. That hopefully meant most people were in class. I left the school grounds, stalked across the parking lot and into the woods. I sat there for the rest of the day until activity buzzed around the parking lot. I intended to catch the bus, but the next thing I saw made me think about spending the night in the woods.

News vans screeched into the lot. Someone must have called them to find out what was in the suicide note. People had been speculating about it and what it said, probably hoping for some literary masterpiece. It was just an angry vent from a sad girl, though.

I clenched my fists together until little moons appeared on my palms. How was I supposed to get out of here without getting trapped by reporters? I looked like shit; it was just hot enough to sweat, and my butt was dirty and wet from sitting on the ground. My hair had frizzed up into a wiry ball; I didn't have to look to know that much.

I refused to let that stop me from getting to *my* house. I trekked through the woods as the sun set and cast a watercolor painting in the sky. Maybe it was a sign things were looking up. As I crossed the road to venture through the woods and towards the house, Troy pulled up. He swerved and blocked the trail on the other side of the road. I went around it, ignoring him. He honked. Rolled down the window.

"Get in," he said.

"No."

"Get in this car or I'll pick you up and put you in here."

I walked faster.

To my shock, he was out of the car, his feet pounding the soft woodsy floor in seconds. He grabbed me by the waist and lifted me up, and before I had time to struggle, he had pulled me around to the passenger side of the car.

"What the hell?"

"I have evidence that Julia drowned the twins in the pond. Come on."

I looked at his profile and said, "What?"

"I can prove your mom had an affair with Theo. He was their father."

I shook my head. "No. Let me go."

I already knew that. The picture I found, the way Theo was

looking at my mom. My beautiful innocent mother, with her large green eyes that soothed. And seduced. If it was true…

"Get the fuck in the car," he said, his expression stony. How could he possibly prove it? I let him pull me inside and waited, my breath panicked, while he jogged around to the driver's side. We pulled away as news vans converged. Troy took a few random turns and parked in the back of a church parking lot. He shut off the car, and the vans roared down the street from afar.

"Have you ever heard of DNA testing?"

I had heard about it on television. They used it to connect crimes. I immediately thought of something morbid—after all, they connected everything with semen, right?

"Okay," he said, reading my expression. "You have. But that's not exactly what I was talking about. It looks like we might be able to exhume them."

I thought about their dead and bloated, drenched bodies haunting me. I shook my head. Panic bloomed in my chest and stomach as I tried to catch my breath.

"I went and got the autopsy results. They had algae on them, the same kind they found on the bracelets. That isn't all. They kept their clothes for evidence. There was hair stuck to their clothing. I gave them some of Julia's hair to see if there was a match, and there was."

"Oh," I said. The panic spreading through my body turned thorny. I felt like I might throw up. Would this have been easier if it were Carter?

"I've been in contact with your parents' band mates who wanted the case reopened."

My skin was cold. Troy's eyes were full of emotion—and I didn't like it. If this all panned out, he would have every reason to leave Julia. And every expectation that he would be with me. But he would handcuff me to the past, something I yearned to be absolved of. I wanted to be with Marcus now, my real family. He was all I had left. Troy was just another reminder of Azalea House. I pulled my knees to my chest and hugged them.

"Aren't you happy?" He put his hand on my knee. I pulled away. "I thought you'd be happy."

"I...am. I am. I just need to process it, that's all. And it still doesn't prove she killed them, Troy."

"She confessed to me she killed Theo. I always wanted to know why. Now I know. This was it." He reached around and grabbed a manila envelope from the back seat. It was labeled Brendan and Benjamin Easton Case. "It's all in here."

I pushed his hand away. "I don't want to see it right now. What are we going to do? Is she still at the house?"

"Yes. There's other stuff. One of the detectives found more hair in their fists. I went into the station and asked some questions and talked to someone I know who works there."

"Who?"

"Someone I went to college with."

The thought of Troy having a life before Azalea House really unnerved me.

"But it doesn't get Leblanc off the hook for all the years he wasted in prison." I uncoiled my body, let my knees drop. I had to start thinking logically. I couldn't let my emotions get to me. It would render me speechless again.

"I'll pay for him to get a degree or something," he said. "We can't make it right. But maybe he'll accept."

"Troy, if you turn Julia in for this, you won't have anything left. Why are you doing this for me?"

"Because it's you. And because I hate her. Her vitriol compared to your kindness is so stark. And I want to be with someone kind."

And younger, I thought.

I took a deep breath but said nothing. What would people think if they confirmed this was really happening? The media was already out of control.

"But what about Marcus?" I asked instead.

"Marcus can take care of himself now. He's a big boy. Come on, Marianne. I'll help you spruce up the house. You can sell it and I can go back to work and support your writing."

Did he really love me? I thought again about what Marcus said. *It's wrong, you know it is*. And it was. He was still my step-uncle. He was married to my aunt. And we were going to try to throw her in jail. How would that look for the case?

"Stop it, Troy. You're being unreasonable."

He pulled my hand to his lips and kissed it, then held it in his lap.

"I know. I can't help it."

He needs love, I thought, *and he'll do anything to get it from someone*.

"I just can't think about it right now. This morning was awful enough with Julia plastering all that around the school," I said instead, hoping to drop all this romance business. It was just another added source of stress for me, which would inevitably end in us having sex again. And I wasn't sure I ever wanted to do that again. With anyone. After reading that suicide note, all those good feelings associated with Troy were beginning to leave.

"Why was that so bad?" There he was with the hand again. I glared at him.

"Troy, everyone at school thinks we're lovers."

He looked at me, his brown eyes as clear as I've ever seen them. "We are."

I tore my gaze away and swallowed back tears. No matter how much I tried to deny it, it was true. He came into my bedroom and I let him. I didn't say no. I didn't fight him off or tell him to fuck off, or do any of the things Momma said to do when I got unwanted attention from a boy.

"Marianne, I know you don't like to be direct," she had told me, her green eyes serious and narrowed, "but you have to speak up if you're to protect yourself."

I hadn't done that. Did that mean I wanted it to happen? Troy was my only ally now. If I didn't have him, there wasn't anyone left. Marcus was all the way in Key West.

"I can't do this, I can't…"

"Stop it. I told you I would help you and I will. Don't you trust me?"

I opened my mouth to answer, but as usual, the words

wouldn't come. I squeaked and put my head in my hands. Troy reached over and tried to pull them away.

"Can't you answer me?"

I did trust him. I didn't trust myself. That was the problem. I realized it there in the silence of the car that day.

"You don't know how embarrassing it was to see her suicide note plastered all over school, Troy," I finally managed to say. I hated the sound of my voice. I sounded so immature and squeaky.

"Vivienne was a weak person," he said. "Julia is a weak person. They both use and use and destroy anything in their paths. Just look at what Julia did to the boys. They were a reminder of your mom and Theo."

I shook my head. "Stop talking about my mom."

"I know you don't want to talk about it," he said, craning his neck to meet my eyes. "But we have to. It's the best way to get her out of the house, and maybe into jail, and for us to be together."

"But what will we *do*, Troy? What are you going to do for work? Or are you just planning to live off my inheritance?" Then I finally looked at him and searched his eyes for the answer. They were lost, confused. "You didn't think about that, did you? Were you just going to use me? You're helping me because you want a free place to live, don't you?"

I couldn't figure out the expression on his face right then. I flung the door open and ran out into the dark outline of the trees.

20

Julia took her time leaving. She left little things around, like makeup and hair products, and would barge in at inconvenient times to pick them up. She and Troy were staying at a hotel outside of the village until they found a permanent place to live. Troy pestered me constantly about building a life at Azalea House, but I tuned it out.

I was on the phone with Marcus as we waited for more news about the case and Vivienne's suicide note. Rumor was that they would release it to the public.

"I wish we didn't have to sit through these videos," Marcus said as we both watched MTV for news. "Every single one of them has some singer with just a chair or something in the background." He scoffed. "They even all have the same lighting."

"It'll come on soon," I said. "I really don't know if I want to watch this."

"Then don't," Marcus said. He was chewing on something, so nonchalant as all this unfolded. "Just come out here. Troy is using you, Marianne. Get away from Azalea House so he can't find you."

"I can't do that. Not yet." But inside, I asked myself when. Was I really in love with him in some kind of way?

We were interrupted by a slamming car door out front.

"Someone's here," I said, more to myself.

"Don't answer it. It's the media, I'm sure. Is Julia there?"

"Hang on," I said. "Just stay on the phone, okay?"

It was Julia. Even before I opened the front door, I could feel her presence, almost as if her anger poured out through black rays that infiltrated the house.

"Julia," I said, not hiding the venom in my voice. "I hope you're here to get the rest of your stuff."

She produced a sarcastic smile. "You'll be pleased to know I'm almost finished, dear." She pushed past me and I watched her ascend the stairs, her heels click-clacking on the steps. I followed her, my arms crossed over my chest.

"This house is too big for you," she said as she tossed nail polish, lipstick, and hair products into a cosmetics bag. My parents' bathroom used to be so neat and pristine, but Julia had littered it with every beauty product under the sun. "You really ought to sell it."

I continued to watch her silently. She tossed the remaining items into the back and zipped it up with overemphasized movements.

"Speak," she snapped. "Say something. I deserve an apology. You and Marcus put Vivienne through hell!"

We locked eyes. She looked at me like I was prey. I kept my arms tucked safely under my chest so she couldn't see the nervous sweat blooming on my shirt.

She pushed past me and stalked out into the hallway. I followed her, close as a shadow, something hot kindling in my chest.

"I'm the one who deserves an apology. Marcus and I deserve one. I know you drowned my brothers."

She whirled around to face me. Before I was able to open my mouth again, to reason with her, to tell her how sorry I was about what happened to her, that it wasn't *my* fault, her claws were around my throat.

"Julia," I choked out. From my room, I heard Marcus's tinny voice through the phone, calling out my name over and over. His voice seemed so far away, so muffled. "Let me go."

"You're just like your mother," she said through clenched teeth. I could feel her weight pushing against me as my heels edged towards the top step.

We were in the same position Vivienne and I had stood in that day she nearly pushed me down the stairs. I reached up and tried to pry Julia's fingers away from my neck. She squeezed harder. I managed to flail and strike her, leaving her lipstick smeared across her face like a bloody arc.

Pounding at the front door. Julia lessoned her grip, but we still teetered on the edge of the stairs.

"Troy," she called. "I'll be right down."

I shoved her against the wall and ran back to my room, the tiny crescent claw marks in my neck pulsing.

"Marianne!" Marcus was screaming into the phone. I picked it up, my hands shaking.

"She's going to kill me," I said. "She's here and she's really going to do it."

"I called the police on the other line. Marianne? Are you injured?"

I didn't answer him. Instead, I listened.

"Julia Easton?" someone said. I heard her talking. I didn't hear Troy.

I told Marcus to hold on and opened the door to listen. Two male voices. I crept to the top of the stairs and peered over the rail. Police officers.

"It's the cops," I told Marcus. I was so out of breath my chest ached.

"Good," Marcus said.

The news blurb came on as I was trying to eavesdrop, but it was on the screen in front of me. There was nothing about the suicide note. But there was something about Julia being under suspicion. I swooned.

"Are you watching this?"

"Marianne, just come down here. I'm serious, okay?"

But I wasn't listening. I watched as the news transitioned into more videos, some new solo female artist with a guitar, crooning on about emotions. I bounced back and forth between wanting to listen to what they were saying in the foyer, versus praying for the best outcome. Marcus droned on in my ear about warm water and nice sunsets while I zoned out. I lit a white candle in my room and watched the flame dance.

After some time, the front door closed. The house went quiet.

"Are you listening to me?"

"No," I said. "I think they took Julia away."

I told Marcus I would call him back. When I descended the stairs, their creaking echoed through the house. Off in the distance, Ghost meowed and trotted down behind me. That meant no one was home. Ghost only came out of my room when it was safe.

As I strolled through Azalea House, I recalled the marble fireplaces, the furniture my parents spent so much time reupholstering, the chandeliers, the built-in bookcases, and all the glorious details that made it so unique. My favorite was the stained-glass windows that cast little patterns on the floor, like painted kaleidoscope shadows, but those were all gone, too. Julia had them replaced with new windows, dressed with frilly curtains.

This place used to retain my parents' spirit, the souls of the twins. But not anymore. I wondered if Julia helped cast some of the good spirits away by changing so many things.

Maybe that was all fine and well. But if I kept it up or changed it around, it was permanently different from now on. Now that I had solved the mystery of the stairs and the sitting spot by the pond, it made me feel sorry for my father. Now that I knew why the twins drowned, because of a horrible mistake Momma had made sleeping with Theo, that charming spot in the woods where they were laid to rest was no longer inviting, no longer a place of refuge. It was only a resting place. The twins wanted it to be covered, to lay together as the wild world went on, to finally have their mystery solved. They only wanted to rest together in peace, not made a spectacle. I would resurrect a site for them in a cemetery somewhere, but their bodies would rest at Azalea House, together, in the woods they so loved.

I counted the money Joseph had given me. It was plenty to get down to Key West. More than enough. I put Ghost and a change of clothes into a large Victoria's Secret bag, one of many Vivienne had left behind.

I had let the white candle burn down to a gooey nub, but I knew what needed to happen. I tipped the flame towards one of the curtains in my room. The Raggedy Ann doll sat still and watched until her complacent stitched grin was eaten away by the wild inferno. In Julia's room, there was a bottle of nail polish remover. I opened it and knocked it to the floor, then touched the candle flame to the carpet. Then, as if in a daze, I went down to the dining room, sending the blue and white patterned curtains and window treatments up in a slow, curling flame. Once they did catch, bits of the fabric fell to the floor and caught the rug, and I put my hand over my face and walked out backwards as the flames engulfed the sitting room.

Out in the front lawn, the sounds of breaking glass jangled my nerves only a little. When smoke billowed out, I imagined it blessing the site of this house and all its atrocities like it was swathed in a smudge stick, like an ancient ritual. The fire came out of the house and window openings like a tentacled monster, and I turned and ran.

Black tendrils of smoke still accosted me, filled my lungs and scratched like fingernails. The nails squeezed until I opened my mouth to gasp for air. I ran past the ditch in front of the property, the one my parents crashed into the night they died. Their screams still lingered there, fainter now with time but still as fresh as an echo.

I ran until the nails gripped my throat so hard, I gagged, a horrible sound that reminded me of the twins' drowning death rattle. As I ran out and through the woods, to the road where others might pass and leave that village, sinister laughs reverberated behind me. Those voices moved in on me like a brick wall caving in, threatening to bury me alive. Even my vision blurred black at the corner of my eyes. Some phantom weight squeezed my body, suffocating me like a thousand wool blankets, but it was just Azalea House holding onto me now. I pushed it away.

When I reached the edge of the property, it left me. I took one last look at Azalea House, a ball of russet fire off in the distance like a setting sun.

I hiked to Carter's house with no moon to guide me. I knew the way.

"I'll die here," he said, coughing out smoke like a choked dragon. "And I'll be at peace. Don't you worry about me." He said it aloud this time, as if he didn't want to keep me too long with prophecies and symbols. "You'll find your way if you trust yourself."

He gave me another ginger root. It already had a tiny green sprout, ready to start anew. I put it in my bag and said goodbye. It would be the last time I saw Carter Leblanc.

I did not go to Florida right away. I rented a room in the city, a place that was okay with a cat that probably shed too much. There was a view of skyscrapers in the background, a stark contrast from all the gardens and the dizzying perfumes of florals at Azalea House. I wrote down everything that happened, stating Julia left a candle burning in the living room.

I hadn't heard from Troy. I heard on the news they arrested Julia, that she confessed to everything. She drowned the boys as soon as she was alone with them, carried their tiny bodies down to the fishing spot, saw Carter's car and tossed them in the trunk. She never admitted to Theo's murder, but deep down, I knew she did it. They probably fought about the twins, and my mom, too.

After about six weeks of being on the road, I saw on the news that Carter Leblanc died at his home in his garden. He had a heart attack.

I wrote to Troy and told him I had to move on, that if I decided to be with him, I'd be keeping a piece of Azalea House with me. I thanked him for helping me. And I thanked him for the space I hoped he'd give me.

In Key West, there is a cemetery haunted not by ghosts, but by green iguanas that scurry in and out of the gray graves. They use the heat from the stones to sun themselves, a stark contrast of anciently derived life and resting death. I watch their green bodies twisting out of the cracks in the concrete graves. Sometimes I like to go there to remind myself things will live on, that nature will always do the right thing and reclaim the land, that things buried will rest peacefully in the deep, cool confines of the musty dirt.

Sometimes, Troy calls me. I never answer, but Marcus sometimes does, and says I don't want to talk, that he needs to find someone new. Sometimes a spike of affection for him stabs me in the chest. But it can never be. I never want to look back like I used to do, dwelling on the past. It unlocks too many secrets, too many things that should stay buried.

Most of the time, though, I sit with Marcus and his beau and write while Marcus codes. Looking out into the blue abyss, along with the Curcuma ginger that surrounds us, provides me with some sense of tranquility, especially with the media circus around Julia and Vivienne and the charred remains of Azalea House.

The Columbine tragedy plays in an endless loop on the news, overshadowing our past lives at Azalea House. I catch Marcus's gaze sometimes, that cold, steely look flashing across his eyes from time to time. The Easton Stare, I call it. But then when I suggest a walk along the beach or when Ghost does something funny, the warmth returns to Marcus's eyes.

People wander in and out of the cemetery where they think the twins are resting, but only Marcus and I know they are out of sight, hidden in the overgrown brush of Azalea House's property. Who knows what will become of the land, but I can't be bothered.

Now, when I look out at the emerald green expanse of the ocean as the sun dips past the horizon, signaling the end of the day, I only look forward to tomorrow. Once I write this book about the band and their challenging history, it will be on to the next thing. I must look ahead. There's a book to write and oceans of a new world to explore.

ACKNOWLEDGMENTS

First and foremost, I have to thank my editor, Michael Dolan, whose advice and belief in this novel continue to amaze me. Thank you for pushing me to dig deep, and for having me *include* things rather than censoring them.

Thank you to those who helped to bring this novel into the world, to everyone at Winding Road Stories for working so hard to make this dark dream a reality.

A big thank you to Sana Abuleil, Ian McKinney, Sam, and J., who read early drafts and whose advice and generosity helped this novel come into its own.

I would also like to thank the following people for their encouragement, advice and friendship: Jamie Weiser, Erica Polzin, James Vincent, PJ and Katie Oubre, Jan Baumer and the best mentor a writer could ask for, Norman Partridge. Thank you to Kory M. Shrum for all your positivity and advice when I was just an insecure smut writer. Thank you to Robert Braverman for your friendship, and for being my creative partner-in-crime for so many years. Thank you, Midori, and my wonderful, powerful friends at FF for helping me find my voice. Thanks to Richard Lamb, Jeff,

Kasey, and Sammi for all the lengthy chats about our shadow selves. It definitely came through in this novel.

A special thanks to my dad and brother, who support me but still think I'm nuts for doing this. Thank you for your unwavering acceptance.

All the love, gratitude and dark chocolate peanut butter cups in the world to J. for reading my work, supporting me, and believing in me.

Lastly, thank you to all of you I've met over the years who have embraced your true selves and inspired me by setting your abusive pasts on fire. This book is for you.

ABOUT THE AUTHOR

Clare Castleberry's horror and erotic fiction has appeared in various zines and anthologies since 2006. She has worked as a writer and librarian in the Republic of Georgia, Thailand, California and New Orleans, Louisiana. Find her on Instagram @femmebionic007 and Twitter @femmebionic.

twitter.com/femmebionic

instagram.com/femmebionic007

Printed in Great Britain
by Amazon

80066026R00135